Blessed are the Meek

By Kristi Belcamino

Blessed are the Dead
Blessed are the Meek

Blessed are the Meek

A Gabriella Giovanni Mystery

KRISTI BELCAMINO

WITNESS
IMPULSE

An Imprint of HarperCollinsPublishers

For my husband and two fierce daughters,
who are my everything.

EPub Edition JULY 2014 ISBN: 9780062338921
Print Edition ISBN: 9780062338938

10 9 8 7 6 5 4 3 2 1

Prologue

San Francisco Bay Area, 1987

HEADLIGHTS ILLUMINATE A small group huddled around a figure on the ground.

Waves slap against concrete, and seagulls silently glide on the wind, white specters in the night. Fog hovers low in stringy fingers billowing across the deserted parking lot.

Heads swivel at tires crunching on loose gravel. A car stops about a hundred yards away. A man in the middle of the group whips his body toward the light and sound. A flash of metal in his hand glints in the headlights before they shut off.

"Who the fuck is that? Who the fuck is that?" The man screams, on the verge of hysterics. "Oh motherfucker, we're so fucked. I knew we were fucked. This is so bad." The man paces, putting both hands up to his face.

Another man grabs him from behind.

"Don't worry. He's one of us. He's with me. It's all good, calm down."

"What do you mean calm down?" the man shouts. "She's fucking dead! It wasn't supposed to happen this way. Nobody was supposed to die. What the fuck? What the fuck? What are we going to do?"

A larger man storms over, sticks his gun to the man's forehead, and in a low voice growls, "If you don't calm down . . . I'll take you out myself. Here's what we're going to do. Listen carefully, or you'll get the first bullet."

Nobody moves. The larger man prods the smaller man along, holding the gun to his temple. "Now, take your gun, aim it, and fire." The two men are now standing above the dark mound on the ground. The bigger man pushes his gun harder into the smaller man's temple. "What the fuck are you waiting for, man. Do it. Either you pull the trigger, or I do."

"I can't," the man says with a sob.

The larger man shoves his gun into the guy's mouth.

"Do it. We're all going to do it."

"I can't," the man says around the muzzle of the gun. Snot drips down his nose.

"Don't get your fucking boogers all over my piece. Fire your goddamn gun now."

The man shakes. He closes his eyes, as if anticipating the explosion in his mouth.

"Fire your weapon," the man says in a low voice. "Now."

The roar of a gun exploding behind them breaks the silence. All heads turn toward the sound. A dark figure steps back into the circle and looks around. "Okay. Who's next?"

The other two men step forward, taking turns firing into the mound at their feet.

"Okay, dickwad," says the big man after he pulls his gun out of the smaller man's mouth and fires his own weapon into the mound. "You're the last one. Your turn. I'm tired of waiting. You either pull the motherfucking trigger, or I pull mine. I'm not going to tell you again." The click of the safety coming off echoes in the silence.

The man trembles as he leans forward. He turns his head away as he squeezes metal to metal. The shot echoes in the darkness. He drops the gun as if it were a lit match and collapses onto his knees, keening and weeping. "It wasn't supposed to be like this. This was never supposed to happen. This is a fucking nightmare. Oh God, forgive us, please. Forgive me."

The man leans over, retching and vomiting. A dim streetlight illuminates the contents of his stomach splashing up from the ground.

"Okay, now, now, it's all better." The big man reaches down and pats the other's head. "Watch out for my shoes. They're frickin' Kenneth Cole. See, now, it's all better. Now, we're all in this together."

"Yeah," another guy mutters. "We're all in it together—up to our motherfucking eyeballs."

Twenty feet away, the driver of the car clenches his gun but is frozen.

A look of horror blankets his face.

Chapter 1

San Francisco Bay Area, 2002

EVERY ONCE IN a while, a breeze lifts the white plastic sheet off the naked body lying in the dirt at my feet. When the wind blows, I catch snapshots of a man's very fit, very naked, and very dead body. I try not to stare. But I can't keep my eyes off it.

Besides, it's my job to look.

I don't want to bring attention to myself by whipping out my reporter's notebook and taking furious notes, but inside I am mentally recording everything I see and hear.

The body lies in a patch of weeds on the side of the rural California highway and is circled by half a dozen pairs of shoes, including the round toes of my black patent leather pumps. A mix of California Highway Patrol officers and local street cops gather in a ring around the dead man. They chat about the sheriff's race and wait for the tow truck to haul the man's car out of the creek bed at the bottom of a steep ravine.

I see the body in flashes as the sheet rises and falls in the wind: A lock of blond hair. Long dark lashes. Full sensuous lips. Smooth, tan chest. Defined abs. Narrow hips. Brief glimpses of flesh are revealed as one officer repeatedly reaches down and pulls the sheet back over the body without pausing in his conversation or taking his eyes off his colleagues. Cars whizz by the wide, dirt shoulder where we stand. I seem to be the only one flustered by the corpse in our midst, but I try to play it cool. If I act like one of the guys, they'll forget I'm a reporter.

I keep waiting for the cops to shoo me away, but they don't. It's a car crash, not a crime scene. Guess that's why the cops are letting me in for the close-up while I wait for the public-information officer to arrive. That, and the fact that the sergeant in charge knows me—he lets me buy him lunch every once in a while on the newspaper's credit card.

The wind flutters the sheet again. The breeze brings with it the heavy scent of wildflowers from a nearby hill. It seems incongruous with the dead body at my feet. I slit my eyes and look down again. A strong gust of wind takes the sheet completely off, so it puddles at one officer's feet. This time when he crouches, he anchors the sheet with a few rocks.

"Hey, Sarge," I say. "Don't you think it's strange there's not blood?"

"I think it's more strange he's bare-ass naked, but who am I to judge? Different strokes for different folks," Sgt. Craig Markson says. "Besides, there's blood all right—on the back of his head."

He puffs out his chest a bit. I get the feeling he's showing off a little by "instructing" the girl reporter on the intricacies of death. "Most die from what you don't see. It looks like they are napping, but inside, the aorta is severed from the heart. That's the way most of 'em go."

Markson is a suffer-no-fools city cop who has probably investigated hundreds, if not thousands, of fatal car crashes during his twenty years on the force. His days at the gym were long ago replaced by visits to the all-you-can-eat buffet, but his eyes are usually crinkled in a smile. He's always done right by me, so I don't take his words as patronizing.

"Guess I expected more blood," I say.

"Sometimes there is. Sometimes it's a freakin' horror show when we show up."

I nod. I once watched blood seep in rivulets out of a smashed passenger door as a tow truck hoisted it into the air.

"Sarge, you got the name?" I say it casually, but in my head, I'm crossing my fingers.

I want to get a jump start on my story. Usually, a traffic fatality is a short story in the paper with the victim's name. That is, unless it is someone famous. The San Francisco Bay Area has its fair share of celebrity faces. Music Promoter Bill Graham died only a few miles from here when his helicopter went down in a storm. It's always worth checking. You wouldn't want to be the newspaper reporter caught writing a two-inch brief about a car crash victim who was the latest *American Idol* star or something. This one might be worth more than a paragraph simply because the guy was driving around naked. Although it's not the first time I've written about nude drivers. The last naked guy I wrote about was drunk and masturbating when he caused a four-car crash.

Markson flips through his own tiny notebook. "You know, Gabriella, I trust you, so don't burn me—don't go with this until it's confirmed. If he was driving his own vehicle, then it shows it was registered to Sebastian Laurent, thirty-four, San Francisco." Then he winks at me, and says, "Plus, that's what his license says, too."

I lean over his shoulder and make sure I get the spelling of the name right. "Thanks, Sarge."

A few minutes later, the coroner's rig—an extra long, unmarked, windowless van—pulls up. Two deputies, dressed in navy jumpsuits with the word CORONER on the back, open the van's doors and unfold the gurney's wheels. The tow-truck operator, cranking a wench, finishes pulling the car out of the ravine. It's a fancy black car. I hear a low whistle from one of the cops. Everyone turns to look.

"Fucking nice ride," someone says under his breath.

"Lamborghini?" another cop says, squinting as he looks at the car, which has mud adhering to all four tires.

"Nope," another cop says. "That beauty is a McLaren F1. Fastest and most expensive car in the world."

A highway patrol officer is crouched down looking into the open door of the car—which is pointed up in the sky like a wing—when he yells, "Hey, Markson, come take a look at this."

With a frown, Markson hitches up his gun belt and walks over. I follow him, trying to be unobtrusive. The officer is pointing to a small shiny thing on the sleek black leather seat. It looks like a bullet casing. Markson's forehead crinkles as he looks at it. He turns to where the coroner's deputies are transferring the body onto a gurney.

"Hold up, guys." When he gets to the body, he looks at a coroner's deputy. "Do me a favor, buddy, turn him over. On his stomach."

The deputies flip the body facedown onto the gurney.

Markson pulls on some latex gloves and leans over. He pushes aside a patch of bloody, matted blond hair. Even from a few feet away, I see it. A bullet hole.

"I'll be goddamned." He is shaking his head. He picks up the man's floppy hands and examines both sides, one by one. I didn't notice before, but now I see that fingernails on both hands are bruised a purple-black, and the knuckles are scabbed over.

"What the hey?" Markson says. He probes the fingers and palms of the hand. "Huh. He must have got in a fistfight with a brick wall or something recently, but I don't see no residue," he mutters to himself. He looks over at one of the detectives walking back from the car. "Any gun?"

"No, Sarge. Car's clean. Nothing but his clothes and these." He dangles a pair of lacy red panties from one finger. A few people snicker.

Markson hitches up his pants again and turns to another officer. "Call homicide."

I'm trying not to be obvious as I pull my notebook out and fire off some scribbles. But I'm not sneaky enough. Beneath a furrowed brow, Markson's eyes meet mine.

"Gabriella, get the hell out of here," he says, and turns to the cop beside him. "Get out the tape, string it up, and mark it off. We got ourselves a crime scene here, folks."

Chapter 2

SEBASTIAN LAURENT WAS a dot-com millionaire. Megarich. Back at my desk at the *Bay Herald*, the news research department gives me an address for him in a posh area of San Francisco known as Ashbury Heights.

The executive editor, Matt Kellogg, swings by my desk as I'm writing my story. He's a huge man, and I crane my neck to look up at him. I'm five-six, and I think I only come up to his armpits. He had a chance to move into an office when he was promoted last year, but he prefers to stay out on the newsroom floor with his "troops." I can't see why. He barely fits into our tiny cubicles. If he flexed his legs, I bet the desk would either topple or shatter into plastic shards. He leans over my small cubicle wall, and it bends from the weight of his arms.

"What you got, Giovanni?" he says, and strokes his beard.

"So far, not much," I say, shaking my head in frustration. "I can describe the accident scene, but homicide has clamped down on any more details. Their press release is only two paragraphs long. I'm digging up background on Sebastian Laurent and his company. His public-relations department released some info, but I don't have anything about his personal life. My sources at the morgue say his whole family lives in France and haven't said when they'll arrive to claim the body."

"France, huh?" Kellogg says. "Well, finish up this story, then Coleman wants you to start working on a follow, more of a feature, to run next Sunday."

"Why does the publisher care?"

"Guess they served on some artsy-fartsy board or something a few years back. Paulson over in business is working his sources. He'll feed you what he learns. Get something on Laurent's personal life. Work your sources. Figure out why someone wanted him dead.

"And, Giovanni, try to get someone to make a stab at explaining why the hell the guy was driving around buck naked."

"He didn't start out that way. I'm sure whoever was wearing those lacy red panties had something to do with getting his clothes off him."

Kellogg snickers and stands up. The cubicle wall flexes back to its original height before he turns and lumbers away.

John Stanford hollers across the room, "Hey, Giovanni, heard you got a close-up of Sebastian Laurent in the buff. Was it worth a million dollars?"

I have no idea what he's talking about and am too busy to care. I don't even look up. But the investigative reporter walks over and drops a copy of *San Francisco By-the-Bay Magazine* on my desk. The cover shot shows Laurent in his Speedo walking out of the surf. A surfboard is tucked under one arm. The headline says, "Sebastian Laurent turns down million-dollar *Playgirl* spread—says he didn't want to embarrass his Parisian grandmother."

I add it to the stack of information on Laurent that news research has dropped off at my desk.

The familiar hum of the newsroom gets louder as more reporters come back from the field and settle at their desks. The musty smell of the newsroom, like moldy paper, burned broccoli, and old books, is comforting. The energy in the room builds as it gets closer to deadline. I hear bits of phone conversations mingling with static and voices piping out of the two police scanners stacked on my desk. After working as a police reporter here for six years, I'm pretty damn good at being able to tune into an urgent voice on the police scanner versus routine radio traffic.

It's the best beat at the paper. The crime beat has everything any reporter could want: stories of intense heartache, drama, and excitement mixed with tales of love that never dies.

And if you dig deep enough, you can often find the beauty in tragedy. For every story that crosses my desk, I make sure I dig. And I make sure people talk. Although I would never trade it for currency, my own tragedy is never far below the surface and could easily be a bargaining chip to get others to open up to me. But I would never trade my own heartache for a story.

My own past lingers like a smoky subtext beneath my words as I interview others who are reeling in grief. They look at me and somehow sense the darkness I fight to keep at bay, deep down inside. They sense that we are kindred spirits. And that makes them talk. They tell me their stories while they turn other reporters away.

Because of this, the bottom drawer in my desk is stuffed with awards stating I got the story and told it better than anyone else. But sometimes I wonder if the price I've paid for this ability will cost me my soul. As each year passes, I feel small pieces of me harden. At the same time, rather than shunning the dark underworld—which would be the healthier way to handle it according to my shrink—I find myself compulsively immersing myself in that world.

Right now, that means writing about another dead person. According to public records, Laurent owned a multimillion-dollar home with a woman named Annalisa Cruz. The owner of the red lace panties? A little digging shows Cruz is a thirty-three-year-old artist known for her sculptures. Most of what I can find online about her is solely about her art, so I just skim the information. Another sheet shows a home number for the couple. The answering machine picks up. A sultry female voice with a slight accent asks me to leave a message.

I leave my name, number, and condolences on the answering machine and hang up. I think about my boyfriend, Sean Donovan, and how I would feel if he had been murdered and a reporter wanted to talk to me. I know my mother didn't talk to any reporters when my sister died. It's ironic, but I sure as hell wouldn't talk to a reporter. At least not that first day.

But I have to try to get people to talk. It's my job. Sometimes it works, and sometimes it doesn't. What I've found is that most of the time people find it cathartic to talk to a stranger about their dead husband, wife, brother, sister, daughter, son, father, or mother. It shows that the death was important to other people, too. Pulitzer Prize-winning police reporter Edna Buchanan once knocked on a door a month after the woman's son was murdered. Instead of slamming the door in Buchanan's face, the woman said, "I was wondering when you were going to come."

My phone rings. It's Sara Stephens, a features writer. When I sit up straight, I can see the top of her head across the newsroom.

"Hey, saw on the budget you were writing about Sebastian Laurent. Got some info on his girlfriend.

"Annalisa Cruz is having a gallery opening tomorrow night in the Castro, a trendy, predominately gay neighborhood in the city. I interviewed Cruz last week for a small write-up about it."

"What's she like?" I ask.

"She's a piece of work," Stephens says. "Wanted to proofread the news item before it ran and had a hissy fit when I told her we don't allow that. Kept saying, 'Do you know who I am? Do you know who my boyfriend is?'"

"Did you laugh in her face?"

"I ended up having to fax it over for her approval."

My mouth drops open. "Are you kidding me? Why on earth would you do that?"

"Coleman."

"Whoa." I think for a minute. Why would the publisher get involved in a news brief? He is usually hands off even the biggest stories. "Is he banging her or something?"

"Who knows, but she apparently has the red phone to him because he called me about five minutes after I hung up with her."

Chapter 3

MY SMALL STUDIO apartment is glowing from all the candles Donovan has lit.

The aroma of a roast and garlic-mashed potatoes hits me as I open the door. Donovan is busy in my galley kitchen, my pink polka-dot apron wrapped around his waist. He notices me standing in the doorway grinning at him like a fool, and he smiles back, wiping his hands on the apron and coming over to give me a long kiss. He hands me a glass of red wine as I slouch onto the couch.

My cat, Dusty, leaps onto my lap. I scratch him behind the ears until his eyes close to slits. I don't really like cats. Dusty's an exception. He's grown on me. He became mine after his owner, my friend, Adele, died. He was kicked onto the street with everything else she'd owned. I will forever have a small piece of guilt lodged in my heart for not being there when she died and for not visiting her more when she was alive. The least I can do is take care of her cat because he was all she had. I push away those memories and concentrate on the good things in my life right now. Like this man in my apartment.

He's seemed a little distant lately—like he's had something on his mind. We haven't spent as much time together as we normally do—work is keeping him busy—and the few nights we have spent together have been rocky. He's woken us both in the middle of the night with nightmares. With all the terrible things he's seen as a cop, I'm not surprised. My own nightmares almost always surface in the dead of night.

Tonight, he seems more like himself, and I'm relieved. I take a long sip of wine and lean back into the couch, closing my eyes and inhaling. "Smells wonderful!"

"It will be. Last year this exact recipe nabbed me this hot-reporter chick I was wooing. Now she's mine, hook, line, and sinker—all because of my secret family recipe."

I roll my eyes. "Hook, line, and sinker, my ass."

"You have to admit, it *is* a good roast."

"Damn good." I raise my glass to him in a toast.

He pops a beer and sits beside me, riffling through the newspaper I brought home. "Nice job on the Orinda fire," he says, referencing my front-page story.

The wine relaxes me, and I sigh with contentment. The doors to my small balcony are thrown open, and the slightest breeze brings in a whiff of the ocean. I inhale and close my eyes. I've got it good.

Donovan has the paper splayed open on the table when he leans in, and his eyebrows draw together.

"Huh. That's too bad."

I lean over, entwining my fingers in his. He's reading the obits. "What's that?"

"Cop I used to know. Jim Mueller. Only forty-five. No cause of death listed."

Donovan folds the paper and stares off into the distance.

"Were you close?" It's as if he didn't hear me. "Donovan?"

He looks up and seems confused. "Mueller was on this task force with me when I was a rookie. We saw some pretty ugly things. Haven't seen him for years."

I don't like the look in his eyes, but I push on. He tells me the task force was ordered to crack down on child pornography in the county. The team had carte blanche to do whatever it wanted, whenever it wanted, as long as it reported results back once a month.

"I was a rookie," Donovan says. "The only reason I was even a part of it was my partner, Will Flora, was appointed to the team—basically, I got to tag along."

I remember hearing about Flora. He was a mentor to Donovan, a father figure to him after Donovan's own dad died. I think Donovan told me that Will Flora was the one who talked him into entering the police academy. I vaguely recall that he died not long after Donovan became a cop.

"Were you guys—the task force—were you tight? Was it just the three of you?"

"No. Six. Us three and Carl Brooke, Mark Emerson, and Tim Conway." He says the names slowly and absentmindedly, looking off into the distance. "We all lived in this undercover house for a while. Yeah, I guess we were pretty close."

He wads up the sheet of newspaper in his fist. His knuckles turn white as he does so.

"How did Flora die again? He wasn't very old was he?"

"He killed himself while we were on the task force. That's why I left."

"I thought he had died of a heart attack or something. He killed himself?"

Donovan nods slowly, pressing his lips together.

"I'm so sorry," I say. I want to wrap my arms around him, but he doesn't look like he wants a hug. "Why didn't you tell me?"

His face scrunches up in confusion. "I thought I did."

He gets up and pulls out my chair at the table. "By the way, your mother called me."

I choke on my wine. Some dribbles down my chin and splashes onto my white blouse, staining it. My mother left six messages on my cell phone today. I haven't returned any of them. Bombarding me with calls was her style. Ignoring them was mine. I know if it is something urgent—like the time my oldest brother got hit in the head with a golf ball—she'd leave another half dozen messages with the newsroom clerks and several on my answering machine at home.

Calling my boyfriend was something new.

"What on God's green Earth did she want?"

Donovan, who is now slicing the roast at the counter, looks down. His voice is low. "I guess she wants you to go to the cemetery on Friday."

"What?" I'm trying to compute what he's just said, and it's not adding up.

"For the . . . you know . . ." His words trail off.

Anniversary.

Of course I know *why*. The date is tattooed on my brain. What I don't understand is my mother's calling about it.

I was only six when my sister, Caterina, older by fourteen months, was kidnapped out of our front yard. Her body was found eight days later in a rural area by off-road bicyclists. My father never got a chance to learn this—he dropped dead of a heart attack three days after she disappeared. The doctor blamed it on the stress of my sister's kidnapping.

My world dimmed that day with the murky darkness that now always lurks right outside my peripheral vision. I've fought against those hovering shadows ever since. Sometimes they briefly take over, fluttering onto my shoulders, squashing any light in my life. Other times, I'm strong enough to push them someplace deep inside.

In my family, we don't talk about unpleasant things. My mother has spent the past twenty-three years avoiding talking about the kidnapping and murder of my sister. I walked the party line until a year ago, when I realized I couldn't do it anymore. I need to know what happened to her. I need her killer behind bars. Or dead.

Donovan and I have only been dating for about a year, but we've spent numerous hours trying to track down Caterina's killer. Donovan succeeded in getting the Livermore Police Department to reopen the cold case, but the detective the chief assigned is a pervy old curmudgeon counting the days until he can retire. I can't count on him to do anything except stare at my chest and patronize me.

I can't help but be shaken by my mother's wanting me to visit Caterina's grave. If my mother is turning over a new leaf—I'm not sure what to think about this. My hand is shaking as I dab my mouth with my napkin. I close my eyes and take a deep breath. "I don't understand," I say, my voice quiet. "Why now?"

Donovan sets down our plates and sits across from me. He doesn't answer. Just shovels a large forkful of roast into his mouth. He knows my mom. He knows our history. He knows my family's dysfunctional attitude toward our tragedies.

"If you want, I'll go with you." He looks at me over the top of his wineglass.

My heart melts a little at this, but I can't do it. I shake my head. Impossible. I haven't been to the cemetery since Caterina's little white casket was lowered into the ground. I'm going to have to think about this—my mother's sudden change of heart. It both scares me and fills me with hope at the same time. Inside, I'm still the little girl who was afraid to talk about Caterina because I didn't want to see despair blanket my mother's face.

I butter a thick slice of sourdough bread and shove it in my mouth. When I'm done chewing, making sure I've chewed until it can't be chewed anymore, until it has dissolved into nothing in my mouth, I swallow.

Donovan watches me until I meet his eyes.

"Went out to a fatal today," I begin, "and when they dragged the body up from the ravine, they found a bullet hole in the guy's head." Dating a cop means that this topic is fair game for the dinner table.

He nods, following my lead to change the subject. He doesn't seem surprised at what I'm saying.

"Did you already hear about it?"

He takes a huge bite of mashed potatoes and nods.

"Of course you did. You cops are the worst gossips around."

We push back our empty plates, and Donovan pours us more wine.

"Sure you can't come Saturday?" he asks. Now he's changing the subject. A muscle in his jaw is clenched. He's still irritated I'm not going to his nephew's baptism in Sacramento. I made some lame excuse about having to finish up a story about a surge in meth production in suburban neighborhoods. The story could be done right now if I really wanted to go to the baptism. But I don't.

"Aren't baptisms supposed to be on Sundays, anyway?"

He clears his throat. "It's called a christening at their church. And I guess they do it on Saturdays."

I bet Donovan's strict Catholic mom doesn't like this one bit, but at least the kid's getting some type of blessing on him. I feel a little bit bad for not going, but the last thing I want is to spend the day with Donovan's six sisters grilling us about starting a family. We're not even married, and they won't let up. Before I met Donovan, I dreamed of getting married and having kids, but now that it's closer to reality, I'm not so sure. The truth is I'm afraid. If I had my back against the wall right now and had to decide, it would be a big fat NO. I'm just not ready yet. But Donovan is. Inch by inch, it's become a source of conflict between us, driving a small, invisible wedge into our relationship.

So instead of answering him, I lean over and fiddle with my boom box. The sound of The Cure's *Disintegration* album filters out. It's our music. It's a signal. Donovan takes my hand and leads me to the bed—conversation over.

Chapter 4

As SOON AS I enter the gallery, I spot Annalisa Cruz. She's barely five feet tall, and her long dark hair falls in a silky sheet down the middle of her back. She wears sleek black leather pants, stiletto-heeled boots, and an oversize, blood red cashmere sweater that is falling off one bronzed shoulder. She holds a glass of wine aloft with elbow crooked, head bent to one side, listening to the man beside her. She doesn't look like a grieving girlfriend to me. She glances down, her long eyelashes casting a shadow on her cheekbones.

I catch a glimpse of my reflection in the large glass windows black with night. Despite the way my skirt hugs my curves, she makes me feel boyish. My long brown hair, which I normally like, seems lank and lackluster compared to her shiny blue-black mane.

She stands by one of her sculptures, which are displayed on waist-high white pedestals scattered throughout the gallery. Big spotlights illuminate them in the dark room. They are glossy black or white female figures, each about a foot long. They all feature a woman reclined, back arched, head thrown back, hair falling behind. One hand clutches a breast, and the other intimately gropes the triangle between the figure's legs. They look like they are . . . yep . . . I see the name of the exhibit—ECSTASY AND ORGASM.

Annalisa Cruz watches me over her wineglass as I make my way over to the crowd surrounding her. She peels away from them and steps a few feet away, turning her back to me, facing one of her sculptures. As soon as I'm near, I'm engulfed by her perfume, a spicy, oriental scent. She talks without turning to face me.

"This one is my favorite," she says with a slight accent, gesturing with her wineglass. "Do you think I adequately captured what it is like to for a woman to have an orgasm?"

She turns and looks right at me.

I blink. Her eyes are blue. Icy. Cold.

I study the sculpture for a second. "Yes, I'd say you nailed it." I stick out my hand. "I'm Gabriella Giovanni. I left a message about a story I'm writing on Sebastian. I'm sorry for your loss."

It's a standard greeting to a grieving person, but she ignores my hand. Instead, she blinks rapidly, not as if she is trying to hold back tears but more like she is trying to summon them. She is rewarded with one fat tear that takes its sweet time squeezing out of the corner of one eye.

"Annalisa Cruz," she says, finally shaking my hand with the barest touch of her fingertips. "*El gusto es mio*"–the pleasure is mine.

"*Encantada*," I respond—likewise.

One expertly plucked eyebrow rises. In the background, people call her name, "Ms. Cruz. Ms. Cruz."

She smiles over my shoulder, then looks back at me. "It's a little crazy here tonight. Why don't you come by my place tomorrow morning at eleven, so we can talk."

She doesn't wait for me to agree. Once again, her attention is captured by something over my shoulder. It's a photographer who begins snapping rapid-fire photos of her. I back away and watch as she poses like a professional in front of the popping flashbulb.

Chapter 5

Sebastian Laurent lived in an ultramodern metal house squeezed in between other multimillion-dollar homes on a cul-de-sac I never dreamed existed, perched 570 feet above the rest of San Francisco.

In the middle of the cul-de-sac is a small park with trees. At the center of the park, a pedestal is all that remains of a statue. I park and walk over to read the marker, which says that years ago, the area, called Mt. Olympus, marked the exact center of San Francisco. In one direction, through the spruce trees, I catch a glimpse of the Bay Bridge and Oakland Hills. In the other, I see the Golden Gate Bridge, which has low-flying clouds covering the top of the span.

Despite the public park, the area feels very secluded and private. I imagine eyes watching me from all the windows.

I steel myself to speak to Annalisa. She didn't even pretend to be upset over her boyfriend's death. Or rather, she did *pretend*. She's a pretty good actress, but I'm even better at reading people. That tear wasn't real. Her performance last night—so devoid of grief—prompted me to leave a message earlier with my best friend, Nicole, our courts reporter, asking her to find out more about Miss Annalisa Cruz.

Laurent's house is the smallest one on the block. It's a small squat box that combines huge shiny metal sheets interspersed with textured wood. But I know the exterior must be deceptive. Property records show the house is fifty-five hundred square feet. It must all be on the back side, sprawling down the hill.

The door to the house is covered with thick iron latticework, and I'm trying to figure out how to knock when it swings open. Today, Cruz is wearing faded blue jeans and a loose, red, embroidered tunic. Her feet are bare. I feel overdone, garish even, in my pink cashmere sweater and white slacks compared to her effortless chic. Her face, devoid of makeup, may be even prettier today than when she had a full face of makeup at the gallery. Huge eyes take in everything from behind black lashes. Her glance lingers on a small snag in my sweater.

"Come in," she says, and makes a grand, sweeping gesture, holding the door for me. The hallway leads to a main room with enormous floor-to-ceiling windows facing downtown and a balcony that runs the length of the room. Across from the windows, a ten-foot-long stainless-steel bar separates the kitchen from the rest of the room.

Annalisa heads behind the bar and indicates a black leather sectional couch with a wave. Across the room is a long table that could feed my big Italian family. A fifteen-foot-high print of Brigitte Bardot standing with her legs spread and her hands on her hips soars above the table.

"Wine?" Annalisa holds two glasses between her fingers. It's 11:00 A.M.

"Sure."

I look again for any sign that she is grieving. Nope. Not even a hint of small dark circles under her eyes. Maybe she's numbed her grief with alcohol.

She hands me a glass of wine and curls her legs up under her on the couch facing a huge fireplace. She fishes for a cigarette out of a shiny blue flat pack and lights it with the flick of a match. She indicates with the lit cigarette that I should sit. The couch is about as long as my entire apartment. I plop down about a foot from her, then rummage in my bag for my pen and reporter's notebook.

She offers me the pack. Dunhills. Expensive English cigarettes. I've been struggling to quit smoking for the past year—occasionally failing miserably—but I reach for one anyway. Screw it. I don't normally drink wine before noon, either. She gestures for me to lean closer, and I do, with the cigarette between my lips. She shields it with one cupped hand as she lights it. Her hand brushes my own, and her eyes never leave mine. I look away.

I take a drag on the cigarette, inhaling deeply, somewhat disappointed by the ashy taste but welcoming the small buzz that shoots through me.

"So?" Annalisa says, raising an eyebrow.

I exhale into the air above me. "Tell me about Sebastian. What did he like to do when he wasn't working? Did he have any hobbies or interests?"

My questions hang in the air like the cigarette smoke in front of us. I let the silence do its job. It's an interview technique to get people to open up. Most people are uncomfortable by silence and try to fill it. Not Annalisa. She looks at me. Then she takes a long puff of her cigarette. Again, her eyes don't leave mine.

"What can I say?" She has the lightest accent. "Sebastian was handsome, successful, rich, everything a girl could want."

Something about the way she says it provokes my next question. "Was he everything you wanted?"

She avoids my question, running her fingers along the back of the sleek couch. "Isn't that what we are all taught to dream of in a man?"

"You don't seem like the type to follow convention. Living as an artist isn't always what good Mexican girls are raised to do."

I seem to have hit a nerve. She narrows her eyes at me. The first sign of emotion I've seen since I walked in. "Why do you think you know so much about *las razas, chica*?"

"*Soy Italiana. Usted es tambien una Catholica. No mucho diferente.*"

She doesn't buy it. "Just because both Italians and Mexicans are Catholic does not mean that they are the same."

"Yeah, but they are enough alike for me to get it. I know what it's like to grow up in a house centered around food and church—how you're an old maid if you're not married with kids by the time you're twenty-five."

Her laughter tinkles like when a child giggles infectiously. I can't help but smile back. "Okay, maybe there are some similarities," she says. Her seemingly normal behavior in the face of her boyfriend's death makes me vaguely uneasy

Annalisa's body relaxes, and she taps the long ash of her cigarette into a black ceramic ashtray shaped like a nude woman's torso. The figure is seductively lounging on her side on the banks of what looks like a pond—the small concave bowl where the ashes go.

"Did you make this," I say, gesturing with my cigarette.

"Do you like it?" she says, exhaling.

"It's fantastic." I'm trying to decide when to bring up her apparent lack of grief over her boyfriend's death when she gets up and opens a long cupboard near the kitchen. I see a shelf filled with similar ashtrays. She grabs a glazed red one.

I fish another cigarette from the pack and light it from the dying cherry on my first one.

"Here. My gift to you." She hands me the red ashtray. I stick it in my bag.

It's generous, but I'm not here to get gifts from grieving—or nongrieving—girlfriends. I need information for my story. I'm waiting for the right moment to confront her about her nonchalant attitude regarding her boyfriend's murder. Maybe she's a sociopath, who has zero empathy for others. Or maybe she killed him.

"Annalisa, did Sebastian have any enemies? Can you think of any reason someone wanted him dead?"

"Lots of people disliked Sebastian. He could be an asshole."

I stay silent, hoping she will continue.

"He even was like that to me." She says this matter-of-factly, with a shrug.

This second cigarette already tastes better than the first, but the jolt of nicotine feels weaker, making me inhale harder.

"Is that why you don't seem too broken up about his death?" I look away when I say this, keeping my gaze on the flames in the fireplace. She takes a moment to answer.

"I am sad. But I don't believe in airing my laundry in public, as they say." Her lips purse as she exhales. Again, she does the rapid eye blinking and is rewarded with two fat tears this time. She doesn't bother to wipe them away but let's them meander down her bronze cheek.

"My family moved here from Mexico City when I was eight.

We may live simply here in this country, but we were royalty in Mexico, friends with *el presidente*. My father lost everything in gambling debts, and so we had to come here to live with my sister's family. She married a rich man—a vintner—we lived in a house on his property, like a servant's cottage, you could say. We may not have had much at times, but we've always had our pride. My family believes your grief should be expressed in private. It's not to share with the rest of the world. So, yes, I'm sad. Even self-centered men don't deserve to be murdered. Sebastian and I . . ." She falters here and stares into the fire. "We have not been . . . close . . . for a long time. So, in answer to your question, yes, I'm sad. I'm sad to lose someone whom I once cared about a great deal."

There is so little emotion there, I can't decide whether to believe her or not.

"If all that is true, why did you stay around?"

"Come now, Gabriella, you know that's not what good Catholic girls do. Especially good Catholic girls living in sin before marriage."

I'm pretty sure she's joking, but I'm a bit confused.

"I'd think your family would throw a party if you moved out."

"No. They said I made my bed and had to lie in it. My art doesn't make any money yet. At least, not enough to survive. I wasn't willing to give up this lifestyle. What would I do? Move back to the sticks in Modesto and live with my parents, become a maid for my sister?" Her body shudders. "Come, let me show you something."

She leads me to a small door off to the side of the kitchen. She flings open the door, and I spot a few steps going down, leading to utter darkness beyond.

My heart begins to race erratically. I was the one who found my father's body in the basement. When my mother came to find out what was taking us so long, she went into some form of shock, and the two of us spent the night on the floor with my father's body until my aunt found us the next morning. Ever since, I've had an unholy fear of basements and underground places. I don't do them.

After a few seconds, Annalisa flips on a light. Relief spreads through me. It's a garage. A red Ferrari flanks one wall. There is an empty space where Laurent must have parked his fancy car.

"I've become accustomed to a lifestyle that most men could not provide for me. This house. This car. Weekend getaways to Paris, London, the French Riviera. Do you understand?" She gives me a cunning look.

"Who gets this now? This place," I say, gesturing to the living room. "That car?"

"I'm listed as an owner on both." Annalisa turns off the light, closes the door, and returns to the living room. She settles back onto the couch and takes a sip of her wine. "After we started having problems, Sebastian never got around to changing that—or his will. I guess in that respect, I am lucky."

"Lucky? Or it makes you look like you killed him before he could cut you off. Did you know the police found a pair of lacy underpants in the car with his body?"

Annalisa has a look of nonchalance on her face and ignores my comment. "The police, of course, think I did it. They have been following me. They even came to the gallery last night. They can look for evidence, but there is none."

This woman has more motive than Catherine the Great. Well, it's now or never. I take a breath. "Did you kill him?"

Her eyes grow wide. I don't know if she plans on answering me or not because we are interrupted by pounding from the front of the house that coincides with a chiming noise that can only be a doorbell.

"It's probably someone from the police department," she says with a sigh, unfurling her legs and standing. "The detectives said they were sending someone over to talk to me again today."

If the cops are here, it's time for me to go. I stuff my notebook in my messenger bag as I follow her to the front door. The ceramic ashtray clinks against my keys in my bag. I wonder if the gift is considered graft or swag. I'm pretty sure it's against newspaper policy to accept it, but I don't make a move to return it.

Annalisa undoes the dead bolt. The door swings open, along with my mouth, when I see who is standing outside.

It is a cop. But not one I expected to see.

It's my boyfriend.

Chapter 6

"Hello, Sean," Annalisa purrs.

He doesn't say a word as we stare at one another.

"Oh, pardon me, Gabriella," Annalisa says. "Let me introduce you to Detective Sean Donovan."

Silence.

Annalisa must sense the tension because she adds, "Don't worry. He's not here to question me. He's here to help. He's my ex-boyfriend."

Ex-boyfriend? It takes me a second to process this information. When I do, I don't like the conclusion I come to.

"Gabriella, I saw your car out front. What are you doing here?" Donovan finally says. We lock eyes, ignoring Annalisa.

"Doing my job," I say, biting the words out. "I didn't know Rosarito police were involved in this case."

Annalisa is looking back and forth at us with one arched black eyebrow.

Donovan looks down for a second at his shoes, then rakes a

hand through his perpetually messy hair. "I'm not on duty." He looks past me, over my shoulder.

"I'll let you explain to Annalisa how we know each other."

Donovan starts to reach for me but drops his arm to his side as I rush past.

I gun my motor as I leave the neighborhood, not even glancing back at the house. I'm gripping the steering wheel so hard, my knuckles are white. Donovan didn't have a single thing to say about Annalisa Cruz the other night when I told him about Sebastian Laurent's death. Not one damn word. He sat there shoving mashed potatoes in his mouth, saying nothing.

Chapter 7

DURING THE REST of my day at the newspaper, I know in my heart that Annalisa Cruz is the girl who seduced Donovan away from a life of celibacy. He doesn't have many ex-girlfriends. She has to be the one.

When we began dating, Donovan told me that after his father died—in an effort to please his grieving mother—he'd considered life as a monk. Before he took his final vows, he met a Mexican-American girl who had come to visit her brother, a fellow monk, at the Berkeley monastery. He had consulted with a priest and, within twenty-four hours, packed his meager belongings and moved in with the girl. I had never known her name. And I was okay with that. I buy into the whole don't talk about your exes thing. But now I don't have a choice. Now I know. Her name is Annalisa Cruz.

When he told me this story last year, I couldn't wrap my mind around the fact that my sexy, tough, cop boyfriend had ever even considered life as a monk. The only part that made sense was when he explained that a girl had lured him away from that path.

The story has always disturbed me, making me jealous of a girl with such allure that she was able to change Donovan's mind—and the course of his life—within hours of meeting him.

Driving across the Bay Bridge toward home after work, I steel myself to talk to Donovan about it. He had today off work, and we had made plans to have dinner together at my place. Now that I know he spent part of his day off with an ex-girlfriend, I'm not really much in the mood to see him. But it will be worse if I show up at my place, and he's not there.

My apartment is in the heart of North Beach, the Italian part of town. My grandparents settled here when they came over from Italy. The landlady gives me a great deal on my tiny studio because she went to Catholic school with my grandfather. I am usually filled with excitement when I hit the streets of North Beach, with all the cafe tables overflowing onto the sidewalks and all the good smells and music, but today my heart is heavy.

Does Donovan's odd behavior and nightmares lately have to do with this woman?

Our bed is a battle zone because my sleep isn't that peaceful, either. I still have nightmares about the day I killed a man—waking up crying and frantically scrubbing at my face and hair until I realize in relief that it was all a dream and that Jack Dean Johnson's guts aren't coating my hands. I don't know if I'll ever get over killing a man. Even one as awful as Johnson.

At the time, I'd thought Johnson was the one who kidnapped and killed my sister, but it turns out Caterina wasn't one of his twenty-four child victims. Until I hunt down the monster who snatched my sister, I know my nightmares will loop on replay.

I pound up the stairs of my apartment building, trying to prepare what I'm going to say. I slam open the door of my apartment.

Donovan is sitting on my beat-up red velvet couch, holding a tumbler of bourbon.

"It's her, isn't it?" I cringe at my own words. It's exactly the opposite of how I had intended to broach the subject. I had coached myself driving home to be calm and rational—not a jealous girlfriend. So much for that.

I throw my bag down and slam the front door behind me. I gave him a key to my place about a month ago. Right now, I'm wondering if that was a mistake. "Annalisa Cruz is that girl—the one that you left the monastery for, isn't she?"

Donovan rakes his fingers through his hair before he lifts his head again. His look says it all. It's her.

"Are you still in love with her?" I'm not breathing, waiting for his reply. I turn away and lean over my chessboard on a side table, pretending to analyze my next move to send to my long-distance opponent, Tomas, in Ukraine. I'm pretending that my whole life doesn't depend on the answer Donovan is going to give me. The board blurs below me as I swallow and blink. *Die before cry.* It's my mantra.

I can't decipher the look on his face as he stands and heads my way. I brace myself. He's going to tell me he is leaving me for her. I know this is absurd. I know because of therapy that this fear stems from my father's dying when I was six and the irrational belief that every man I love will eventually leave me. But I'm frozen, waiting for his answer. Does he still love her?

"I still care about her," he says, "but I'm not in love with her."

Relief floods through me.

He paces my small studio apartment. "But I am going to help her. They want to pin the murder on her. The underwear they found in Sebastian Laurent's car were hers, she admitted it. They think she was"—he looks up at me—"pleasuring him in the car and that's why his clothes were off. They think she shot him and put the car in gear, sending it over the embankment."

"Sounds pretty plausible to me, especially now that I've met her and seen how warm and loving she is."

He ignores my snarky comment.

"It sounds like the evidence against her is pretty strong, even without their finding a gun, but I don't think she killed Sebastian Laurent. I can't let her take a murder rap."

I brush past him into the kitchen and slam cupboards around, hunting until I find my favorite rocks glass—an old vintage one with tiny gold stars. He says he doesn't love her, yet he feels compelled to be her knight in shining armor. I yank the vodka bottle out of the freezer, upsetting some frozen-chicken-noodle-soup containers. My studio apartment is tiny, stuffed with bookshelves and big plants, and that usually doesn't bother me, but right now, I'm not interested in being in the same room as Donovan.

"Maybe your feelings for her are clouding your judgment." I pour myself three fingers of vodka and take a large gulp that makes my lips tingle and sends a fiery trail of heat trickling down into my core. "She seems perfectly capable of killing someone to me."

"You don't know her." Wrong. Thing. To. Say. I storm into the bathroom and slam the door. It's childish, but it's the only place I can go to get away from him without leaving the apartment. Donovan knocks. I'm slumped on the floor near the door, staring at the chipped black, blue, and yellow mosaic floor. The 1940s tile is missing many pieces, but I refuse to replace it. I ignore Donovan's knocks a few inches away on the other side of the door, draining the vodka in my glass.

"Okay, that came out wrong," he says through the door. "I know Annalisa seems cold at times, but I don't really think she's capable of putting a bullet through someone's head. Don't get me wrong. She's no angel, but she'd rather manipulate the guy into doing it to himself. I just can't see her pulling the trigger."

"That doesn't mean she isn't guilty," I say to the door. "She could've paid someone. Did you know she stands to keep the multimillion-dollar home, a Ferrari, and God knows how much of a life-insurance policy?"

"That's why I think she might take the fall for it," Donovan says. I can hear that he is sitting on the floor on the other side of the door. "No alibi. Claims she was home alone asleep. Nobody can verify that."

I don't say a word.

Donovan clears his throat. "Ella, you have nothing to worry about." He slides something under the large gap under my bathroom door. I stare at it. But don't pick it up. It's a picture of us that my favorite photographer at the paper, Chris Lopez, took. Donovan and I are standing by some crime-scene tape talking. It's shortly after we got together, and it's obvious in the way we're looking at each other that we're already in love. I made Lopez print out two wallet-size copies. I kept one and gave the other to Donovan. I stare at the photo, my ear pressed against the door. Donovan stands, and I can hear his footsteps as he walks away.

I pick the picture off the tile and stare at it. He had me from day one. From the first second I saw him, I knew. I do some deep-breathing exercises my therapist taught me. Thinking of my therapy sessions makes me realize I'm overreacting.

He doesn't deserve my jealousy. That's one thing I've been working on in therapy—my flying off the handle. It's a constant theme. Okay, screw it. I'll try to handle this the "mature" way. I make the sign of the cross, crack open the door, take a deep breath, and try to sound as calm and rational as I can.

"What else they got on her?"

I don't meet his eyes but head to the kitchen to start making *pasta carbonara*. I fill my big pot with water, dump a small palmful of salt in, and set it on a burner. The bacon-and-egg pasta is Donovan's favorite. This morning before I left, I had promised to make it for dinner. He gets out the butcher-cut bacon, eggs, and cheese, acknowledging my peace offering.

"There's a string of domestic-violence calls to her address," Donovan says, beginning to grate the big hunk of *Parmigiano Reggiano*. "The most recent one was last weekend, neighbors called 911. They said they heard a woman screaming, 'Please don't kill me.' Annalisa told police Sebastian Laurent held a knife to her throat. He said she tried to push him off the balcony. He hung by his fingers but was able to haul himself back up while she hit his fingers with a fireplace poker. Annalisa's got a bit of a temper."

I remember Sebastian's Laurent's bruised and scabbed-over fingernails and knuckles.

"You think?" I add some red-pepper flakes to the bacon chunks sizzling in my skillet.

Donovan continues. "Sebastian Laurent apparently has—or *had* I should say—some type of pull with the SFPD because neither one was arrested in the incident."

Domestic-violence calls are a mandatory arrest in California with probable cause, and it sounds like cops had plenty of probable cause.

I fish a spaghetti strand out of the pot with a fork and test it with my teeth. It's almost *al dente,* so I nod at Donovan, and he starts beating the eggs with a whisk, adding in a ladleful of the hot pasta water.

LATER, WE'RE ALMOST finished eating when I remember something.

"Maybe it's not Laurent. Maybe it's her. Maybe the cops didn't arrest them because Annalisa has the pull." Twirling my last bite of pasta and taking a sip of my cabernet, I tell him what the news research department dug up this afternoon—a gossip-column photo showing San Francisco Mayor Adam Grant and Annalisa Cruz having dinner together a few months ago at a fancy Union Street restaurant.

Grant is a hotshot thirty-five-year-old lawyer who is being groomed for the White House.

"Cheating on her dot.com-millionaire boyfriend doesn't help her case, either," I say, hiding my smirk with my wineglass. "Or maybe it does. Let the mayor help her."

He ignores my comment.

"Doesn't look good," Donovan says. "Lot of circumstantial evidence, but there is definitely motive." He clears our plates. I head to the living room with the last of my wine. "She's going to need more than his help," he says. "I'm sorry if you don't like it, but she needs my help, too. It's something I have to do."

He means it.

Heat rushes into my face. He's drawn the line. Two can play that game.

Perched on the edge of my couch, I rummage in my bag and retrieve a crumpled pack of old cigarettes.

"I thought you quit," Donovan says, his eyes narrowing.

I pull Annalisa's naked-woman red ashtray out of my bag and

plop it on the coffee table. That shuts him up. I put a match to my bent cigarette, shaking it out with a flick of my wrist and tossing it across the coffee table, where it lands smack in the ashtray.

Donovan starts to say something. He stops when I lean back, put my feet on the coffee table, raise an eyebrow, and let out a long stream of smoke.

Chapter 8

THE NEWSROOM IS humming like a beehive this morning.

A new report from Cal Trans came out reminding everyone that until construction on the eastern span is complete, the Bay Bridge could collapse in the next earthquake that registers more than 6.0.

"Just great," says Rich Olsen, who is hovering by my desk. "I already do a Hail Mary every time I go across that bad boy. That's it. I'm moving to the East Bay. I'm not going to take my life into my hands getting to work every day."

He's from Minnesota.

I laugh. "I've been in about ten earthquakes, and I'm still breathing. You've got to play the odds, my friend."

"Screw that."

The replacement, which has been planned for decades, just started this year. Meanwhile, hundreds of thousands of commuters are driving across the span each day—some as nervous as Rich. The mayors of both Oakland and San Francisco are still taking cheap shots against one other about who was to blame for the delay, mainly caused by arguments over design and whether the bridge should have a bike path. Finally, the governor stepped in, and said, "Bay Area, get on with it already!"

But the mayors are still bickering. This time over some issues with the integrity of construction materials, whose fault it is, and how that might delay the project. Every television in the newsroom is tuned to the argument. San Francisco Mayor Adam Grant's smile, broadcast on the newsroom's wall-size big screen, is so large it seems a bit sinister.

Seeing Grant reminds me that I need to find out why he was having dinner with Annalisa. I'll go talk to Lisa Shipley, our longtime political reporter. I'd rather do that than figure out how I'm going to juggle covering two robberies, a four-car pileup on the 680, and a grass fire before deadline.

I welcome the newsroom chaos today. Today is the twenty-third anniversary of Caterina's little body's being found. It's horrifying that we don't even know the exact day of her death. Only the day some off-road bicyclists found her little body under a bush.

I ignore the tears forming at the corners of my eyes. I muted my cell phone when I woke this morning to avoid my mother's calls. As an added bonus, I won't know if Donovan calls, either. Good. I'm still irritated with him.

It's eleven thirty. My mom wanted me to meet her at the cemetery at noon. Well, I'm too busy to go. But I know I'm lying to myself. The truth is, I'm afraid. I pick up Caterina's picture from my desk. For years it was hidden in a desk drawer. Now it reminds me every day why I make those difficult phone calls to make sure every victim I write about is more than just a name in the paper. I kiss my fingers and gently touch the picture. With her dark hair and small pink lips, she looks like an angel.

"Lisa, what can you tell me about Mayor Grant?"

She's eating lunch at her desk. My stomach grumbles when a whiff of a half-eaten cheeseburger and French fries drifts up to me.

She answers in a staccato voice, still typing, without taking her eyes off her computer.

"From big money. Mother's family is East Coast, blue-blood royalty. Father's family descended from a San Francisco railroad tycoon. Think the Kennedys, but conservatives. Republican Party loves him. On fast track to the White House. Against gay marriage. But appointed several gay staffers. Walks right down the middle, which makes him a very viable presidential candidate for the GOP. Only thing holding him back is being single, but I heard that the plan is before the election, he'll find his dream girl. The spin doctors will use it to conjure a romance and engagement the likes of this country hasn't seen since Grace Kelly married the Prince of Monaco. He'll be like our own royalty—Princess Di will have nothing on him." She takes a breath and looks up. "How come?"

"Think he's capable of murder?"

She stops, shoves a fry in her mouth, and gives me a look over her huge round glasses. "He's a politician."

"I'll take that as a yes."

"Politicians will do nearly anything to get what they want," she says. "With that said, Grant is probably too smart to murder someone. You talking about Sebastian Laurent?"

I nod. "Maybe Grant wanted boyfriend out of the way? Maybe Annalisa Cruz is the girl he's going to woo and marry in front of the world. She's got the looks for it." I hand Lisa the photo of the couple having dinner.

Annalisa Cruz's hair is pulled back in a chignon, and she's wearing a slinky red dress—big diamond earrings dangle from her small earlobes. Grant is in a dark suit. The pair sits at a restaurant table bathed in candlelight.

Lisa gives the photo a fleeting look. "I heard about that, too, but that's par for the course in politics. And, trust me, Grant wouldn't have to resort to murder to steal another guy's girlfriend. You've obviously never met him. Want to?"

Lisa takes another bite of her cheeseburger, dips her frizzy black-and-gray hair, and flips through a stack of papers. Unearthing one, she hands me a letter on fine parchment paper with the seal of the mayor's office at the top.

She holds a finger up, asking me to wait as she finishes chewing her bite. Finally, I see her swallow. "I can't make it to the annual press-club dinner tomorrow night. Kellogg wants someone from the paper there. Call Grant's assistant and confirm. You'll get to see the mayor in action, and, at the very least, you'll get a good meal out of it."

I thank her and walk away.

"Giovanni," she calls after me. "Like I said, Grant has no problem with the women. Watch yourself. He's partial to brunettes."

Chapter 9

THE PRESS-CLUB DINNER is black tie. Crap.

"The women will be wearing formal, floor-length gowns and the men tuxedos," the mayor's press assistant says when I call to confirm.

"Gotcha." I hang up, thinking, what kind of people actually own "floor-length gowns" for crying out loud? Not reporters, that's for sure.

On Saturday morning, with the dinner in T minus ten hours, I realize I need help. I pick up the phone.

"Mama, want to go shopping?"

"I'm on the next BART train."

Just like I expected, she doesn't even mention the anniversary at the cemetery yesterday or that I've avoided her calls for the past week. I barely slept last night thinking of Caterina. I still wonder what triggered my mother's change of heart. It makes me uneasy, but I'm afraid to ask.

Today, as we shop at Union Square, my mother has slight dark circles under her eyes, and I wonder if she spent a sleepless night, as well. If so, only someone who knows her well would notice. She looks as stylish as ever in pressed jeans and a silky turquoise blouse. Her black hair is either in a tidy bun, or like today, a sleek ponytail. Her dark eyelashes seem even blacker with the slash of her signature red lipstick. She taught me *la bella figura*—the Italian philosophy to present your best self always—but I've always managed to bungle it. She's always had men flocking to her, but never remarried after my dad died. It was only after we kids moved out that she began dating another widower she's known since childhood.

Three hours of shopping later, I have a massive headache from trying on a variety of "floor-length gowns" in silver, gold, and black. I kept getting sidetracked by the frothy chiffon sundresses in pretty oranges, turquoises, and pinks that would go great with my new strappy stiletto sandals. Finally, I settle on a black velvet halter dress. It's modest in front but has a plunging back side and is formfitting without being clingy or revealing. I fork over a month's salary at my mother's encouragement.

"You look like an angel in that dress," my mother says over lunch at Scala's Bistro.

"Since when do angels wear black?"

"You know what I mean," she says in exasperation. "Donovan will drop to one knee for sure when he sees you wearing it."

I close my eyes and count to ten, so I don't explode. "Mama, please! Can you get off the marriage kick," I say, holding my hand up to my throbbing head and waving away the waiter who is trying to refill my wine. "Plus, he's not going to see me in this anyway."

"What? I don't understand." My mother's hand freezes, with a forkful of expertly twirled linguine-and-clam pasta halfway to her mouth.

"The mayor's dinner is for reporters, not cops. Donovan's not invited. Besides, he's up at his sister's house in Sacramento this weekend for his nephew's christening."

"He didn't invite you?" Her brow furrows. "Are you two having problems?"

"Mama, he did invite me, but I have to attend this dinner, so I couldn't go." A blatant lie, which fills me with guilt.

I ignore her question about us having problems. I don't know if we are or not. I *do* know I haven't invited him to stay the night at my apartment since I caught him swooping in to rescue his old girlfriend from a murder rap. I look away, pushing around my shrimp risotto so it looks like I ate more than I did. I'm not hungry. For a girl with an appetite like mine, that's saying something.

"I pray every day that someday you realize work is not as important as love," my mother says. "When you are on your deathbed, are you going to remember some horrible story you covered or the love you had with someone else?" She raises one eyebrow. I keep my face deadpan. "You have to be careful you don't lose this one because you put your job first."

"Donovan's different," I say, but flash back to the string of boyfriends who called it quits because of the demands of my job, including the one who did so on the morning of our wedding. Or rather, I broke it off but only because he told me he didn't want his wife to be a reporter.

"I hope so. He's a good man," she says, dabbing her lips with the big linen napkin. She waits until she has my full attention before she says what she does next. "And Ella, you are . . . getting older. If you want to have children, you may not want to wait too long."

I bite my lower lip and look away. What can I say? In a corner of the restaurant, several small children run and squeal, chasing one another around as their parents finish their meal. I can feel my mother's eyes on me like searchlights. I dip my head and rummage in my handbag for my lipstick. It's better than admitting what I feel deep down inside—that lately, I can't bear the thought of becoming a mother.

After lunch, I drive my mother back to her home in Livermore, in the East Bay south of Contra Costa County, where my newspaper is located. We pass by the cemetery. I sneak a glance at my mother out of the corner of my eye. She is sitting ramrod straight, staring straight ahead.

Chapter 10

THE FAIRMONT HOTEL was the first place Tony Bennett sang, "I Left My Heart in San Francisco" and is possibly the nicest hotel in the city. The beaux-arts-style massive white building sits atop Nob Hill. Tonight it is lit up in all its magnificence. I pull up to the valet stand in my beat-up old Volvo sedan. At least it's clean. I spent an hour vacuuming and waxing it.

Normally, I would've walked or taken the bus from my place. But I knew my dress would've provoked whispering from the older women on the bus. Tromping up the hills of San Francisco in black velvet and stilettos would've been absurd.

The valet, a boy with freckles and close-cropped hair, opens my door for me. As I get out, my sandal's spiky heel catches the hem of my dress, and I trip, falling right into the valet's arms. His face is as red as his uniform as he helps me regain my footing.

When I look up, it's my turn to blush. The mayor is a few feet away on the sidewalk, smoking. By the amused look on his face, he obviously saw the whole thing. Figures. Heading toward the door, I hold up the torn hem on my dress so it doesn't drag on the ground. I'll find a bathroom and assess the damage.

"Maybe I can be of some assistance," the mayor says, coming over and offering me his arm. "Adam Grant."

The jig is up.

"Gabriella Giovanni."

The look on his face is blank.

"I'm with the *Bay Herald*. I'm attending your dinner this evening."

"Aha! Well, then, how fortunate I had the chance to meet you beforehand," he says, taking my elbow and leading me inside. "Shall we?"

The doorman tips his hat as we enter. Grant leads me to the concierge's desk. "Ethan, Ms. Giovanni has had an unfortunate accident. Do you think we can fix her up?"

"Yes, sir. In a jiffy. I'll send housekeeping right over."

Grant leads me to a tufted chaise lounge nearby. "Sit. I'll keep you company."

"Are you serious?"

"Why, yes." He pats the seat beside him.

"Thank you. You've been very kind, but I can take over from here." The thought of him watching someone sew my dress is humiliating.

"Oh, I would be remiss if I left you alone here. I like to think my mother raised me better than that."

"But you're going to be late for your own dinner," I say, and glance at my watch.

"That's one of the perks of being the host now, isn't it? The party doesn't start until I arrive." He reaches into the inside pocket of his tuxedo and takes out a small phone. "Denise? I've been delayed a few moments, so can you keep everyone entertained? Maybe offer another round of champagne and aperitifs? Fabulous. And one other thing, can you do a bit of rearranging at the dinner table? I'd like you to move Gabriella Giovanni's seat so she's at my side. Thank you kindly." He snaps the phone shut.

"You didn't have to do that."

"It was my pleasure." I look away from his eyes, crinkled in a smile.

A woman in a gray uniform arrives with a needle and thread, distracting his attention from me. I sneak a peek at him while he's not looking. He has silky black hair and Elizabeth Taylor blue-violet eyes. Up close, his skin is lightly pockmarked, but this one small flaw makes him more attractive.

I thank the woman as she deftly mends the tear in my dress. She smiles but keeps her eyes on the fabric. When she finishes, I reach for my silver clutch, but Grant has already reached for her hand. I see a flash of green and what looks like a one with two zeros behind it. My face flushes. I was about to give her five bucks.

UPSTAIRS, A TUXEDO-CLAD waiter offers me a salmon canapé that I try to nibble at delicately. The bruschetta crumbles in my hand and I end up dropping a tiny flake of salmon down the front of my dress. The mayor has his back to me a few feet away so I turn toward the window and try to fish the pinkish flake out, but it slips deeper into the land of no return.

The dining room offers spectacular panoramic views from floor to ceiling of the Golden Gate Bridge on one side and the Bay Bridge on the other. I sense someone at my side and know before he speaks who it is.

"I argued with my staff about which room we should hold the

dinner in. They said the Venetian Room is more fitting, but I find it stuffy and ostentatious." I cast a glance to my side. Grant stares out the window as he speaks. "I prefer the Crown Room for its views."

Before I can agree, an assistant whispers in his ear, and the mayor leads me to my seat. Others in the room follow his lead. The meal begins with oysters on the half shell. I sigh with pleasure as I taste one. Grant watches me. I'm self-conscious under his gaze, trying to eat them in a ladylike manner.

"They say oysters are an aphrodisiac," he says, lowering his voice so nobody else can hear.

My face grows warm. I've already had two glasses of champagne and nearly forgot why I was here—to find out more about Mayor Adam Grant. *In case he had anything to do with Sebastian Laurent's murder.*

"Have you read any interesting books lately?" I change the subject.

"I have actually," he says. "I'm right in the middle of a few—Jimmy Carter's latest and *Stupid White Men* by Michael Moore."

"But you're a Republican!" I say, then regret it.

He laughs. "I'm also reading *The No Spin Zone* by Bill O'Reilly."

"Well, that makes more sense."

"I take it you're not a Republican?"

"Not even close. But don't tell anyone in my family." I splash some Tabasco sauce and squeeze some lemon juice on a fat juicy oyster. "They'd disown me."

"My lips are sealed," he says. "I think we can still be friends even though I presume you didn't vote for me."

I shrug, but he sees something on my face. "You did, though, didn't you?" He smothers a laugh.

He is poised as he tips the oyster shell up to his lips. His eyes never leave mine. I give a wry smile. "Yeah, I voted for you. We needed a change around here." Then I see my opening. "Plus for a Republican, you're surprisingly supportive of the arts."

"This *is* San Francisco," he says, taking a small piece of garlic bread to mop up some juice on his oyster plate. "I would be foolish not to support the arts, now wouldn't I?"

"Yes, but you are personally supportive, too, aren't you? I thought I saw a picture of you at an art opening last week. For Annalisa Cruz."

There it is.

He looks at me for a minute, and I catch the shadow of something flash across his face. "Oh, yes, Annalisa. She's a good friend of mine. We've known each other for years."

"She's quite a talented artist," I say, taking a sip of water but not taking my eyes off his face.

"Do you know her work?"

"I only just met her. I'm writing an article about Sebastian Laurent."

I watch him carefully. Nothing unusual crosses his face this time. Instead, his eyes grow somber.

"His death was a damn shame."

LATER, AFTER THEY'VE served dessert, I try again.

"You said Sebastian Laurent's death was a shame. Were you friends?"

"No, not at all," Grant says, pushing back his plate of raspberry torte and taking out a thin, silver cigarette case. He's obviously immune to the city's antismoking laws. A waiter materializes by his side with a crystal ashtray. I guess if you're the mayor, you can pretty much do whatever the hell you want in your city. But I think it is brave of him to light up in front of a group of reporters who all have the means to spread negative publicity. Maybe just arrogant.

He exhales before he answers. "Sebastian was the jealous sort and resented my friendship with Annalisa. Despite that, I don't believe anyone deserves to die a violent death."

"He was jealous of you? So I shouldn't interview you about my profile piece on him?" I eye his cigarette case, secretly sending him vibes to offer me one. He doesn't.

"Probably not, but my press office might be able to come up with a statement about his death and the loss to the community as a result. He brought a lot of business to the city with his company."

I nod. He changes the subject.

It's late, and everyone else has left. Grant and I have talked for hours about everything—except Annalisa or Sebastian Laurent again. I've run out of time and have nothing to show for my evening except some champagne and good food in my belly.

Grant walks me to the elevator. His staff members wait in the doorway behind us.

"I'll be right there," he tells them.

I press the DOWN button and turn to him, looking up into those blue eyes.

"It's been such a pleasure," he says, and gives me a slow smile that sends shivers down my bare arms. "I don't want it to end. I have an idea, and it might help with your story—do you have plans tomorrow?"

I blink. "Uh, the usual Sunday routine—Mass, then supper at my grandmother's house with my family."

His hand reaches out toward me, and for some reason, I hold my breath. A current of electricity zips between us. Our eyes meet.

Then his gaze drops, and I feel the slightest brush of his hand in the hollow beneath my neck as he pulls my necklace out of my dress and holds my Miraculous Medal between his fingers. It's light blue with a small silver etching of the Virgin Mary in the center. He caresses it between the pads of his fingers. His fingers grazing my neck combined with the suggestive gesture sends a thrill of desire through me that startles me and suffuses me with guilt.

"I saw this earlier and knew you were a good Catholic girl," he says. "Would you have to do penance for missing Mass tomorrow?"

I blush and look away.

"I'm sorry if I offended you," he says.

"You didn't," I say, looking up at him again. The moment is gone, and I feel a surge of relief, thinking of Donovan.

"Would your family be terribly heartbroken if you skipped this Sunday?" he asks, taking a deep drag on his cigarette. I notice it is a Dunhill blue, like Annalisa Cruz smokes. He exhales before he finishes. "I commissioned Annalisa a few months ago on a larger piece for my house in Napa. The installation party is tomorrow, and I'd love for you to be there. Have some wine, food, and fun."

I try not to hide my excitement. The chance to see Annalisa Cruz and him together is too good to pass up. Maybe, if one of them killed Sebastian, they'll let something slip. Maybe they were in on it together. I'm suspicious of his motives. Is he a player who hits on every woman he meets, or is his attention toward me part of a more cunning plan? Either way, I'm going.

"When you put it that way—I think my family would be okay without me for one Sunday."

The elevator door slides open, and I step inside, pushing the button for the lobby.

"Be sure to bring a swimsuit," he says. And then, right before the door closes, he winks at me, and says, "By the way—I wasn't at Annalisa's art opening last week."

The door slides shut. Busted.

Chapter 11

Beyond a black iron gate, I steer my Volvo up a long, winding driveway. The gravel road is flanked by olive trees and grapevines that snake up the yellow Napa hillside. Blue sky stretches forever.

What the hell am I doing here? I agreed to come last night but now feel awkward. I think back to dinner last night. There was something about Grant—a streak of intensity beneath his outward poise that sent a shiver of excitement through me. He has an element of bad-boy danger to him—breaking his own city's laws by lighting up that cigarette in front of an army of reporters, talking about how oysters are an aphrodisiac, reaching for my necklace and rubbing it somewhat suggestively. The memory makes a flush spread up to my ears. There is more to him than meets the eye. I remind myself that I am there to hunt for a killer.

Careful, Giovanni. Sure, he's handsome and charming, but so was Ted Bundy.

The dirt driveway meanders to a cluster of buildings. The main house—small white stucco with bright blue accents—looks like it was plucked off a Mediterranean hillside. Petal pink flowers in giant terra-cotta pots border the entryway.

The big wooden door swings open, and Grant himself comes to greet me. He wears beige linen pants, cuffed to reveal his ankles, and a shirt with the sleeves pushed up and the buttons undone halfway down his chest. His tanned feet are bare. He kisses me on each cheek.

"Come along. Everyone's out by the pool in back. I'll show you where you can change."

The murmur of voices drifts through the house from the back, along with a woman's tinkly laughter. I thrust a small box toward Grant. "Hope you like biscotti. My own recipe."

He eyes the box like a little boy and holds it up to his nose, inhaling. "I love biscotti. I can smell the anise. Thank you. But, I'm warning you—I'm not sharing. I'm going to hide these in the kitchen and eat them with my coffee tomorrow morning." He leans over to kiss me, and I turn my head, so it lands on my cheek.

For someone who has as much money as he reportedly does, he is either an incredibly great actor or has somehow managed to stay remarkably unaffected.

Remember Ted Bundy.

We make a stop in the kitchen. A corner of the countertop has a jumble of olive oils and spices in old glass bottles. A worn oak table still holds a jar of jam and crumbs from breakfast and the scattered remains of the *New York Times.*

Grant points me to a bedroom right off the kitchen. "Feel free to change in here. I'm ready for a swim, too. I'll meet you back here."

I close the door and pluck my six-year-old swimsuit out of my bag. I don't do the beach—at least not in a swimsuit—so although it's a little faded, the suit is still serviceable.

"I know I've kept you in a drawer for a very long time," I say to it, tugging it on. "But I promise if you be nice to me today, I'll take you out more often."

Luckily, there is a full-length mirror. The first thing I do is check my backside to make sure it is covered. I'm at my best weight in years, but no matter how thin I get, I've always got "back," as they say. It's the Italian thing.

Now I check the front? *Mama mia.* I'm not super excited about how small the white triangles seem right now. Should have brought my even older, black one-piece. Too late now. I wrap my towel around me and crack the door.

Grant is waiting with a big smile when I emerge into the hall. I pull the towel tighter around my chest. I sneak a glance at him. He has on a black Speedo. Jesus, Mary, and Joseph.

Somehow, over the past few days, I've been thrust into a foreign world where the men wear teeny, tiny European swimsuits. If I brought home a guy who wore a swimsuit like this, my Italian-American brothers would want to kick his tiny Speedo-clad butt.

"Can I take your towel?" Grant asks. I quickly shake my head.

He leads me past the kitchen. French windows reveal a backyard filled with small palm trees and a giant curving pool with at least two waterfalls. About two dozen people are mingling around the edges of the pool, some with their feet dipped in the water. Caribbean music is playing, and a light breeze brings with it the scent of barbecue and chlorine. I hear that laughter again and immediately recognize it and search for its source. Annalisa Cruz. Her back is toward me. She dips her head in laughter once again, and I see who has made her laugh.

Donovan.

Chapter 12

MY FACE GROWS warm. A woman in a maid's uniform hands me a glass of wine and whispers something in Grant's ear.

"Excuse me for a moment." I watch him walk away before I dart a glance at Donovan, feeling foolish. Acid fills my stomach, and I realize I am sick with jealousy seeing him with Annalisa. It is irrational, I know, but all I want to do is run away.

I wonder if I can sneak back through the house and out to my car without anyone's noticing? But Grant, who is standing at one of the French doors looking at me while he talks on the phone, is watching. Damn. He smiles at me and holds up his finger, gesturing for me to wait.

"Gabriella, what the hell are you doing here?"

Donovan grabs my arm. I jerk away. I didn't even see him walking up.

"I should ask you the same thing. Thought you were in Sacramento."

"That was yesterday. I stopped here on my way home." His eyes flash with annoyance.

"Funny you didn't mention it to me." I turn a little away from him, crossing my arms across my chest, and watch the other people having fun. I see a silky head bobbing in the water. Annalisa.

"Annalisa called this morning." He lowers his voice. "She's afraid. She thinks the killer might be targeting her. Someone called her last night, said he was looking forward to her party today. She was hysterical, worried the killer might show up here, so I told her I'd stop by."

"How gallant of you." I take a big gulp of wine and feel it hit my cheeks in a warm rush.

"Why are you here?" He stares at the people splashing and laughing in the pool. "Annalisa didn't say she had invited you."

"She didn't."

Grant appears at my side, slipping between the space I've made between Donovan and me. "Gabriella, I'm terribly sorry to have left you alone, but I see you have no problem making new friends."

Donovan's eyebrows lift in surprise.

Grant looks at Donovan with a perplexed look. "I'm sorry. I know we met earlier, but could you remind me of your name again?"

Now it's Donovan's turn to be pissed. He looks at me, as if he's waiting for me to explain our relationship. I'm too angry with him. If he wants to sneak around behind my back seeing Annalisa, I figure I don't owe him anything. We lock eyes. Slowly, I unwrap my towel and, without looking, hand it to Grant. Donovan's eyes sweep over my body in the skimpy bikini, and the muscle in his jaw clenches. The silence grows.

Grant frowns. "I'm sorry, your name was?"

Finally, Donovan looks at him. "Detective Sean Donovan, but you'll have to excuse me. I'm on my way out. I need to get back to the city."

"A detective? I hope there isn't anything wrong?" Grant says, his eyebrows rising. I see a glimmer in his eyes, a spark of what looks like defiance. Or a challenge?

"No, everything is fine." He grits the words out and turns to leave without a backward glance.

Grant has that same curious look in his eyes as he watches Donovan leave, but then he turns back to me, and it is gone. "Let me introduce you to some other people here."

He takes my arm and leads me through the crowd. The electricity from his touch shoots through me at the same time I'm trying to process a surge of anger and disappointment about Donovan. Why was he here, and why do I feel betrayed? It doesn't help to realize that Grant's touch is dangerously alluring. He idly runs his fingers down my forearm, sending faint tremors through my body. I try to subtly elude his grasp, but he holds firm.

Across the backyard, Annalisa takes in Grant's proprietary clasp of my arm with a frown as she climbs out of the pool. She maneuvers through the crowd, her tiny red crocheted bikini actually making my suit feel a bit matronly. We both are more than ample in the chest area, but if hers are real, I'll hold up the white flag.

When she is a few feet in front of me, I feel her glare before I see it. Slowly, she scrutinizes my body, from my bare toes to the tendrils of hair sticking to my temple in the heat. Her eyes narrow to slits. I meet her gaze, and, for a split second, I can almost see the daggers in her eyes, but the look disappears so fast I wonder if I imagined it as her teeth spread into a wide smile.

"Adam, you didn't tell me we had another guest," she says, grabbing both my arms as she kisses my cheeks, releasing me from Grant's hold. She knows exactly what she is doing. She pulls back, weaving her own arm through Grant's. Her head only comes up to his armpits. She presses her wet body close to him, slanting a glance at me. "Adam, did you scare Gabriella's boyfriend away? Sean seemed upset. Is something wrong?"

Grant looks at me. "Boyfriend?"

I ignore the question in his voice. "He had some urgent business back in the city. Important things. Cop stuff."

"Oh, I *know*," Annalisa says with a small smile. "I remember those days. Good God, that was so boring, having him leave in the middle of the night because work called."

She hits her mark. The image of Donovan in her bed sears my brain. I take a big gulp of my wine, so she won't see my reaction. But when I look up, I know I didn't fool anyone.

Grant laughs. "Annalisa, he's another one of your conquests? Your track record never fails to amaze me."

Her look sours. "He wasn't one of my conquests. He was my first true love."

That's it. "Excuse me. Where's your restroom?" I need to escape before I slap her.

"I'M SORRY IF I upset you." Annalisa is waiting for me outside the bathroom. "It's hard for me to see Sean with another woman. It's not that I don't like you. It's just that I've always assumed that one day we would get back together. I've always imagined us growing old together."

I say nothing. She looks forlorn. But I know she's a good actress.

"If it makes you feel any better," she says, turning to me with sad eyes, "he told me today that it would never happen."

I take a minute to process this. She reaches into a small bag and takes out a compact mirror and a tube of blood red lipstick.

"I'm not the first woman he's been with since you. He was married, after all."

"Oh, her," Annalisa laughs. "Teresa never was any competition for me. He would have left her for me in a heartbeat if I'd said the word. But I wasn't ready for him yet. I'm more mature now and ready to settle down." She pouts her lip in the compact mirror and takes a manicured finger to a small lipstick smudge. "Believe me, Teresa wouldn't have stood a chance."

She stops and looks right at me. "You, on the other hand, seem to have a bit more of a hold on him. And there's not even a wedding ring on your finger."

She sounds puzzled. I can tell that she is trying to figure out what it is about me that Donovan would prefer over her. This true-confessions thing is pissing me off. "Why are you telling me this?"

"Because I want us to be friends."

"I don't know if that's possible," I say with ice in my voice.

Her eyes widen as I walk out. She may be a viper—may even be a killer—but I'm Italian.

THE LATE LUNCH consists of a buffet of fresh seafood and fruit. People fill up their plates and find spots on lawn chairs or plop down on the grass to eat. I've tried to keep an eye on Grant and Annalisa without making it too obvious. For a while, they rough-house in the pool like teenagers. Grant keeps picking Annalisa up, holding her over his head, and tossing her in the water. She squeals with delight.

I don't know why, but I feel something that doesn't make any sense—jealousy. I feel like Grant threw me aside as soon as Annalisa walked up. It's absurd. I have a boyfriend. This is not a date. And besides, he could be a *killer*.

Maybe it's because Grant has one of those magnetic personalities. He's able to make you feel like you are the only person in the world that matters to him at that moment. It is so intense and flattering that it feels like something is missing when he directs his attention to something or someone else.

I strike up conversations with other people at the party, trying to find out more about Grant and Annalisa without making it obvious. Nobody seems to know anything about Annalisa beyond the fact that she is the artist being honored, but everyone talks about how Grant is a great guy. Donovan said Annalisa was fearful the murderer would show up at this party. But what if the murderer is the one hosting the party?

I feel bad about the way Donovan left, so I sneak into the house and dial him on my cell. He should be home in Oakland by now. His phone rings and rings, but his voice mail never picks up. This seems odd, so I redial his number. This time it goes straight to voice mail. I hang up without leaving a message.

When I come back out, Grant has Annalisa backed up against a wall in the pool, leaning in close to talk to her. She doesn't seem to mind one bit. Maybe they *are* in on it together. They're awfully cozy for a woman who just lost her live-in boyfriend. How convenient to have him out of the way.

Grant pulls Annalisa out of the pool and leads her to the patio. They seem deep in conversation, with Annalisa gesturing fiercely, casting a glance back at the pool.

I look where she is gesturing. At first, it looks like everyone is frolicking, swimming, or sitting on the edge of the pool as they drink, but then I notice a woman in a black bikini casting dark looks at Annalisa and Adam Grant. She's sitting in a beach chair, scowling and sipping on her drink. For a second, it looks like she's mumbling to herself. I had talked to her earlier, and she had dismissed Annalisa with a wave, saying, she'd never heard of her or her art, and she was only there because she was a longtime friend of Grant's. She went on to tell me how she was a famous interior designer who had "done" Grant's penthouse apartment in the city.

Now I give her a second look. Who said the killer had to be a man? A scorned woman could have seduced the pants off Laurent, shot him, and sent his vehicle plunging over the ledge. I'm about to go pull up the chair beside her when I notice another guy, a man with dirty blond hair and a rugged attractiveness.

It looks like he is paying too much attention to Annalisa, but it is hard to tell exactly where he is looking because his gaze is hidden beneath dark glasses. He stands out from the crowd because he's the only one dressed, and I don't remember seeing him here earlier. He's sitting with his feet in the water, wearing a tight T-shirt and rolled-up cargo pants. He has an intense look on his face, his lips clamped together.

After a few seconds, he says something to a woman in the pool directly in his sight line between him and Annalisa. The woman swims over and stands between his knees. He leans down and gives her a long kiss. He must have been staring at his date, not Annalisa.

I search the other faces, but nobody seems to stand out. What made Annalisa so agitated? I start to head over to the lawn chair, but the woman in the black bikini is gone. I search the heads in the pool but can't find her anywhere.

Grabbing a towel, I head toward the house, pretending to use the bathroom while I snoop for the black-bikini woman. The house isn't big, so I try every door on my way to the bathroom. Off the kitchen is a hallway with about five doors. All closed. I try the first one. As soon as I see the stairs leading down, probably to a wine cellar, fear spurts through me. I shut the door. No way.

All the other rooms are empty. Where did she go? When I come across the bathroom, I decide to take advantage of the facilities. When I come out, I fling open the door and scream.

The man from the pool in the dark sunglasses is standing there. He's Robert-Redford handsome with dirty blond hair brushed back and a strong jaw with a cleft in his chin.

A low chuckle erupts from his throat. "Sorry. Didn't mean to startle you. Isn't this the bathroom?"

I burst into nervous giggles. "You scared the daylights out of me."

He looks over his shoulder. "I'm surprised the whole party didn't rush in to see what was the matter. You've got some pretty good lungs on you."

Even though he wears dark glasses, I feel his gaze rake over me, taking in every inch of my bare flesh. It sends a shiver down my spine. I grab my towel from my arm and wrap it snugly around my torso.

He gives me a wry smile, the side of his mouth curling up. He takes a step closer, and I involuntarily shrink back.

"That's too bad. I was enjoying the view." His voice is low and seductive and sends a tremor through me. His body blocks the doorway. I swallow and look down.

"What's your name?"

"Gabriella."

He is silent for a moment, then steps to the side.

Rushing by, I barely catch his murmur: "Nice to meet you. I'm Mark."

NOT LONG AFTER, Grant asks for our attention. After everyone quiets, and a maid passes out flutes of champagne, Grant whips away a black velvet cloth to reveal a five-foot-long white marble sculpture on a huge pedestal. The art piece is much like the smaller ones by Annalisa at the gallery, but this one's a fountain. It features a voluptuous woman with long flowing hair leaning back with her back arched. The figure is lying on the edge of a pool of water, with one hand dipping into the water. It takes me a minute to figure it out, but the fingertips are resting on what looks like a whale's head emerging from the water.

"When I first met Annalisa, she told me a beautiful story from her childhood in Mexico that warmed my heart," Grant says. People grow quiet. "I asked her several months ago to bring that story to life in a sculpture for me, and I'm honored to unveil it today. And I'm honored that Annalisa is here to share that story again."

Annalisa moves to Grant's side.

"When I was a little girl, my mama told me this story," she begins.

"There was once a prince who set off to find the most beautiful woman in the land to marry. He found her in a palace near the sea. She only showed him her face once, then quickly covered it with her veil. He fell in love and wanted to marry her that instant, but her father, a wealthy merchant, demanded a large dowry, so the prince had to return home to fetch the gold.

Meanwhile, a gypsy girl who worked for the beautiful young maiden had been hiding nearby. When she saw the prince, she became enchanted and obsessed with him. That afternoon, the maiden went swimming in the sea. When she came to the shore, she asked the gypsy girl to comb her hair. While the gypsy girl was brushing the maiden's hair, she pricked her with a magical needle and turned the maiden into a whale. The whale rode out on the next wave.

The gypsy donned the maiden's veil and pretended to be her when the prince returned. After the wedding ceremony, the prince lifted the veil and discovered he had been tricked. He tried to get the gypsy girl to tell him what happened to his maiden, but she refused. The merchant father threw the gypsy girl in the dungeon, but she refused to speak.

That night, the prince had a dream. He dreamed that a giant, gray whale was calling to him. He couldn't shake the feeling, and the next morning he immediately set out to sea in the merchant's finest ship, outfitted inside as if it were a floating castle, with silver and gold and velvet and furs.

It took three days, but the prince finally came across a whale. A large gray one. When the ship drew near, the whale surfaced right near the deck where the prince was standing. The giant head came up out of the water, and the whale's big eye stared at the prince.

The deckhands shouted that the whale was possessed by the devil and tried to scare it away. But the whale stayed, staring at the prince. Even when deckhands grabbed harpoons and were about to spear the whale, it remained still, so the prince called off the attack. That's when he knew. It was his maiden.

From that day forward, for the rest of his life, the prince never again stepped foot on the shore. He stayed on the ship, so he could be near his true love. The whale never left the boat's side, and the two grew old together.

"They say the maiden whale still lives today," Annalisa continues, "and that those who are fortunate enough to see her will be given a special gift. If ever you see a whale, and it looks you in the eye, then you must immediately return to shore and go to sleep so you can dream."

"Or so you can do something else in that bed! I've seen your other sculptures," blurts out a red-faced, hairy-chested man who's obviously had too much to drink. A blond woman falling out of her swimsuit top giggles. He's broken the spell that Annalisa's story has cast, and the party erupts into nervous laughter and titters.

I'm surprised by how captivating Annalisa's story was and disappointed this buffoon interrupted her at the end. She's upset, too, and stomps off. Grant follows her to an area under the palm trees. He is rubbing her arms, talking, and leaning down to look into her face. Her eyes flash with anger.

Listening to Annalisa's story, I felt like I got a glimpse into a part of her that people rarely see—the deepest part of her—a part of her that maybe I could be friends with if she wasn't Donovan's ex-girlfriend.

Near the corner of the house, Adam Grant holds both of Annalisa's shoulders as if he's trying to calm her down.

Right then, a woman screams and points to the pool. The red-faced man is floating face down. Within seconds, a blur of color flies by and dives into the pool. It's Mark, the man with the dark sunglasses. Within seconds, he's pulled the larger man out of the pool and propped him on his side. He places his hands under the man's jaw and presses. Water dribbles out of the man's mouth.

Mark leans down and puts his ear to the man's mouth and nose. Then gently puts the man flat on his back and, holding the man's nose, begins rescue breathing. He stops and puts his finger on the man's wrist, muttering something.

The music has stopped, and the only sounds are a few whispers. Finally, after what seems like forever, Mark jerks up and turns the man's head to the side. The man vomits a pinkish neon froth, then begins coughing and trying to sit up.

People rush over with towels and a glass of water and soon I can't see the man at all. After a few seconds, the crowd parts, and leaning on another man's shoulder, the red-faced man heads to the side of the house down a path leading to the driveway.

Mark stands alone in dripping clothes.

I make my way over there.

"Nice work."

"Was worried there for a minute," Mark says. "He's lucky."

"Is he going to be okay?"

"He's headed to the hospital to get checked out, but yeah, I think so." He turns and smiles.

The blond woman Mark was talking to in the pool rushes over and wraps him in a big hug. "Thank God you were here!" Without a backward glance at me, she drags him off to a lawn chair near hers, where he strips off his wet shirt and rolls up the cuffs on his pants even more before turning his face to the sun.

Once everything has settled down, I realize I'd forgotten all about Adam Grant and Annalisa in the commotion. I glance over to where they had been standing.

They're gone.

I quickly slip through another door, winding my way through the house, with my towel clutched over my bikini. But I don't hear a sound. I tiptoe around the terra-cotta floors, trying to figure out which direction Grant and Annalisa went. Small drops of water drip from my hair onto the floor. I pause, listening. Nothing but the sounds of laughter outside.

Then, faint voices off the room closest to the kitchen filter out. I think that was the room where Grant said he was going to change earlier. On instinct, I grab someone's empty glass off the kitchen counter as I pass and creep to the adjacent room. Slowly, I crack the door. It's an empty bedroom, the one where I stashed my clothes among other people's totes and purses. I slip in and lock the door behind me. I press the glass against the wall, then my ear against the glass. Perfect. I can hear every word in the other room.

"Why would you bring him here? A police detective?"

"I was scared."

"You don't think I'm capable of protecting you?"

"You don't understand," she says. "He's helping us. He wants to prove I'm innocent. It's under control. He will do anything I say. Anything. Trust me."

"Why are you acting so skittish now? You must tell me what's going on? You were fine, and now you act like you've seen a ghost?"

Annalisa *had* looked frightened when she glanced at the pool.

"It's nothing. I just don't want to go back out there."

"I don't understand. It's your party."

"Please, please don't make me go back out there?" She is pleading. She sounds terrified.

"There, there." Grant's voice is soothing.

"Besides. I *miss* you," she says with a purr in her voice. "We can have much more fun in here, anyway. I can think of lots of things for us to do. Nobody will miss us."

I hear Grant's low laugh. Then silence. I wait, listening, with the glass starting to hurt my ear. Then I hear a moan.

"Oh God," I hear Grant say, groaning.

I am startled by the sudden turn in conversation, and my grasp on the glass loosens. It falls to the floor and shatters on the stone floor, the loud noise piercing the silence.

I freeze, pressing my ear against the wall, ready to bolt and hide in the closet. But the only sound I hear is the squeaking of bedsprings. I grab my clothes and sneak out to my car.

Chapter 13

THE NEXT MORNING, I'm the first reporter in the metro section. Kellogg's computer is on, so he must be here somewhere. My desk phone rings across the room, and I hurry toward it. As I pick up my phone, something catches my eye on the small television set suspended from the ceiling above my desk. Police cars and news vans in front of a familiar house—Adam Grant's Napa Valley home. Seeing the house sends a small shock through me.

The sound is muted. Every TV in the newsroom shows the same thing. Even the big screen, tuned to CNN, is broadcasting aerial footage of Grant's house.

The phone is up to my ear, but I forget to say anything. I'm reading the words scrolling across the bottom of the smaller TV hanging above the cop reporter's station. "Body found in Mayor Grant's home . . . police are scheduled to hold a press conference . . ."

It doesn't say if it was a man or woman. Annalisa? Jesus, Mary, and Joseph. Maybe she was telling the truth. I think of the woman in the black bikini who disappeared right before Annalisa and Grant went into the house. And I heard Annalisa practically beg the mayor not to make her go back outside. She'd seen the killer, hadn't she?

I distantly register a voice calling my name from the phone at my ear. In the background, I hear the crackle of the police scanners on the desk nearby. I focus on the voice on the phone, which is becoming shrill. "Hello? Is anyone there? Gabriella?" It's the receptionist at the front desk.

"Sorry. I'm here."

"There are some police officers here to see you."

At her words, my face feels tingly, and a ripple of dread rolls across my scalp.

Chapter 14

MY VOICE IS wobbly and my hands are shaking as I lead the officers into the big conference room off the reception area. They introduce themselves. Harry Gold, an older man with a stain on his checked blazer and his belt pulled up over his belly, is a detective from Napa. Jack Sullivan, a wiry man with thick lips and close-cropped red hair, is a San Francisco Police Department investigator.

"Is this about Adam Grant's house?" I'm so nervous I spit out the words without thinking. They are here because they knew I was at his house yesterday. How did they know?

"Who's dead? What's going on?" I ask.

"That's what we're trying to figure out," the redheaded cop says as he pulls out a chair at the big conference table. "Why don't you start by telling us about your visit there yesterday."

Of course, I think. They want my help. I sink into a chair across from him.

"Can you tell me who . . . the body is?"

"We'll get to that," the older detective from Napa takes out a small pocketknife and starts cleaning under his nails. "First, tell us about your visit yesterday."

I briefly summarize how I met Grant at the press dinner and was invited to his party. I get more detailed when I start talking about my time at his house. I stammer when I get to the part about eavesdropping. The redheaded detective who is leaning forward with his elbows on the table and his fingers steepled in the "power position" gives the other cop a look. It's subtle, but I realize my hesitation is sending up a red flag with him. At the same time, I realize they aren't talking to me because they think I'm on their side. I try to explain.

"I was trying to find out something about Annalisa Cruz and Adam Grant and maybe"—I decide just to spill it—"figure out whether they had anything to do with Sebastian Laurent's death—the guy found dead last week, the dot.com millionaire?"

They give me blank looks. The older cop is now pushing his cuticles back without looking up, just nodding at what I'm saying every once in a while.

"Keep going," the redheaded one says, tapping a finger on the table. Don't these guys take notes? Their offhand demeanor makes me flustered. I wonder if that's their intention?

"I was in that bedroom, and I was kind of . . . well, I was trying to listen in to their conversation."

"What did you hear?" the older cop asks without looking up from his grooming.

"The mayor seemed angry that Annalisa had brought a detective to the party. That's my boyfriend, Sean Donovan, he's a Rosarito cop —" I trail off.

"Is that it?" The redheaded cop lifts an eyebrow. His fingers stop tapping.

"Well, actually, they started, um, doing some more private stuff, so I, um, left."

"You left?"

"Went home."

"What time was that?"

"Probably six o'clock."

"Did anyone see you leave?"

"No, I sort of snuck out," I say. "Now, can you tell me what's going on?"

The older cop tucks his pocketknife away and stands.

"We're going to need you to stay in town for a while," the redhead says casually and locks his gaze on me.

Need you to stay in town for a while.

The redhead stands and holds the door for me. I start to walk away and turn back.

"You haven't told me who the victim is."

He gives the other cop a meaningful look.

"Who is it?" I nearly whisper the words. I wait for him to say Annalisa's name.

"Adam Grant."

I feel the blood drain from my face, and my entire body is bathed in a chill that sends tremors down my spine. Adam Grant? He was so charismatic and vibrant, it is hard to imagine his body lifeless. The cops walk past me and turn without saying good-bye, leaving me standing in the doorway watching their backs.

And then the realization strikes me—the police think I murdered the mayor of San Francisco.

Chapter 15

BACK IN THE newsroom, everything seems surreal, as if I'm dreaming or hearing everything from underwater. Reporters are filtering into the newsroom. The volumes on the smaller televisions have all been turned up. Pictures of Adam Grant flash over the screen—pictures of him with Annalisa. Also, pictures of Annalisa with Sebastian Laurent.

The TV coverage cuts to a blond woman spilling out of her low-cut top. A diamond pendant dangles in her cleavage. She's standing in the doorway of a home with giant pillars. TV reporter: "Candace Davenport was at the pool party yesterday."

That's where I recognize her. Although we didn't talk, she was hard to miss, falling out of her strapless swimsuit top and giggling, always with a big froufrou drink in her hand.

"My husband, Jeffrey, and I left around five thirty so we could get home and get ready for our dinner party. We had the board of the San Francisco Opera over for our annual planning meeting . . . my maid gets fresh scallops, oh sorry, well anyway. It's such a shame. The mayor is such a nice man." She starts to get teary. "I mean he was. What is our city going to do without him? I don't know why he was hanging out with that woman, anyway. I mean, it's like she's a Black Widow. Her boyfriend died last week, now she comes to the mayor's house, and he ends up dead, too."

The reporter cuts back to the newsroom.

"That *is* an odd coincidence," the anchor says to the reporter.

Hell yeah it is. The cops are wasting their time with me. They better be questioning Annalisa. Black Widow is right. I can't figure out why Annalisa would kill both Sebastian Laurent and Adam Grant, but that doesn't mean she didn't do it. What would she gain from Adam's death? She practically gave motive for Sebastian's death at her house, showing me how she didn't want to give up her luxurious lifestyle. My thoughts are interrupted by the reporter's voice on the TV.

"We'll stay on top of this story and let you know what else we find out. The police are holding a press conference at the Napa house at ten, and we'll be sure to get all the details for our viewers."

I stare up at the TV hanging from the ceiling, frozen, unable to move.

"Until then," the anchor says, "we'll be cutting to national news. Our correspondent is at the White House interviewing the president about the death of San Francisco Mayor Adam Grant. As many people know, this is not only a sad day for San Francisco, but it is a sad day for the Republican Party. Mayor Adam Grant has long been thought of as the Republican Party's next hopeful. He's even been dubbed "President-in-Training." It's going to be a political blow for them to lose this promising candidate."

Small groups of reporters are gathering in front of the big-screen TV that takes up one wall over by the photo department. When the news cuts to something about the Bay Bridge, I make my way over to my desk, trying to avoid meeting anyone's eyes. My phone rings again.

"Holy shit!" It's Nicole, the courts reporter for the newspaper, based in our Martinez office. She's my best friend.

"Yeah." My voice sounds like it is coming from a long way away.

"I can't believe the mayor of San Francisco was whacked! It's on every station, CNN, BBC, everywhere. The judge called a recess because nobody in the courtroom would shut up. He kept banging his gavel, and people kept talking. I'm sure he's back there in chambers watching it himself. Oh, gotta go, it's Phil on my other line."

Phil is her editor. She hangs up before I can tell her what happened—that police just questioned *me*. When I place the phone back in its cradle, her words finally sink in. She's right. This story is huge. International news. And I was there. Right at the heart of this huge story. I can't help it, but as a reporter, it sends a thrill through me. At the same time, I'm chilled that the charismatic man who rubbed my arm yesterday is now dead. I barely knew him but was intrigued by him. It stung to hear Nicole use the word "whacked," but that's what we do in this business—gallows humor, I guess. Something that helps us deal with the horrors we cover, making light of death at times, using words like "offed" and "decomp" and "stiffs" like we aren't talking about someone's husband or son or father. Or sister.

I remember with a jolt that the cops actually think I might be involved. I shake it off. I must have imagined the way that one red-headed cop looked at me. Me? A suspect? That's just plain crazy and a waste of time. They must be crossing their t's and dotting their i's. But why did they tell me to stay in town? Maybe they say that to everyone they talk to on a case? I'm not sure. That's something I should ask Donovan.

My heart sinks, realizing we are still in a tiff. He hasn't called since I saw him at Grant's house. I rummage through my bag until I find my cell phone. I haven't missed any calls. He was so intent on defending Annalisa Cruz. What does he think now? Can he defend her now?

Maybe the police will tell us more at the press conference. I look at the clock—it's only eight thirty. I can make it to the press conference in Napa if I speed. I grab my bag, a new notebook, and my jacket before someone touches my elbow. Kellogg.

"Gabriella, you can't cover this one."

"What?"

"You were there. You can't cover this. Especially since the police questioned you this morning."

He knows I was there? He knows they talked to me—and he called it "questioning." Mother Mary. But still. That doesn't mean I can't do my job. "You're kidding, right?" I say, digging for my keys. "This is the biggest story the paper has seen in a year, if not longer."

"I realize that, but you can't cover it. I'm sorry. I'm sending May."

May is the night police reporter. We used to be sworn enemies—she was after my job. We patched things up after she got moved to the education beat. Even though I don't particularly like her, she's a good cops reporter, so I went to bat for her, and Kellogg moved her back to night cops.

I stand still. Keys in my hand. "But I was there . . . you said it yourself," I say. "We'd be foolish not to use what I saw yesterday. I was *at the house*." I think fast. "I can write a first-person account of the party and everyone and everything I saw until I left. Nobody—nobody else—will have that."

Kellogg scratches his beard, and his eyes narrow to slits. He nods slowly. "You're right. But you're still not going to Napa. Let's talk to Coleman."

AN HOUR LATER, Greg Coleman—the publisher—and the newspaper's attorney have given the okay for my story although the attorney is going to review it before it runs.

I write up a first-person account of my time spent with Adam Grant, much like what I told the cops this morning, but I leave out the part about my eavesdropping and the details about Donovan. I begin with meeting Grant at the press dinner and end with my leaving the Napa party without being able to say good-bye to him because he had gone into the house. I don't say he went into a bedroom with Annalisa Cruz.

When Greg Coleman reads it, he orders Kellogg to edit all but one small mention of Annalisa Cruz—that it was a party to unveil her art piece. I had forgotten about Sara Stephens's telling me Cruz had the red phone to our publisher. What the hell? Kellogg argues that he can't censor the story like that. Coleman won't back down. Kellogg huffs and puffs and mutters threats to quit under his breath, but then calms down and settles into his desk. In the end, Kellogg makes me do the changes. Lame. I'm furious. Annalisa's name is all over the TV news, but we can only say one small sentence about her. I don't get it.

MAY COMES BACK from the press conference with a few new details. Grant died from a single gunshot wound to the head. *Same as Sebastian Laurent.*

Because it was such a high-profile murder and Napa is a small, sleepy-wine country jurisdiction, San Francisco Police offered mutual aid, making the murder a joint investigation, May says. That explains why detectives from two different agencies visited me this morning. I was so stunned I didn't even realize how odd it was that they were from different cop shops.

Police were questioning all ten of the guests who were still at the party that afternoon when Grant disappeared into a bedroom, May said. That fills me with a tiny bit of relief. I wonder if they told everyone else to stay in town, as well? Or just me?

According to the public-information officer at the press conference, most guests left after a maid told them the mayor wasn't feeling well and had gone to his room. Annalisa left not long after, the maid said. I quickly figure out that besides Annalisa, I might have been the last person to see Grant alive.

I try calling Annalisa's house. No answer.

Hearing about the cops questioning all the remaining guests reminds me that I forgot to mention the woman in the black bikini to the cops. She was giving Annalisa looks to kill. But now that I think about it, how do I know she was looking at Annalisa? She could as easily have been shooting daggers at the mayor. Plus, she disappeared right before Annalisa went into the house. I rummage around in my bag looking for the business cards those detectives had given me, telling me to call if I remembered anything.

Before I can find them, my desk phone rings.

"Giovanni."

"Is this the Gabriella Giovanni who had a sister taken?" a gruff voice asks.

My vision closes in, and my heart begins pounding in my throat. I hit the RECORD button on the tape-recording machine hooked up to my phone.

"Yes."

"I got some information about that."

"What do you mean?" I grit my teeth.

"Just got out of the can and heard some stuff, you know," he says. "I'm no saint myself, but it ain't right to do something to a kid."

"What's your name?" My hand, holding a pen and hovering over a scrap of paper, is frozen.

"That's not important, but if you want to meet, I can maybe tell you more."

"Where? When?" Nothing will stop me from meeting this man.

"Berkeley Pier. Wednesday morning. Nine o'clock."

"Fine. I'll be there. How will I know you?" A surge of excitement courses through me. This man might know something about Caterina's kidnapping.

"I'll find you."

I'M ABOUT TO log off my computer later when my cell rings.

It's Donovan. I'd been so busy writing my first-person story, I hadn't had time to worry about him. Seeing his number sends a wave of relief flooding through me, but I'm still nervous when I answer, saying a meek, "Hi."

"I would've called earlier," he says. "But I've been tied up. Was at SFPD. Detectives wanted to find out if I saw anything when I was at Grant's house yesterday. Hear they asked you the same thing. I guess Annalisa told them we were there."

I don't even question how he knows this. We both are pretending like we didn't have a tiff yesterday even though I kept my cell phone nearby all night last night waiting for him to call. "They told me not to leave town. What does that mean?"

"Several witnesses said last time they saw Grant, he disappeared into the house with Annalisa." He pauses. "And that you disappeared close to the same time. You two were the last ones to see him alive."

"I know. That's bad, isn't it?" I don't wait for him to answer. "Donovan, I got a call. From a guy who says he knows something about Caterina."

"Does he sound legit?" Over the past year, once it became public knowledge I was hunting for my sister's killer, I've received my fair share of crank calls about her. Some freaks. Some psychics. All dead ends. But nobody who has asked to meet me in person.

"He sounds sane if that's what you mean. I'm meeting him at nine Wednesday morning at the Berkeley Pier."

"I'll drive," Donovan says.

There is a long silence.

"Working late?" he asks.

"No."

"Why don't you head over here after you get off."

Chapter 16

A<small>FTER WORK</small>, I drive straight to Donovan's apartment on the shores of Lake Merritt in Oakland.

I'm still a little bit irritated about finding him swooping in to rescue Annalisa in Napa. I know what my therapist, Marsha, would tell me. I can even hear her soothing voice in my head: "Don't run away. Talk to him about how you feel. Tell him you are jealous and feeling insecure."

See, that's the part that kills me. Admitting I'm jealous of Annalisa goes against every fiber of my being. But, I know it's probably the right thing to do. Marsha's advice is engraved in my head—I can't truly love unless I make myself vulnerable. My track record of running away instead of facing my emotions hasn't gotten me very far over the years.

The sun is setting by the time I park in front of Donovan's place. All his lights are off. I knock for a few minutes, but nobody answers. I grab my phone and punch in his cell number.

"I'm outside your door," I say when he answers.

"Sorry, should've called. I lost track of time. I'm at St. Joan of Arc's down the street. Come on over."

What's he doing? Confessing his sins? I peer down the road, and two blocks away, I see the white church overlooking the lake. When I get there, the front doors are locked.

"Over here." Donovan is standing over to my left on top of stairs that lead to the rectory. "I want you to meet someone."

Inside, an elaborate chandelier lights a giant painting of the Virgin Mary. Donovan takes my coat and hangs it on the antique mirrored coatrack.

I look at him with a question in my eyes.

"This way." He takes my arm and leads me up carpeted stairs. I pull away, and he gives me a look. I'd planned on settling in at his place with some wine and maybe some make-up time in the bedroom. And instead, he asks me to come to church? Why didn't he tell me he was going to Annalisa's party yesterday? Is he trying to avoid that conversation?

At the top of the stairs, we enter a room lit by a roaring fire in a giant fireplace. To my left is an elaborate mirrored bar built into the wall. Dozens of sparkling crystal glasses—from rocks glasses to champagne flutes—line its glass shelves and reflect the firelight.

A man rises to greet me from his plush armchair.

"Ah, it is the lovely Gabriella Giovanni," he says with a thick Irish accent. "I've heard so much about you. I am thrilled to finally make your acquaintance."

The man looks to be in his early forties, with a thick head of hair swept back from his sparkly eyes. He reaches over and gives me a kiss on each cheek, European style.

"I'm Father Liam Allegro," he says, and heads over to the bar. "Please call me Liam. Can I offer you a drink? Sean and I are having bourbon."

This guy doesn't mess around.

"That sounds lovely," I say. "You have an Irish accent, but your last name is Italian?"

"My father is from Italy," he says, turning his back to pour my drink. "He was working in Ireland when he met my mother at the bus stop. Needless to say, he never made it back to Italy. Please have a seat."

I give Donovan a questioning look, and he pats the couch beside him. I perch on the edge. He rubs my back through my shirt. I'm still perturbed. What are we doing here?

"I've been telling Father Liam about Annalisa and these murders," Donovan says.

I try not to roll my eyes. Does everything have to do with that woman? Can we not mention her for two seconds?

"The reason I wanted to talk to Father Liam is because he knows Annalisa. But more important than that, he's not only my priest—he's my friend—and I need his advice."

Father Liam hands me my drink.

"You know Annalisa?" I take a sip of the fiery liquid that warms me to my core.

"Yes. Donovan and I have been friends for years. He came to me when he was a monk and met Annalisa."

"Were you a priest then? You don't look old enough to have been a priest that long ago."

He chuckles. "I had just begun my priesthood. In fact, the congregation jokingly called me 'the boy priest' behind my back."

"Were you the one who told him to leave the monastery for Annalisa?" I try not to sound hostile, but I hear an edge of bitterness in my question.

"Annalisa is possibly the most physically beautiful woman I've ever met," he says. "But sometimes the most beautiful people on the outside become ugly very quickly when you see what they are like on the inside."

Oh brother. Even the priest has something to say about her looks. Enough. And it hasn't passed by me that he's expertly avoided my question. I've cracked tougher nuts than him. I repeat my question.

"Were you the priest who told Donovan to leave the monastery?"

His eyes glint merrily. "Ah, I forget I'm talking to a reporter. No, I did not tell him that. But I did tell him to listen to his heart."

Donovan said he'd come here for advice.

"Did you give him that same advice today?"

"I can see why you're good at your job," he says, laughing.

"I'm sorry," I say, finally softening. "I'm having a hard time with Annalisa's intrusion into our lives."

Father Liam nods as he takes a seat in an upholstered armchair by the fireplace, hitching up his jeans delicately. His jeans are Armani. I spotted the label when he turned. They have neatly ironed creases down the middle. He is wearing Italian leather loafers and a light blue sweater. Cashmere?

"Let's say he helped me clarify a few things," Donovan says. His eyes are mischievous as he grabs my hand and kisses it. He's not usually so affectionate in public. I think I like it.

In the distance, the doorbell rings. Father Liam doesn't move an inch. I wait for him to get up to answer the door, but he reclines even farther back. Off to one side of the parlor is a study, lined with books and a big wooden desk. A small CD player with big speakers is piping Vivaldi into the room. I lean back and relax, as well, nearly forgetting about the doorbell until I hear voices downstairs and boisterous laughter. Donovan and Father Liam get up to greet three men who walk into the room.

Introductions are made. They are all priests. Father Liam fixes them drinks.

"Gabriella, we usually don't have women sit in on our poker night, but you're welcome to stay," Father Liam says. "We start the game in about half an hour."

I remember that occasionally Donovan has said he was playing poker with some friends, but I never knew it was with a bunch of priests.

"Oh, no, thank you. As soon as I'm done with my drink, I'll be going."

"Yes, good idea," says Donovan, smiling and rubbing my arm. What's gotten into him? While I like it, I can't help but feel a little wary of him being so lovey-dovey since the last time I saw him, he stormed away in a fury.

"Liam! I brought my *Lord of the Dance* CD," says one of the priests.

"No, no, not tonight," Father Liam protests.

I raise my eyebrows at Donovan. He shrugs.

"Come on. Dance for your friends," another priest says.

"No, they don't want to see an old man dance."

I laugh. I somehow can't picture the dignified priest dancing in front of a group. Or dancing at all, for that matter.

But the other priests won't let it go. Interspersed between conversation about books, movies, and tales about Ireland, they continue to egg him on.

One young priest with a mop of curly black hair turns to me. "Have you seen him dance?"

I shake my head.

"Liam, are you going to deprive this young woman of entertainment at your residence? I thought you were a better host than that."

Father Liam shakes his head, but then Donovan prods him. "I, for one, want to see this. Come on, for an old friend?"

"I suppose if I don't, I'll never hear the end of it," Liam says in a fake-annoyed voice. His wink and smile to me betray him. "Well, I would never refuse a lady. What is your desire, Ms. Giovanni?"

Without a second of hesitation, I answer. "I'd love to see you dance!"

The priests erupt in hoots, and one walks over to the CD player. The room grows silent. Donovan looks at me in expectation.

The music begins, then, in front of the fireplace, with the flames behind him, Father Liam begins to dance. Arms flat at his side and eyes closed as he feels the music. His feet are a blur of tapping and movement, Irish dancing. I realize my mouth has dropped open, and my eyebrows must be up at my hairline. I don't even turn to see how Donovan is reacting. I can't take my eyes off the dancing priest. The spell is broken when the song ends, and Liam opens his eyes and bursts into laughter. The room erupts in applause, whistling, and hollering.

"Wow." I can't find any other words. Donovan is sitting beside me, grinning idiotically.

"Father Liam used to compete with Michael Flatley in Ireland, before he got the call," says the priest with the black curls.

Of course he did.

Not much later, we say our good-byes and walk back to Donovan's house. Despite my initial irritation, I had a great time at the rectory and hope Father Liam meant it when he said he'd have Donovan and me over for dinner soon.

Instead of the sidewalk, we cross the street to the walking path that circles the lake. Donovan holds my hand, swinging it and whistling. Instead of leading me home, toward his place, he turns and takes me to the end of the lake that is set up like a small Greek amphitheater. He leans against a smooth white porcelain pillar as we look out into the night. The lake is circled with strings of fairy lights, and the downtown Oakland skyline twinkles across the lake. A warm night breeze lifts my hair off my neck and sends pleasant chills down my spine. Gently, Donovan cups my chin in his hand and turns my face toward him.

"Gabriella, after I talked to Father Liam, he helped me figure some things out." He pauses and takes a breath. I swear he's acting nervous, and this sends butterflies fluttering about in my stomach. "I have to confess something to you."

Here it comes. Did he cheat on me? I hold my breath, waiting.

"As you know, my first marriage had some difficulties. When I marry again, I'm going to do everything I can to prevent those problems from cropping up again. Before I met you, I wasn't even sure I ever wanted to get married again. "

His voice is starting to waver. Get married? My stomach, already gurgling in apprehension, does somersaults. *Holy Mary, Mother of God. He's going to propose? Not here. Please. Not here. Not now.* I don't know why the thought sends waves of panic through me, but it does. All I want to do is run away. I quickly try to stop him before he says the fatal words. Or does something like get down on one knee. I speak fast.

"Don't you think maybe this is something we should talk about later? It's been a rough couple of days for us. Things have happened really fast, and, frankly, I'm still trying to get over being angry with you."

He steps back. I see a glimmer of disappointment in his eyes before he looks off at the downtown Oakland skyline. A flock of geese waddle up on the grass nearby, making loud, honking noises.

"You're right," he finally says. "We should probably head back to my place. We can have this conversation another time." He puts his arm around me. He probably thinks I'm gun-shy because I was engaged before. But that's not it.

I know I should feel elated, like any normal woman would if the man she loved was about to propose to them.

But I don't.

A big invisible rock slowly settles into the pit of my stomach.

Chapter 17

LAST NIGHT, AFTER we got back to his place, Donovan and I kissed and made up, as they say. It was what I needed. No thinking. Only feeling. He told me not to worry about the police questioning me, that it was just standard procedure. I was filled with relief, and every bit of jealousy and anger oozed out of me.

This morning, I feel a renewed sense of hope about our relationship and know that Annalisa is no threat to me. He loves me. And Holy Mary, Mother of God, I think he was about to propose as we walked by the lake. I make a note to call my therapist. I need to talk to her about the panic and irrational fear that shot through me when I suspected that was about to happen.

When I get to the office, I make my cop calls, checking in with all the police and fire departments on my beat.

As soon as I hang up from my last check, my desk phone rings.

"This is Harry Gold, from Napa PD."

"Hi, Detective," I say. "What can I help you with today? Got an arrest in the Adam Grant murder to report?"

I know I'm verging on cheeky, but the warning for me to stay in town rubbed me the wrong way. And besides, Donovan says I have nothing to worry about. It's Tuesday, two days since the mayor was murdered. I bet the cops are starting to get a little desperate. "No, no," he sounds distracted. "Just wanted to go over a few things with you again."

"Right now?" I say it with a huff. I hear the rustle of papers on his end.

"If you don't mind."

"Fine, I was meaning to call you, anyway."

The rustling stops. "Is that so?" He waits.

"Yeah. I remembered something sort of fishy."

He remains silent.

"It was this woman. She was giving Annalisa Cruz and Adam Grant looks that could kill. And she was sort of talking to herself, mumbling, like she'd sort of gone off the deep end. I thought maybe I'd go talk to her and see what her story was, but when I turned back around, she had disappeared."

Gold clears his throat. "Disappeared?"

"Couldn't see her anywhere in the backyard."

There is silence as if he is thinking about that or taking notes.

"Could you describe her?"

"Possibly. I wasn't very close."

"Okay. We'll come back to that in a sec. Let's go from there. You said you followed Adam Grant and Annalisa Cruz into the house?"

I tell him again how I couldn't find them at first, then heard their voices coming from a bedroom. I know I'm being terse, but I have no intention of making this easy on him. He's wasting his time. I've told him about the suspicious woman, yet he still wants the focus to be on me and what I did.

"And then what did you do?"

Good Lord, I'm going to have to say this out loud in the newsroom? I lean down, ducking my head below the top of my cubicle wall. "I picked a glass off the kitchen counter and went into the adjacent bedroom."

"And then it says here you were listening in by holding the glass to the wall?" I can feel my face growing warm.

Just then, the hulking form or Kellogg appears above me. He leans on the wall of my cubicle. Shit.

"Yes." I hold up a finger to Kellogg, who is holding a sheaf of papers.

"Do you think that glass will have your fingerprints on it still?"

"No. It fell to the ground and broke." I shrug at Kellogg.

"Did you clean up the broken glass?"

Now I feel like a loser. "No. I was in a hurry to get out of there."

I hear him draw in a breath. "And why were you in a hurry again?"

I let out a loud sigh, and I know my voice shows my exasperation. "Because I didn't want to get caught." My voice catches on the word *caught*. "Caught *eavesdropping*. It's not something I'm proud of."

Kellogg's eyebrow rises, and he walks away. *Thank you,* I mouth silently to his retreating form.

Gold is silent on his end. Is he waiting for me to fill the awkward silence? I fiddle with the cord on the phone. I can outwait him.

"Can you describe that woman you say disappeared?" He says "disappeared" like it's in quotes, and he doubts my words. I give him a description, as vague as it is—pretty, shoulder-length brown hair, average weight, average height, black bikini. I don't think it narrows anything down much.

He clears his throat when I finish. "Okay, then, I guess that is all for now."

"Don't you want to ask me if I saw anything else suspicious?"

"Uh, yes, sure. Did you see anything suspicious?" He parrots back at me.

"No," I say, and hang up.

KELLOGG SEES ME hang up and meanders back to assign me a story—an obituary—about a prominent Mexican-American defense attorney who has died. The story is interesting. The lawyer actually talked a judge into sentencing a former gang member to college instead of prison for a theft conviction.

I'm relieved I have a story to keep me busy today, to keep my mind away from the meeting I have tomorrow with the man who says he knows something about Caterina's kidnapping.

After I spend the day talking to a few judges, Mexican-American groups, the attorney's family, and the reformed gang member, who is now an attorney himself, I file my story, feeling good about my day. It's gone fast. I've barely thought about tomorrow's meeting with the man who knows about Caterina—the meeting that could give me the answers I've been waiting for my entire life.

Chapter 18

TONIGHT, DONOVAN IS working late, so I'm going to make a yummy dinner, change into my pajamas, pour a glass of wine, and curl up on my couch with a good book. After work, I cram my old Volvo into a parking spot a few blocks from my place, grab my market basket out of the trunk, and head for Columbus Avenue. I stroll the streets of North Beach, past people eating and drinking at the sidewalk tables.

"Gabriella!"

It's Gino, one of my grandfather's oldest friends. He sits with a bunch of other Italian men from that generation. The sidewalk cafes of North Beach are their own social club. It's comforting to know I can find these men here nearly every weeknight at this time.

"*Facciamoci un aperitivo!*" Gino says, gesturing to a plate of appetizers and inviting me to join them. "Sit down and eat. Maybe you need a Negroni! *Scusi, cameriere,*" he starts to call the waiter over despite my protests. "Eat! *Mangia! Mangia!* Look at her"—he gestures to me, looking at his friends—"nobody likes a skinny Italian girl."

They grunt in agreement.

I laugh and lean down, kissing Gino on both cheeks. "*Perché no?*" Why not? I've got time. I shrug and pull out a chair. And I need something to take my mind off my meeting tomorrow about Caterina.

BY THE TIME I leave Gino's table, I scratch the idea of making dinner. I'm full drinking beer and munching *antipasti*. It was fun talking to the old neighborhood guys, and it's always good to brush up on my Italian. It helped me push back thoughts about my meeting in the morning with the man who might have something to tell me about Caterina. I look at my watch. Still early. It's going to be a long night. I realize now that I will go crazy sitting on my couch reading. I'm too restless and anxious about the meeting tomorrow morning.

I need a distraction. Maybe a game of chess? Although I play a long-distance game with Tomas, sometimes I need a fast-paced game. Market Street is just the place for it.

Thirty minutes later, I'm down on Market and Powell Streets in my baggiest jeans, a hoodie, and a stocking cap pulled low over my eyebrows. It's my uniform for the game. Trash litters the sidewalk, and noisy buses, vehicles, and streetcars are the sound system for the line of tables flanking Market Street. Nearby, a man wearing a Sherlock-Holmes-style hat is playing the saxophone. I drop a few quarters in his case as I pass. Even though it's warm out tonight, another man stands against a pole wearing a puffy down jacket down to his ankles. He's sporting a fur-lined cap. I don't make eye contact.

A red-and-orange streetcar screeches to a halt nearby as I take a seat at one of the dozen rickety blue tables painted with green-and-white chessboards. My back is to the street. I face the big window of an old-fashioned beauty shop. Women sit under hair-dryers talking animatedly. To my right, another row of tables has canvas chessboards duct taped to them. I dig in my jeans pocket for two dollars.

"Natasha!" says Georges, the Bulgarian who runs the games. "I've got the perfect opponent for you. New guy." Georges leans in and lowers his voice. "I don't think I like him. I wouldn't mind seeing him lose."

I nod. Down on Market Street, other than saying, "check" or "checkmate," I don't speak. When Caterina was murdered, I didn't talk for six months. My uncle tried to coax me out of it by teaching me chess. It worked. After clamming up for months, the first word out of my six-year-old mouth was "check" one day when I lost myself in the game.

Georges started calling me Natasha after I'd been playing down there for a year without talking or volunteering my name. I like the anonymity of being a chess player on Market Street. It's the place I go when I don't want to think anymore and need an escape. Right now, all I can think about is my meeting in the morning. It even overshadows Adam Grant's murder and the fact that the cops are questioning me about it. But I have to relax. I'm not meeting the man until tomorrow. Twelve hours away.

Three games later, I've won fifty bucks from the new guy, a New York stockbroker who just transferred to his company's San Francisco office. The sun has dipped behind the business district's sky-scrapers, and the shadows have brought a chill with them. I nod my good-byes. I'm tired, so I hop the bus at Chinatown instead of walk. A little girl, around four, sits across from me. Her big black eyes are round with mischief, and she sings a little song to herself. I can't help but smile at her, but she ignores me—singing and swinging her little legs in their ankle socks. She isn't paying attention and nearly misses her stop. Her grandmother has to reach back and grab her, scolding her in Chinese.

I'm walking up the stairs in my apartment building when Nicole calls to fill me in on the Grant story.

"The D.A. told me off the record that he heard Napa isn't even close to identifying a suspect in Grant's murder."

A wave of relief sweeps over me. I knew they couldn't possibly be looking at me seriously.

"What about Annalisa? Did you ever find anything on her?"

"Not much. Her trail goes cold before she started dating Sebastian two years ago. As far as the mayor's murder, yeah, her name came up, but they've got nothing solid on her. She's one of several people they're looking at."

"Nothing on her except the fact that Grant died the same way her boyfriend did—single bullet to the head."

"Gabriella?" Uh-oh. Something in her tone makes my mouth suddenly dry. "The real reason I called is to warn you. Apparently, *your* name came up, too. The D.A. said he would bet his last dollar you had nothing to do with it, but some San Francisco detective's got a hard-on for you."

Donovan told me it was standard procedure to question me? Must be that arrogant little redheaded putz. He's obviously got something to prove. But I'm a dead end. It's natural for some cops to hate reporters, but that doesn't mean he would seriously try to pin a murder rap on me. That'd be stupid. And a waste of time. I remember what Nicole said first—no suspects—nothing solid on anyone.

"They questioned me at the newsroom and called me again today."

A trickle of anxiety surges through me as I say these words. I close my eyes. Ever since Annalisa entered the picture, things have gone from bad to worse. "Why would they even consider me a suspect?" I finally manage to ask.

"Someone told the cops you were acting jealous at the party," Nicole says. "They said there was some kind of argument between you and Annalisa, and it was over the mayor."

"What?' My stomach sinks. There was no argument, but I *was* feeling irrationally jealous. That sliver of truth sends a shiver of apprehension through me.

Nicole went on. "The theory is that you and Grant were an item, and when you found out he was seeing Annalisa on the side, you offed him."

"That's ridiculous," I say.

"Tell me about it."

"I have a boyfriend."

"No shit."

"I just met him Saturday, for Christ's sakes."

"Uh-huh."

"That theory won't hold water."

Nicole doesn't answer. I wait. The silence stretches on for several seconds. My stomach roils with fear. I ignore it. There is nothing a cop—even one who was out to get me—could find that would pin Grant's murder on me. Nicole clears her throat.

"Gabriella, they're looking at someone else, too—Donovan."

Her words make my breath catch in my throat.

"I don't understand."

"It doesn't make any sense to me, either," she says. "I'll try to dig up more on that. They really clamped down because he's a cop, though."

"Thanks."

They are looking at Donovan? Isn't it absurd for detectives to nonchalantly look at another cop for the murder? There's no evidence whatsoever. I mean, isn't there some unspoken code to protect the blue line or something? Why would they so quickly look at him? It doesn't make sense.

I brush away these thoughts and fall asleep thinking about the meeting the next morning. That man might have the answers I've waited for my entire life. Surprisingly, instead of dreaming about Caterina, like I so often do, I dream of a whale—a big gray one that keeps flipping its tail out of the water. I'm chasing it. In my dream, I'm on an air mattress, of all things, and no matter how hard I paddle, until I'm panting with exhaustion, I can never catch up. It always remains out of reach.

A few hours later, pounding on my door awakens me. I glimpse at the clock—5 A.M.

"San Francisco PD."

I throw a robe over my silk chemise before opening the door, squinting at the two men in uniforms before me.

"I don't understand. I already talked to some detectives today—yesterday."

"Don't know nothing about that, ma'am," the one cop, who has a crew cut and bulging muscles, says. "We were told to escort you down to the station."

Nicole's info was good. Some dickhead detective does have it out for me. Well, good luck with that. I'm not some naïve young woman who is going to be intimidated by some punk cop.

"Am I under arrest?"

"No, ma'am."

I think about that for a second. I've got nothing to hide. I'll go. If something I saw, or know, helps them find Adam Grant's killer, I'm willing to talk to the cops again. But I'm calling a lawyer first—just in case.

Chapter 19

RUSSELL TROUTMAN MEETS me at the station. I only called Donovan's cell phone twenty minutes ago, but somehow the defense attorney beat me to the cop shop. Donovan sounded distracted, saying the attorney would be waiting at the police station. He seemed in a hurry to hang up, saying he was in the middle of something and that he'd meet me at the station. With the cops eyeballing me from my doorway, I didn't realize until later that Donovan didn't seem surprised by my call.

Troutman, who, with his bushy white beard and square-framed glasses, looks like a mall Santa Claus on a diet, gives me a friendly smile when he introduces himself. His pin-striped suit is rumpled. When he sits, I spot one brown and one black sock.

I look around, but Donovan is nowhere in sight.

Even though Troutman is friends with Donovan's family, I'm a little surprised that Donovan called in such a heavy hitter to sit with me. Troutman is a top-notch defense attorney who gained a reputation after he got a famous Bay Area restaurant owner acquitted for first-degree murder despite the man's having confessed under oath to killing his business partner. I don't remember what Troutman's argument was, but I do remember people were shocked when he won the case. Since then, he's had several other victories in the courtroom that have made the record books.

"Nice obit on Rodriguez today," he says, shaking my hand. "He was a lawyer's lawyer, that's for sure." His other hand has a rolled-up copy of our newspaper. He's not only been awake, he's had time to read the early edition. Huh.

"Thanks."

He leads me into what looks like a boardroom. Inside, a long table and several chairs fill up the room. The only window is a long one next to the door that leads into the hallway. At least it doesn't look like the sterile rooms that suspects are questioned in on TV, and there's no big mirror with cops on the other side watching. It smells like coffee, making me instantly crave a cup. I grab the chair farthest away from the door and plop down in it. Troutman sits a few chairs down and turns his chair toward me.

"We have a few minutes to talk before the detectives come in. Why don't you tell me when you first met Adam Grant?"

"Is this place bugged?" I eye the walls and ceiling.

"This isn't one of those rooms where they can record you. You're good."

If there was a big wall of black glass, I wouldn't say a word, but there's not.

I lean back and tell Troutman everything I know—even before I met the mayor, in case any of it helps. I begin with Sebastian Laurent's body being found and how it led me to Annalisa, and how the picture of her and the mayor led me to Adam Grant.

Troutman takes notes, doing a lot of grunting but not saying much, except asking a few questions to clarify, such as "What time was that? What day was that?" and so on.

Finally, we are done, and we still sit, waiting. Silent. Troutman leans back and opens his mouth wide, cracking his jaw. I shoot him a startled glance, and he immediately closes it.

"Sorry. It's been a long night," he says with a grimace.

I yawn widely, forgetting to cover my mouth.

"Want some coffee?" he asks, and stands. I nod eagerly. His hand is on the door when I ask the question that has been nagging at me.

"Do you think they have anything on me? I mean, I didn't do anything, so how can they call me in for questioning like this? Isn't it against the law or something?"

"They're grasping for straws. It's best just to cooperate. Tell them what you told me, and you'll be fine."

"I already did. Apparently it wasn't good enough."

Troutman nods and leaves.

A few minutes later, he's back with two cups of coffee.

"Donovan's waiting for you in the lobby."

I start to stand.

"We better stick here in case they come in. He said he's going to run an errand and will be back in a bit. Sooner we talk to them, the sooner we can all go home."

"Can Donovan be in here when they talk to me?"

Troutman shakes his head.

Later, we've both made headway on our coffee and are still waiting for the detectives. Is this some form of torture? A form of interrogation? Making a suspect wait until they are so crazy they'll confess to anything?

Troutman taps his fingers on the desk, then rifles through his notepad.

It is now seven in the morning. I am fidgety and anxious. I'm supposed to meet my source—the guy with info on Caterina—in two hours. I cross and uncross my legs. I adjust the cuffs of my shirt. I chew my lip. I start nibbling on the Styrofoam coffee cup, leaving a circle of little bite marks around the edges.

I didn't do anything, but just being here makes me feel guilty. Of what I don't know. At this point, I'm ready to confess to the lip gloss I shoplifted in third grade. I turn to Troutman, who seems calm and patient. I guess I would feel the same way if I were being paid by the hour to sit and wait.

Finally, at seven thirty, I can't help it and say something. "What the hell are they doing?"

"Not sure," Troutman says, flipping through a yellow legal pad. "I told them we needed time alone since we hadn't spoken yet. I think that didn't sit well with them, so now they are going to retaliate by making us wait. By the way, when they question you, if you're not sure whether to answer or not, look at me, and I'll step in. Since we have time, why don't you go ahead and tell me everything you told me before. Tell me again. I'll refer to my notes as you are speaking"

So I repeat it. For the fourth time in as many days.

When I finish, I'm tired, irritable, and frustrated. I get up and start pacing. "They can't seriously think I had anything to do with Adam Grant's death? This is ludicrous."

Finally, the door opens. Sure enough, it's the same two detectives who questioned me at the newspaper. That punk, redhead, Jack Sullivan, and the older one from Napa—Harry Gold.

"Miss Giovanni," Sullivan says as if he's being polite, but it comes out sounding like an insult. Detective Gold gives me a nod, which somehow seems so respectful in comparison.

"I guess my story was so scintillating you wanted to hear it again?" I say, kicking my feet onto the table. Troutman gives me a horrified look, so I immediately swing my legs to the floor and feel my face flush. Lack of sleep is getting to me. I better pull it together. This is a *homicide* investigation. Those two words sober me up.

"I didn't mean to be flippant. I'm just really tired and have a meeting in a few hours, so if we can get this started, I'd be happy to answer your questions."

Harry Gold whips out a small tape recorder and plops it on the table. "Don't mind if I record our conversation, do you? My memory isn't as good as it used to be."

Out of the corner of my eye, I see Troutman give a nearly imperceptible nod of approval.

"Fine."

Gold presses record and begins, giving the time and date and names of everyone in the room before clearing his throat.

"Okay, Ms. Giovanni, sorry to keep you waiting. If you could, please start again when you first met the mayor on Saturday night."

I go into the whole embarrassing story of how I met the mayor after ripping my dress and end with me driving away from the mayor's Napa house. Again, I avoid anything personal about Donovan.

They stop me a few times to ask clarifying questions, much the same way that Troutman did. I try to stifle a yawn and slump farther down into my seat.

When I finish the part about leaving Grant's house, Sullivan asks me where I went from there.

"Home."

"Did you see anyone when you got home?"

"I live alone."

"Did anyone in your building see you that night or did you go out later?"

I shake my head no. Sullivan stares at me for a long moment. I stare back.

Are they baiting me with the silence? Hoping I'll be uncomfortable and blab that I killed the mayor? I probably have as much interview experience as they do. I can wait them out. Or better, I'll steer the conversation the direction I want, like asking them about the *real* suspects.

"So, did your partner here tell you what I said about the woman in the black bikini?" I direct my question to Sullivan. He stares at me like he's trying to figure me out. Then he shoots Gold a look.

The Napa detective clears his throat. "I'd like to ask you a bit about your boyfriend, Sean Donovan."

"What does he have to do with any of this?" I sit up straight. I saw the look Sullivan gave Gold. They did the handoff. Bad cop, good cop. Sullivan is the bad cop. Gold is the good cop, the one who is supposed to be "my friend," the one who I "want" to talk to. It's utter bullshit.

"How did you meet Mr. Donovan?"

"Detective."

"Excuse me?"

"He's a detective. Detective Donovan."

Sullivan actually rolls his eyes. I cross my arms across my chest. Now, he's starting to piss me off.

"How did you meet Detective Donovan and when did you meet him?" Gold says.

Troutman nods that it is okay for me to answer.

"We met on a story. He was the lead detective in the Jasmine

Baker case—that missing little girl last year—and I was writing about it for my paper. I still don't see how my relationship with him has anything to do with the mayor's murder."

I know my attitude is not making friends, but at this point, I could care less. All I want is to get the hell out there. And wipe that ugly smirk off Sullivan's, face. If he's not looking smug, he's covertly looking at my chest, which I try to hide by pulling my jacket tighter.

"And did you know when you met him that Annalisa Cruz was his ex-girlfriend?"

"No." I grit the word out.

"When did you find out that Ms. Cruz and your boyfriend had a previous relationship?"

I lean my head back until I'm staring at the ceiling and the close my eyes, exasperated.

"Miss Giovanni?"

I keep my eyes closed.

"Gabriella?" It's Troutman.

I open my eyes and bring my chin back down. "Last week."

"What day?"

"Thursday."

"How did you find out that they had a previous relationship?"

Oh my God. Are they going after Donovan through me? I wait, thinking fast. What do I say? I don't want to say I found out because Donovan showed up at Annalisa's apartment.

I give Troutman a beseeching look. "Can we talk for a second?"

I figure asking this makes me—and Donovan by default—look guilty, but I need to consult with Troutman. I'm terrified of saying the wrong thing.

Both men push their chairs back, Sullivan stretches and yawns before he very slowly pushes his chair back in and saunters toward the door.

"The recorder, gentlemen." Troutman doesn't miss a beat.

Sullivan winks. "Whoops. I forgot." He leans over and hits the STOP button.

Sure he did.

"I'm sorry," I say to Troutman as soon as the door clicks shut.

"No, that's the right thing to do. You need to ask me if you have questions."

Chapter 20

As SOON AS the door slams shut, I tell Troutman my concerns—I don't want Donovan to look bad—or like he is in cahoots with Annalisa, God forbid. I talk quickly. It's already eight fifteen. I have to leave in the next half hour to get to my meeting at the Berkeley Pier on time.

Troutman bites his lip for a minute, thinking.

"I think that Sean's showing up at her house offering to help shows his good character, so you spin it that way. Tell them that your boyfriend is the kind of guy who will go out of his way to help old friends," he says.

"They'll know I'm 'spinning' it, as you say."

"True. But if this did—and this is a big if—ever go to trial, we can refer to this interview and use that in our case."

My face grows warm with the realization that a trial is even a possibility. I don't even ask whether he means my trial or Donovan's. Nicole said Donovan's name had come up in this investigation, as well. I swallow and nod. Eight thirty comes and goes.

The detectives are taking their sweet time coming back into

the room. Are they doing that to try to wear me down? Taking smoke breaks? Having breakfast? Whatever they are doing, I'm beyond irritated.

At five to nine, my irritation turns to anger. I'm going to miss my meeting with the man at the Berkeley Pier unless I leave *right* now. It might be my only chance to meet with this man who claims to know something about what happened to Caterina. Instead, I'm stuck in a grimy interview room answering idiotic questions.

I pace. "Do I have to stay here? I'm not under arrest am I?"

"Let's be cooperative for now. But when they come back in, I'll tell them it's over."

I sink back into the chair. What the hell has that redheaded cop got against me? I think he hates me because I'm a reporter. Plain and simple. And maybe because I'm dating a cop. I've infiltrated their inclusive little world. Nicole said the cop had it out for Donovan, too. That's probably why that cop hates Donovan, too—for dating a reporter. It's not the first time I've seen this.

One of my worst experiences dating Donovan was when he invited me to a birthday party for a fellow officer. The cops had rented a union hall for the party. When I showed up on Donovan's arm, everyone stared. All the cops' wives' glances toward me might as well have been daggers through my heart.

The worst part was that so many cops I considered friends acted like I was invisible. They sat there with their wives and brushed off my attempts at normal conversation, even going so far as to walk away. These cops, my good sources, whom I talked to on the phone daily, pretended like we'd just met. I was furious. Wimps. Every last one of them.

And forget trying to be nice to the wives. My efforts to strike up a conversation were ignored. They acted like they didn't even hear me and started talking to each other about something else. It was humiliating. Even though I came on the arm of a cop, I was a pariah.

A reporter! Who dared to dress up for a party by wearing high heels instead of loafers! Treason! There was one wife who was nice to me. Unlike the other wives, she wore a slinky dress, and her laughter could be heard throughout the room. Everyone loves Claudia. She's friends with all the cops *and* their wives. At one point, she took me aside and whispered drunkenly in my ear, "Oh fuck those bitches if they don't like you. I think you're swell."

I'll be forever grateful to her.

The door opens, and the detectives walk in. I push back my chair so forcefully it tips over. Troutman grabs my arm.

"Listen, I'm out of here," I say, shrugging my jacket on. "I'm missing a very important meeting."

"I'm sorry, miss," the older cop, Gold, says. "We think a murder might be a little more important than any appointment you might have. Time is of the essence. There's a killer out there, and it's our job to stop him."

"Or *her*," adds Jack Sullivan, giving me a nasty smirk. He presses RECORD on the machine and continues his questions. Troutman gently puts his hand on my arm, and I sink back into my seat, feeling the frustration and anxiety and anger boiling up inside me. I jiggle my leg and tap my fingers on the table. I need to get the hell out of here. Before the man leaves the pier.

The clock strikes nine. I still have a sliver of hope. Maybe if I leave right now, the man will still be there waiting. I fidget in my chair as they think up more inane questions to ask me. Troutman holds up his palm to calm me. It doesn't work. Going over what I've already told them three times. I stand and pace, refusing to sit down again.

By nine thirty, when they finally are done, I know it's too late. I wouldn't make it to the Berkeley Pier until ten. And that is if there is no traffic. Which, of course, is highly unlikely. If I speed, and there's no traffic I could maybe, maybe make it an hour after I was supposed to be there. Nobody, especially a wary source, would wait that long.

"I told you everything I know yesterday." I say, glaring. "Why don't you just find the woman in the black bikini? Why don't you concentrate on talking to Annalisa Cruz? She saw him last, not me. I'm sure her DNA is all over him."

Troutman places his hand on my arm. "Only a few more minutes, love," he says, and turns to the detectives. "My client is right. Unless you have another question to ask right now, it's time for her to leave. She's been here long enough."

"We'll decide what long enough is, pal," says Sullivan in a huff.

Troutman remains unruffled. "Unless my client is under arrest, I see no reason for you to keep her here any longer. She's been extremely cooperative and done everything she can to help you in your investigation."

Harry Gold, the detective from Napa, gives the other cop a look, and says, "Okay. Thank you. We'll be in touch."

"I hope not."

And just as quickly, they both leave the room. I'm free to go.

DONOVAN IS WAITING in the lobby.

"Good Lord! I thought that would never end. I can't believe we missed the meeting. I'm *furious.*"

"I thought about going anyway," Donovan says. "But it probably would've scared him off if you weren't there."

"Yeah, he seems skittish. I can't believe they think I had something to do with—you know . . ." I say, trailing off when I see other people in the lobby staring at me. Troutman shakes his head in warning.

But Donovan knows what I mean.

"They've got nothing. Don't worry."

I nod. I hope he's right.

"I need to get to work."

He wraps his arm around me. I shrink into the embrace, relief seeping through me. I'm not in this alone. Still, anxiety surges through me. *I was just questioned by detectives in a murder case.* I scream it inside my head. Jesus, Mary, and Joseph! I need something to tamp down the fear and nervousness coursing through me.

"Can you please take me somewhere to get a drink?"

He raises his eyebrows. I glance at the clock. Not even ten.

"How about some caffeine?"

At the door, we both shake Troutman's hand.

"Thanks for coming," Donovan says.

"No problem, but I'm not sure they're done with her," Troutman says. "You're going to have to find another attorney next time—if there is a next time," he adds, seeing my startled expression. "Otherwise, it might be considered a conflict of interest."

His words don't really sink in until we are in Donovan's small Saab.

"Wait a minute, what did he mean conflict? He's representing Annalisa Cruz?" Did Donovan bring him in to help his ex-girlfriend, too?

"No. Annalisa hired some high-powered Los Angeles defense attorney."

Donovan turns away as he maneuvers out of his parking spot.

"So what's the conflict of interest?"

"He's already representing me."

Apparently, the San Francisco police were being kind waiting to question me in the morning. They didn't give Donovan the same consideration. They hauled him in at midnight and were finishing up with him when I arrived. That's why Troutman beat me there. He'd been there all night.

Chapter 21

I WANT TO go back to bed, but instead, I order a triple shot of espresso at my favorite North Beach cafe, kiss Donovan goodbye, and head to work. Once there, I finish my story on Sebastian Laurent. I'd been waiting to talk to his family, but nobody has returned my calls, so I'll have to run the story without their comments. Which sucks. His family swooped into town from France, had him cremated, and left town with his ashes. No memorial service. Sadly, my big story on him is now old news in light of the mayor's murder.

Adam Grant's murder—and its repercussions—will take up the bulk of this Sunday's front page. Four reporters in our newsroom have been assigned stories on Grant. I don't tell Kellogg I was called in again for questioning, so he's still letting me write a story about the mayor as a person, not a politician. Lisa's got the political angle.

Maybe if I don't say that I was brought in for questioning out loud, that big leaden weight in my stomach will go away faster. Every time I think about this morning, an adrenaline shot of fear races through me. I quickly shake it off, reminding myself that the cops are desperate, but that doesn't mean they can find anything to make a murder rap stick. Because there's nothing there. You can't arrest someone for murder without solid evidence, right? At least that's what I've always believed covering the cops beat. But what if I'm wrong?

And why are they after Donovan? How can they be looking at him in connection with the murder? He left the party hours before I did. Then, I remember trying to call his cell and his not answering. He would never kill someone.

But he has, a tiny voice says. *And so have you.* But only bad guys. But who or what is a bad guy? It's a term children use. Bad guy or not, does anyone deserve to die at the hands of another?

To shake off these thoughts, I focus on work. I make a list of people to talk to about Grant, including Annalisa. This time when I call, she picks up on the first ring. Choking on her sobs, she tells me how Adam Grant was one of the finest men she's ever known.

"He didn't deserve to die," she says. "He was going to be president. He was going to change this world."

I'm not so sure about any of that, but I bite my tongue. She bursts into tears and hangs up without saying any more. It sounded pretty convincing over the phone, but I suppose if you were facing a murder rap, you'd put on the best performance of your life.

Later, at my desk, I hear Code 3 calls from fire and rescue squads in Moraga. I turn up the scanner. It sounds like a trench collapsed around a worker laying pipes at a construction site. I dial Chris Lopez's cell phone.

"C-Lo, hear that?" He's never without a small earbud headphone trailing down to the police scanner clipped to his belt.

"Yo, man," he says. "I'm on it. I'm in the side lot smoking a heater. What's your 10-20?"

"Meet me at my car. I'll drive."

I'm relieved that there is something to do besides wait around, hoping that the guy with info on Caterina calls back.

Lopez and I share a special bond.

He's ex–Green Beret and packs heat wherever he goes. Rumor has it he saw some nasty shit in Vietnam. He's one guy you want on your side. He's wasting his talents at the *Bay Herald*—he should be off in foreign countries covering war zones. But after a three-month stint for the paper in Afghanistan, he decided he missed his elderly mother too much to be that far away.

Lopez was with me the night we hunted down Jack Dean Johnson at his lair on Fort Ord, an abandoned military base. At the time, I thought Johnson was responsible for Caterina's death. Donovan ended up at the scene, as well, but Lopez was the one I called. He's had my back for years. Sometimes I think my relationship with Lopez makes Donovan jealous although he'd never admit it.

Lopez and I are the first newspeople to arrive at the scene. Construction workers were digging a long, waist-high trench when the dirt shifted and buried one man up to his armpits. From where we are, across a small grassy area, we can see the man's shoulders and head sticking out of the dirt. People crouch down beside him, monitoring his vital signs.

"Extracting him is a little tricky," Rick Mason from the Moraga Fire Department tells the reporters gathered on the lawn. "They're afraid if they shift the dirt too much or too fast, the trench will collapse even further. They're trying to dig around and free him up, but it's a lot more difficult than you would think. We're calling in our special trench-rescue team."

I've been with the newspaper for six years but never knew there was a team trained for trench rescues. I scribble a note to do a story on them another day.

The media is kept about thirty feet away. Lopez, who has more energy than a three-year-old hopped up on Halloween candy, can't sit still. Frustrated that he can't get closer to the scene to take photos, he paces, smoking cigarette after cigarette and muttering to himself. My fingers itch to bum one from him.

I hide from the sun under a leafy tree. Lopez climbs the tree and fires off snapshots with his telephoto lens. Even from afar, the man's face looks pained as rescuers tilt back his head to give him water.

A long, slow hour passes. I can't understand what's taking so long. A few reporters I know are here, so we make small talk, joking about a recent prostitution sting and how one young, hot-blooded deputy went undercover and was teased mercilessly about it afterward. Heads swivel at a commotion by the hole. Bodies are a blur, running, moving, crouching. Then, all movement stops. I arch my neck, trying to see, but legs rooted near the trench block my view.

The sudden silence hits me right in the chest. The legs step away seemingly in slow motion. A small white tarp covers a mound where the man's head had been. The men look down as they walk away without speaking, shaking their heads, some swiping at their eyes.

I can't even comprehend what I am seeing. I sat there, joking around and laughing. All of the reporters did, waiting for the man to be rescued, not realizing it was a life-and-death situation. Not realizing it for one second. How could he have died? We all just watched a man die.

Rick Mason comes over, grim-faced, and says he will fax over a press release by the end of the day. He walks away in a daze. He's not ready to talk about it, either. He just watched a man die. Up close.

Lopez and I are somber as we walk back to my car, parked on a nearby street.

"Man, that's a shitty break for that guy," Lopez says, putting a cigarette between his lips and offering the pack to me. "Want a heater?" I shake my head. "Guess the pressure on his chest was too much. Shut him down."

I nod, afraid to speak. When we get to my car, it takes me a minute to process what I see. My car is slumped low to the ground. All four tires are slashed. I see something glinting in the sunlight. A shiny police badge is trapped under one windshield wiper. For some reason, it gives me the chills. It says ROSARITO POLICE DE-PARTMENT. Donovan's department.

Is it a sign? A warning? Is it from someone who thinks I killed Adam Grant? Some cop from Donovan's department making a statement? If they thought Donovan was dating a murderer, I could think of half a dozen cops at Rosarito who would be rub-bing their hands together, waiting to see me behind bars.

I slip the badge out from under the windshield wiper and stick it in my jacket pocket. I finger it. It feels weighty, real, but I've heard about people getting caught with fake badges before.

Lopez lifts an eyebrow. "What the hell, man?"

THE TOW-TRUCK DRIVER drives us to the newsroom. The me-chanic promises that the garage will drop off my car in the paper's parking lot by six tonight. I've been going to the same garage for years because of little individual touches like this.

The Moraga Police Department was not the least bit interested in my punctured tires. A bored beat cop came out to the newsroom to take a report, but only after I insisted. "Probably some punk kids," he said. His lackluster attitude made me clam up about the police badge.

But I know. Somebody is trying to send me a message, and it's not a message I want to receive.

Chapter 22

AFTER I WRITE and turn in the trench story, I've got a few hours to kill until my car is ready. I'm writing up briefs about identity-theft tips when something on the scanner catches my attention.

"Fell five stories." With all the crackling, I can barely make out what is going on. I catch snatches of conversation. It sounds like a guy fell five stories off a downtown building. That's not going to be pretty. I grab my bag, dial Lopez, and am halfway across the newsroom when he answers.

"Pick you up at the back door."

We race down the main drag to downtown Walnut Creek, Lopez punching the dash whenever the light turns red. The building they are talking about on the scanner is right across from the downtown mall.

When we pull up, a fire truck and three police cars are leaving.

No ambulance. No coroner's van.

Nobody anywhere. It's baffling. We circle the building, toward the back, I see a few guys standing around a cable company van. One guy is in the middle, and they are patting him on the back and laughing. We stop and introduce ourselves.

"I heard something about a guy falling off a building."

The men are giddy, as if they've been drinking.

"That's old lucky Bob, here," one guy says, slapping another guy on the back. "Thought he was a goner."

"Wait? You fell off this roof?" I peer up to the top of the building, my eyes widening. Lopez gives me a look.

"Yup."

"We need to talk," I say, whipping out my notebook.

They take us up on the roof to tell the story, with Lopez taking pictures the entire time.

Apparently, Bob Nelson was walking backward, laying out cable, and walked right off the edge of the roof. His partner, Dale, tried to warn him, but by the time the words came out of his mouth, it was too late.

"My heart was pounding. I thought for sure he was a goner," Dale said. "I crawled to the edge of the roof, scared sick about what I was going to see."

He pauses, either for drama or to let me catch up on my note taking. I finish and look up, waiting.

"So's I look over the edge, expecting to see the nastiest thing I ever saw, and sure as shit, Bob is down there walking on the sidewalk, walking around like nothing happened."

"No kidding," I say, eyebrows raised.

Bob explains that when he went over the edge, the cable looped around his ankle. It stopped him about four feet off the ground, right in a bush. He extracted his ankle and fell into the bush, uninjured. "Some lady came running outside all frantic," Bob says. "I was just sitting here on the ledge, trying to figure the whole damn thing out, and she runs up to me and is all panicky, and says 'Oh my God, oh my God, I just saw some guy fall off the building.'"

"What'd you tell her?" I ask.

"I says, 'Yup. That'd be me."

Bob and Dale say good-bye. They're off to buy lottery tickets.

"I figure today is my lucky day," Bob says.

I finish the story in record time. It practically writes itself. It's a good distraction. I haven't thought about the badge or my flattened tires at all. The garage calls me to tell me my car is in the parking lot, and the keys are at the reception desk. I make a note to send a giant box of biscotti to the garage at Christmas.

When my desk phone rings, I jump, hoping it's the man who has information on Caterina.

It's not.

It's Nicole. "Hey, lady, want to meet at The Bear after work? I'm craving their garlic fries. I can leave right now. The Larson case was continued."

"Awesome. I've had a hell of a day. I desperately need a drink. Plus, I've got something to show you." I eye the book on my desk.

The deck at our favorite sports bar overlooks the bustling downtown Walnut Creek streets. The entire downtown area has a cool, European vibe, with its big trees and wide sidewalks. The restaurants have cafe tables outside, and people stroll the summer streets laughing and talking as they visit boutiques and bookstores carrying bags from Pottery Barn and Saks Fifth Avenue.

I've ordered my signature drink, Absolut vodka, straight up, chilled in a tumbler. Instead of her usual frosty Honeyweiss beer, Nicole has what looks like a soda in front of her.

"What's up with your drink?" I lift my glass toward hers.

"Giving my liver a break," she says. She raises her glass to clink mine. "Cheers! Saw the storyboard, you're right—you've had quite a day. It's not every day that both your stories are slated for A1."

"No kidding. Bizarre stuff. But that's not the half of my crazy day."

I tell her that both Donovan and I were brought in for questioning this morning at the San Francisco PD. I also tell her about the tipster who said he had information about Caterina and how I had to miss the meeting.

"I don't get it," she says, her brow furrowing as she munches a garlic fry. "Why are the investigators wasting time pestering you? Let me talk to the D.A. again and see what he's heard. They must really not have any leads. I know the pressure is on because this murder is huge. It's all anybody is talking about at the courthouse."

"I just can't understand why they are brushing me off when I tell them to find the woman in the black bikini." I say, dipping some fries into a small dish of malt vinegar.

Nicole finishes chewing before she answers. "'Cause they found her. Alibi. Rock solid. She was arrested for drunk driving about a mile away from Grant's house. Spent the night in the Napa clink. According to time of death and when the maid last saw Grant, she was already in custody."

"Shit."

Nicole laughs. "Don't worry. They don't have anything on you. Let's talk about something else. What's the surprise?"

I rummage around, then pull a book out of my bag, holding it up for her to read: *Homicide Investigator's Handbook.* "This came in the mail this afternoon. Brand-new! I haven't looked at it yet. Waited to share it with you."

"Cool!" There aren't a lot of people in the world who would react this way. That's one reason we're friends.

"Ready?" I ask.

She nods. I close my eyes and crack the book near the binding. When I look down, I see a picture of a charred burn victim. It looks like something out of a horror movie with its empty eye sockets. Both of us involuntarily squeal.

I pass it to Nicole, "Your turn."

She flips a few pages, chomping on garlic fries. "Holy shit, look at this one —what a way to go," she says, pointing out a page where the guy's dog had stepped on the accelerator, pinning his master between the truck's bumper and a fence.

Nicole shakes her blond bob and wrinkles her freckled nose as she thumbs through the book. "Wow. Never thought about what a body would look like after an explosion—it's just a pile of mush."

We close the book when the waitress returns to check on us. After she walks away, I pick up the book again and come across a photo I never needed to see—an up-close shot of a guy with half his head blown off by a .50 caliber bullet.

"Okay, you win. That one is horrific." Nicole says, grimacing and looking away.

"Yeah," I say. "I don't think I ever need to look at this picture again in my life." I take a Post-it note out of my bag and stick it over the picture so I don't accidentally turn to that page again. But I've seen worse.

"Sorry about that," I say to Nicole. "That one was pretty bad."

"Yeah, but it's nearly impossible not to look at."

"I know." I look off in the distance. Nicole picks up on my worry immediately.

"Okay, fess up. Besides all the other crazy shit you dealt with today, what else is bothering you?" Nicole's probing gaze is kind, but I can tell she is worried.

"Boy problems."

I tell her everything—including my irrational fear that Dono-van is still in love with Annalisa—gulping my drink a little faster than usual. Nicole knows the history of my rocky love life, picking one wrong guy after another. Until I met Donovan.

"Sometimes I feel like I'm just waiting for the other shoe to drop," I say, and look away, wishing I had a cigarette. Nicole waits, watching me with a furrowed brow as I continue. "Sometimes I worry that maybe . . . maybe he's out of my league."

It is the first time I've ever said this out loud, and I'm a little embarrassed to hear the words come out of my mouth. Nicole startles me with a big laugh.

"You're crazy," she says, waving my concerns away with her hand. "Do you ever look in the mirror? You got that Sophia Loren thing going on."

"No wonder I like you so much," I say. Talking to Nicole always makes me feel better.

I think *she's* the beautiful one, classy and poised, with her Grace Kelly looks. She's, also, an ace reporter. She never fails to dig up dirt on suspects that even the best detectives have some-times missed, which has earned her grudging respect from both defense attorneys and prosecutors—even when her information ends up clearing a suspect of wrongdoing. And, not many people know it, but she has the Contra Costa County district attorney's personal cell-phone number and is invited to his family's annual Fourth of July party.

Besides all that, she's a hell of a lot of fun. She's the closest thing I have to a sister. I wonder what my life would have been like if Caterina had lived. What would she look like now? Would we be best friends?

"Gabriella?" Nicole's voice brings me back.

"Huh?"

"Never mind," Nicole says. "I was prattling on about Ted's job search. He finally got a new one. No more long-distance relationship."

Nicole's husband's job in medical device sales required him to spend five out of seven days on the road.

"That's great news!" I held my glass up and clink hers. "Tell him congratulations!"

She smiles at me. We are both quiet for a moment.

"I'm just worried he's still in love with her." I look down when I say this.

"Besides that one time, has he ever talked about her?"

"We haven't really talked much about our past relationships with each other." It seems we've both done a damn good job of avoiding anything like that. I guess I didn't realize how bad it was until now.

"And you haven't talked to him about this fear?"

I shake my head. This morning we talked about Caterina and getting questioned by the cops, but not my jealousy, which is the last thing I want to talk about.

Nicole drains the last of her soda and signals for the waitress. "You need to go home and talk to him. Now."

I don't want to admit it, but she's right. I sigh and get out my wallet.

Chapter 23

WHEN I GET to Donovan's place he's already in bed.

It's only ten thirty.

Although he was at the cop shop all night getting questioned, I'm still surprised. I've seen him work all-nighters and not go to bed before midnight. Something is wrong.

I don't know what else to do, so I wash my face and brush my teeth and crawl into bed with him although I know I'll be staring at the ceiling for a good long while.

He mumbles something and wraps his arms around me. I want to wake him and talk. I want to confess I'm jealous of Annalisa. I want to tell him that someone is threatening me—popping the tires on my car and leaving a police badge as a calling card. How did someone get a badge, anyway? It's not like you can buy them at the store?

At the same time, I feel relieved to postpone those conversations until the morning. I'm sure my shrink would have something to say about it. Thinking of my therapist, Marsha, makes me feel guilty. Ever since Annalisa has come into our lives, I've missed my appointments and ignored Marsha's phone calls. I'm not sure what I'm trying to avoid, but even to me, it's obvious I'm dodging something.

The night passes very slowly. I get very little sleep. Donovan makes it nearly impossible by tossing and turning all night long. A few times, I wake and hear him moaning, as if he's in pain. At one point, he starts swinging when I try to wake him, and I jump out of bed, hugging the sheet to me, pressed against the wall.

"Donovan! Stop it! You almost hit me!" My shouting wakes him. He looks disoriented, rubbing his eyes, then sees me cowering in the corner.

"Sorry. I was having a bad dream." He turns and starts snoring. I crawl back into bed. My eyes are heavy, so I roll over and go back to sleep.

When I wake at dawn, he's gone.

I CAN BARELY concentrate at work. I'm dead tired and keep thinking about missing that appointment with the man with information on Caterina's killer. Unlike yesterday, the news this morning is so slow, I have plenty of time to think.

I try to distract myself by working on a story about Adam Grant. His funeral is tomorrow, Friday. It's not often I've written a story about someone I know who died. I once had to write a story about a cop I knew who died coming home from a bar. He was drunk and flipped his car.

So, I have mixed emotions when I sit down to write about Grant. I'm a little sad, but I barely knew the guy. It's hard to realize that less than a week ago, I was having dinner with him at the Fairmont Hotel.

I call the number listed for Grant's San Francisco apartment, hoping to reach family members in town for his funeral later today. The woman who answers the phone, Grant's sister, Daphne, agrees to talk. Although she is clearly grieving, she is happy to share her memories of him. She talks about what a great sense of humor Grant had and how, in many ways, he never lost his child-ish delight at what the world had to offer.

"He always knew how to appreciate everything, especially those little things we forget to pay attention to," she says. "In some ways, that makes me happy—that when he was alive, he truly lived. And in other ways, that breaks my heart that someone who loved life so much had it cut short."

I highlight this quote. It's a good one. It reminds me how I caught a glimpse of what she is describing when I gave him biscotti—he was sincerely excited and appreciative.

I wonder if his sister knows I was at Grant's house the day he was murdered. Obviously, she doesn't know the police are ques-tioning me about his murder. I'm worried she will hang up or yell at me, but I have to tell her.

"There's something you need to know," I say, then blurt it out in a rush. "I was at the party. In Napa. Your brother invited me. I met him the night before at a press dinner. The police questioned me—because I was there. I feel awful about what happened—that someone did that to him. He seemed like such a great guy . . . I'm so very sorry."

For a few seconds, she is silent, and I brace myself. She has every right to scold me for not telling her this up front.

"Thank you for telling me that." Her voice is quiet.

Before she hangs up, she gives me phone numbers of others who might want to talk to me about Grant, including his cousin and a childhood friend.

After several interviews, I begin crafting a story about a man who appeared to be loved by everyone who met him. When I have the skeleton of a story, I hit SAVE and close the file.

Writing the story has made me melancholy. Life cut short too soon always does. I remember what he said about Sebastian Laurent: "I don't believe anyone deserves to die a violent death."

I open my file on Sebastian Laurent. He was murdered nine days ago and is quickly fading from the public's eye and attention span. I don't want that to happen. I told Kellogg I'd have a follow-up story for Saturday's paper, but I need the autopsy results. My source at the morgue, Brian, told me tox was a rush job, and the autopsy report would be available today. He said he'd shoot me an e-mail when he got to work. I check my in-box.

There it is. The message itself is empty. The only writing is in the e-mail's subject line.

It says, "I see dead people."

Chapter 24

DEATH HAS A very distinct smell.

Once you've smelled it, you'll never forget it. It'll linger in your olfactory memory like a shadowy dream. And I can't explain it, but now that I know the smell, I sometimes catch whiffs of death in the oddest places—on the breeze as I walk to the corner market, on a stranger sitting nearby on the train, a faint hint in the hallway of a decrepit apartment building.

I punch the accelerator on my old Volvo and head toward the morgue in Martinez. With the windows down and the scent of summer in the air, I remember the first time I smelled death—during an autopsy. Dead man about my age who had overdosed on smack. Unfortunately, he had the same exact build and coloring as my boyfriend at the time, which messed with my head. So to avoid looking at his naked body, I ended up staring at the man's head the entire time. Now his lifeless eyes and slack face are ingrained in my memory.

The most poignant part of the autopsy was for the first time in my life—even though I had attended several open-casket funerals and am Catholic—I realized that the body truly is merely a shell, a carcass. What lay before me was not a person anymore. An enormous sense of peace came over me as this heavy realization set in. When my sister and father were lowered into the dark ground, whatever had made them alive wasn't there anymore. They were already gone.

During the autopsy, I was surprised to see the forensic pathologists use a tableful of tools that looked like they came from someone's garage or kitchen—a vibrating circular saw to cut through the skull, what looked like a bread knife to slice samples of organs, pruning shears to cut the rib cage apart, a hammer with a hook to help pry open the cut skull, and a pair of everyday scissors. Later, I found out that frugal—and savvy—forensic pathologists will save money by buying ordinary tools instead of more expensive autopsy accouterments.

I first smelled death when the forensic pathologist sliced open the chest with what looked like a big butcher knife. The pungency of the smell that arose from the internal organs made the smeared Vicks VapoRub under my nose a total waste.

Later, the pathologist used a circular saw to cut through the top of the skull. To get at the brain, the doctor peeled the skin from the forehead to the chin, so it flopped down over the face like a mask. I flinched at the suction sound the skull plate made when the doctor pulled it off. I can still hear that sucking noise if I try.

That day, I also learned about the linger factor of the smell of death. After the autopsy, I was covering a swearing-in ceremony of some new cadets when I smelled the dead guy again. And it was strong. Discreetly, I took a piece of my hair and held it up to my nose to see if the smell had gotten into my hair like smoke sometimes does. No, it smelled like my hair conditioner. Driving back to the office, the smell was so strong I began to fear I was actually losing it, some strange side effect of seeing the autopsy. I called Nicole, our resident expert on autopsies.

"Oh, yeah. It sticks around for a long, long time," Nicole reassured me. "The scent gets in your nose hairs or something. It might be there for a while. Don't worry, it's real. It's not in your head."

When I pull into the morgue parking lot today, I dial Brian on my cell because the morgue lobby is closed for lunch.

He tells me to pull around to the big bay doors at the garage in back. The doors are open, and I see Brian stoking the coals on a small black barbecue to the side of the garage where the big vans drop off the bodies. One van is gone.

"Jim out on a call?" I ask.

"Yeah. T.C.," Brian says.

Traffic collision.

"Hungry?" Brian asks. "We got bratwurst."

"No, I'm good."

I've attended barbecues at the morgue before to be social, but having to carry my plate through the autopsy room into the inner offices always gives me the heebie-jeebies. I usually secretly make the sign of the cross, praying that some screwy airborne meningitis or flesh-eating bacteria don't land on my burger.

Today, Brian leads me through the empty autopsy room—past the freezer of dead bodies and the storeroom with jars of organ samples—into the inner offices.

In the county I cover on my beat, Contra Costa County, the coroner is the sheriff. He assigns deputies to the morgue—two-year stints of working twenty-four-hour shifts. Their job is basically to go pick up bodies that the coroner's office needs to autopsy.

Usually, that involves anyone who died a suspicious death but also includes victims of fatal traffic accidents and drug overdoses. The two deputies on duty sit in cubicles with walls reaching nearly to the ceiling. A big white board on the far wall lists all the bodies they've brought in over the past twenty-four hours. It's sort of a "Dead of the Day" list. I scan it briefly.

Davidson, Luke, #341, Antioch PD, homicide
Doe, John, #342, Martinez PD, unknown
Smith, Anne, #343, Danville PD, traffic collision

The homicide was a gang retaliation from last night. May already wrote about it for today's paper.

"Want to see my latest?" Brian asks.

Brian keeps a death book. Although the deputies have to photograph the scene as part of their job, Brian keeps copies of the Polaroids for his own personal scrapbook. I've browsed it before. I still can't get some of the images out of my head, especially the father of five whose head was crushed by a six-ton dump truck as he worked on its brakes.

"Another time. On deadline."

Brian hands me the Laurent file, and I sit at an empty desk.

Most autopsies include the coroner's determination of the cause and manner of death, then specifics of the autopsy findings. I'm looking for anything that sticks out.

Opening the file, I set aside the postmortem photos—after all, I'd seen his dead body in person—and flip to the report.

AUTOPSY REPORT
Department of Coroner

Autopsy performed on Sebastian Laurent
at the Department of Coroner, Martinez, Calif. June 23,
2002 @ 1000 hours.

FINAL DIAGNOSIS AND FINDINGS:

1. Perforating Gunshot Wound of the Head

A. Entrance: posterior cranial, intermediate range

B. Path of the projectile: Skin, left occipital region

C. Direction of projectile: Diagonal, front to back, posterior cranial to occipital lobe

D. Exit: None. Fragments of projectile recovered in parietal lobe, cephalic region, frontal region

E. Associated injuries: Entrance wound; perforations of posterior cranial region with bilateral hemorrhage

F. Postmortem radiograph: Metallic fragments of projectile identified

Cause of Death: Gunshot Wound of Head

Manner of Death: Homicide

How Incident Occurred: Shot by another person

CIRCUMSTANCES:

On June 21, 2002, the decedent left his San Francisco residence at an unknown time in the early-morning hours and drove to Kirker Pass Road in eastern Contra Costa County. At approximately 0800 hours, a neighbor walking her dog on the hills above the road saw the decedent's vehicle in the ravine below.

California Highway Patrol officers responded to reports of a traffic collision and found the decedent's body inside the vehicle. They initially believed the death was accidental.

An officer examining the vehicle called homicide after finding evidence of foul play in the form of a .40 caliber shell
casing found inside the vehicle and an entry wound at the
back of the decedent's head.

EXTERNAL EXAMINATION:
    The body is secured in a blue body bag with Coroner's
Examiner seal #0000523
    The body is viewed unclothed. The body is that of a nor-
mally developed, white male appearing the stated age of 34
with a body length of 72 inches . . .

I skim the external examination since I saw the body myself.
Up close. I pause at the part where the forensic pathologist iden-
tifies the slug. The bullet was fired from a SIG .40 caliber duty
weapon—the gun most cops, FBI, DEA, and Secret Service members carry.

My stomach flip-flops. I don't know why. I continue to read,
skipping the sections on the endocrine, cardiovascular, respira-
tory, and other systems so I can get to the tox report. I make a note
to ask why the tox was a rush job.

TOXICOLOGY:
    Blood, bile, urine, liver tissue, and stomach contents
were submitted to the laboratory.
    Findings: Toxicology studies indicate high concentra-
tion of sodium pentothal in the blood.

Sodium pentothal. The drug is famous for being a "truth serum"
because it can decrease the higher brain function needed to lie.

But after covering an execution on Death Row—I know its other use—lethal injection. It's a rapid-onset knockout drug—the first of three drugs used in lethal injections. It's not an easy drug to get your hands on, either.

Did someone inject the drug into Laurent before his car went careening over the edge of the road? Did the killer strip the body of clothes before sending the vehicle plunging, or did it happen later, when he was in the ditch? And what was Laurent doing out on that deserted stretch of rural highway in the middle of the night?

In my car on the way back to the newsroom, I call one of my best sources. Lt. Michael Moretti and I bonded on the Italian-American thing. Plus, he knows I would go to jail rather than tell people he fed me information. We Italians can be loyal sons of guns.

"Hey, kiddo." I don't know why, but it always makes me feel good when Moretti calls me this.

"Any new dirt on the Kirker Pass Road shooting?"

"Don't I even get a 'Hey, how's it going, Moretti?'"

"Sorry. Saw the autopsy report. The slug was from a SIG .40 caliber."

"Yeah. Heard that," Moretti says. He waits, clearing his throat.

"What is it?" Fear shoots through me.

"Did you see the list of belongings taken from the car?"

"No." I slam on my brakes. "I'm heading back to the morgue right now."

"Slow down. You didn't hear this from me." Famous Moretti words.

"Of course I didn't," I quickly reassure him.

"They found a badge. A police badge."

"What the hell?" I can feel the shiver streaking down my arms, raising the small airs and making me feel weak. "Let me guess? Rosarito?"

Now it is his turn to be quiet. I tell him about my tires being slashed and finding the badge on my windshield. *Which means the killer is the same person who slashed my tires.*

"I don't like it," he says grimly. "Not one bit. I want you to be extra careful, Gabriella. This doesn't sit right with me at all. Why don't you come by the station later, I've got an extra bulletproof vest here. Size small. You could borrow it."

I change the subject.

"Did you see the tox?" I ask. "He was drugged. Knocked out. And why do they have tox already?"

"They probably made tox priority because the guy was a big shot. Ended up finding the hypo on the shoulder, in the weeds. Clean. No prints."

They found the needle? "I can't figure that whole scenario out," I say, pressing my foot down hard on the accelerator. If I don't hurry, I'm going to be late to Grant's funeral.

"No skid marks going over the side," Moretti says. "Plus, some old boozer was driving home from the bar and says he saw the McLaren F1 parked on the side of the road. Another car was behind it, but he has no clue what kind of car it was. Too busy ogling the F1."

"Yeah, that's one car that's hard not to notice. Kind of like when a bank robber wears a clown wig so everyone remembers the wig and nothing else," I say, navigating a hairy turn on the long road up to the cemetery.

"*Capisce.* Same thing. Detectives even brought the old guy in for hypnosis to see if he had some details buried in his memory that could help him describe the second car, but it was dark that night, and the old geezer's eyesight isn't that great anyway, so no dice."

I think about Annalisa's car, parked in the garage.

"So, probably if it was a red Ferrari, he would have remembered it."

"You'd think."

"Was the car in PARK when they found it?"

"Nope. DRIVE. Someone pushed it, maybe with another car. By the way, they did find some red paint on the bumper."

Chapter 25

ADAM GRANT WILL be buried in a family plot on a stretch of the Oakland Hills cemetery called Millionaire's Row. Although the section is gorgeous with palm trees, ornate Greek- and Roman-style crypts, and stunning panoramic views of the San Francisco Bay, it seems like he would've been embarrassed to be interred in a place with that name.

The funeral is a media spectacle. At least four helicopters circle overhead. All the major news stations have reporters on scene. I spot Andy Black, my competition from the *San Francisco Tribune*. Even the BBC is here.

Kellogg was distracted when he agreed to let me cover the funeral. I'm sure if he knew the cops had questioned me a second time, he'd have forbidden it, but he seems preoccupied with editing a Bay Bridge story coming out this weekend.

Lisa Shipley is somewhere around here, covering the funeral as part of her story about the political impact of Grant's death. I spot her across the lawn, with notebook in hand, talking to official-looking people.

The church service was closed to the public, but they couldn't block off the graveside service, so the mass of mourners and reporters congregate on the cemetery's green slopes watching the hearse pull up. I feel a little like a vulture, but I keep telling myself that it's my job to be here.

Lopez and I both stand back, letting the television reporters storm the cemetery, inching as close to the burial site as they can. I stay back and quietly take notes on the scene, so I can describe it later in my story. I don't need to be graveside. I have too much respect for Grant's family members to disrupt the service with my presence. I do keep an eye on them, though, in case anything unusual happens.

It wouldn't be the first time. During one funeral I was covering, a mother threw herself on top of the casket after it was lowered into the ground. I'm still haunted by the sound of her wailing. I'm scanning the crowd when I see two people who make me cringe. Across the lawn, the detectives who questioned me—Sullivan and Gold—are hanging back from the crowd, leaning against a tree. The redheaded cop must see me looking because he lifts his two fingers in a salute.

I know that homicide detectives often attend funerals because they have this theory that killers like to attend the funerals of their victims. Nice try. I lift my notebook in response to his salute. *I'm here doing my job, sweetie.*

If they think they can pin Grant's murder on me, they are out of their minds. All my fear about being considered a suspect churns into rage. Incompetent morons have no suspects, so they are focusing on me while the real killer skips around doing a jig because he or she is getting away with cold-blooded murder.

Lopez must notice my face turn purple because he lays his hand on my arm.

"Jerk-off cops over there staring at me." I jut my chin in their direction.

He knows the whole story.

"Fuck 'em," he says, taking a drag off his cigarette. "Want me to go have a word with Mr. Big Butt Detective?" He does a funny walk with his butt sticking out, and I laugh. The older cop does have an extraordinarily large backside. Lopez's impersonation gives me the dose of laughter I need to relax. The anger whooshes out of me. *Pull it together, Giovanni. You've got a job to do.*

I spot Annalisa Cruz in the line of mourners at the front, next to the grave. She has her arms entwined with a woman I recognize from TV as Daphne, Grant's sister, the one I spoke to on the phone. Annalisa wears a tight, pencil skirt and balances on impossibly high black stilettos. A wispy veil attached to her big black hat covers half her face. Every once in a while, she dabs her eyes with a handkerchief. I swallow hard as they lower the shiny black coffin into the ground and release dozens of doves that take flight, soaring in the blue sky above.

The mourners file away from the grave and get into big black cars. The line of cars is nearly gone when a stretch limousine stops in front of us. The driver, wearing a black suit and old-fashioned chauffer's cap, rolls down his window.

"Annalisa Cruz would like to offer you a ride to the reception," he says.

Lopez and I look at each other in surprise. We weren't invited to the reception in the first place.

"The front seat please," he says, leaning over to open the passenger door.

We climb in quickly, so we don't hold up the funeral procession. I try to peek in the back, but the thick black glass prevents me from seeing anything. But I know. I can feel her.

The wake is at a private home in the Oakland Hills. Nobody says a word during the drive. When the limo pulls in front of the sprawling house, the chauffer hops out. He holds the door as a fishnet-stocking-clad leg emerges from the car. Annalisa's shoulders are quaking as she turns and walks up to the house without a backward glance.

I shrug and nod for Lopez to follow. Inside, a butler leads us to an elaborately furnished sitting room that is bigger than my mother's entire house.

Lopez keeps his camera snug in its case. We find a quiet corner to hide in, feeling out of place and conspicuous. We are the only newspeople in the room. I still can't figure out why Annalisa wanted us there. So far, she's avoided speaking to us.

The nook where we are sitting only has the two seats and gives us a view of the entire front room, packed with people in black dresses and suits, holding glasses of wine and nibbling from plates of hors d'oeuvres carried around by white-coated catering staff. I scan the crowd and spot the red-faced man who was rescued from the pool. A few minutes later, I see the blond woman on the opera board. I cast a quick glance around looking for the black-bikini woman. Makes sense the same people would be at Adam Grant's funeral. They were his friends.

Annalisa flits in and out of the crowd, swigging wine and casting an eye in our direction at least every five minutes. Men are constantly at her elbow. It looks like they are consoling her. Lots of hugs and kisses ensue. At one point, I see her surreptitiously wipe a tear from a corner of her eye.

A man wearing dark sunglasses takes her elbow. She jumps. Then when she sees me watching, she smiles and wraps her arm through his. She leans her body close, pressing her chest up against his side, then stands on tiptoe as if to whisper something in his ear.

When he turns his head I recognize him. It's the man I ran into in the hall at Grant's house. Like a magnet, my gaze is brought back to the man. Even though I can't see the direction he's looking beneath his sunglasses, it almost seems like he's looking at me. It's confirmed when he leans down and says something to Annalisa, and her head jerks toward me with a scowl. She flails her arm in my direction, with a nasty sneer on her face. I can just imagine what she is telling the man on her arm, but whatever it is, he still gives me a slow smile and raises his chin to acknowledge me.

Seeing him smile at me, Annalisa actually takes his arm and turns him physically, so he's facing away from me. What the hell? I don't understand why she acts so territorial. I have a boyfriend. I don't cheat.

The man unfolds her fingers from his arm and starts to slip through the crowd. I find myself craning my neck to see where he is going. He stops to talk to the blond woman. At one point, he turns, catches me staring, and gives me another slow smile.

Annalisa sees our exchange, and her mouth flattens into a thin line. She tosses her hair and stalks off into another room. What is her deal?

And why did she give us a free ticket to this private and intimate gathering anyway? I've absorbed enough of the atmosphere and taken enough notes that I can write a decent story about both the funeral and reception. I'm ready to leave. So is Lopez.

"Let's blow this joint, man. This scene is too bizarre," he says.

"Yeah, totally. Can you call a cab? I'll meet you out front." I have to use the bathroom. Which is too bad because, all at once, I'm desperate to get out of this house. I wonder if Annalisa invited us just so we would feel out of place. So I would know just how much I don't fit into this world? Well, I already knew that.

When I come out of the bathroom, Annalisa is slumped on a chair outside. Her legs are curled under her, and her head is lolling back on a velvet cushion. She absentmindedly fingers a silky red scarf slung across her shoulders. She was waiting for me.

"Gabriealllllaaa." Her words are slurred. She's drunk. "Did Sean tell you he was over at my house last night?"

I freeze. A jolt of jealousy streaks through me. I didn't see him last night because he said he had to work late. He didn't say he was going to Annalisa's, but there's no way in hell I'm going to tell her that. "I feel bad when he has to work in the evenings like that." I place a heavy emphasis on the word "work."

"Oh, honey, he wasn't working." She smirks.

So, *this* is why I was invited here. This conversation. My blood is boiling at her words, but I won't give her the satisfaction of knowing that.

"I don't know what you're implying, Annalisa, but I'm not buying. I trust Donovan."

"His name's *Sean*." She practically spits the words out. And then she crosses her legs seductively, and a smile comes across her face that makes me worry about what she's going to say next. "We did a little reminiscing when he was over. You know, down memory lane. We were having so much fun we decided to look at some old pictures of us as a couple."

I clamp my mouth shut tight. *I will not react. I will not react.*

"He was so surprised I still had an old picture of his. A drawing. You see, when he was fifteen years old, he drew a picture of his dream woman. Did he ever tell you that?" Her words are slurred, and she has a little smug, self-satisfied smile on her face. She looks off into the distance. "Well, he drew this picture of his dream woman—the woman he wanted to marry. And guess what? When he met me, he about keeled over because I was the spitting image of the woman he had drawn."

A sour taste fills my mouth.

"Did he ever tell you about that? It looks exactly like me. Someday, I'll have to show it to you. I actually had it framed. It was so sweet. It proved to both of us that our destiny is to be together. It is written in the stars."

Her words hit their mark once again. It hurts. But I will die before I let her know that.

"Isn't puppy love fun? Too bad it never lasts," I say.

"It is fated. It cannot be altered." Her voice rises in pitch, and she speaks even faster. "You cannot change destiny. And now, with the other men I've loved gone—" A sob escapes her, and she closes her eyes tightly for a moment. "Now it is even more clear what path I am supposed to take."

I swallow. I must not react. It takes me a few seconds to pull myself together. She is attributing the murders of Laurent and Grant to fate and believes it is a sign that she is supposed to be with Donovan. I'm dealing with a crazy woman. She could've killed both men. Despite what Donovan says, I know it. Time to leave before I lose my temper. But not before I show her my own brand of craziness. I start to walk away, then turn back.

"By the way, Annalisa, when Donovan was at your place did he tell you our good news?"

She's not as good an actress as I am. She practically chokes on her wine.

"Oh, I can see he didn't tell you." I pause dramatically and watch her eyes widen. "He wants to get married. Isn't that romantic?"

Her eyes narrow to slits, and her lips purse. Not prettily.

It's a blatant lie. I'm nearly as astonished as she is at the words I've said. Although I'm pretty sure Donovan was about to propose as we walked around the lake, I stopped him before he did. So maybe instead of a lie, it's a bit of an exaggeration. I know I've taken poetic license to a whole new stratosphere, but it is so worth it when I see the look on her face before I walk away.

"That can't be. Sean is supposed to be mine." She is mumbling to herself, but then her words next stop me dead. "That's not what the plan was. He's protected. The others . . . not my fault. I didn't know."

I whirl back around.

"Sean is protected? What are you saying?" I grab both her arms and look into her eyes. "Speak. What the hell are you talking about? What *plan*? Was your *plan* to kill all your boyfriends? Was it?"

She stares at me, her mouth wide open in amazement.

"Answer me," I say.

People are starting to stare. A woman who had introduced herself earlier as Grant's cousin rushes over, extracts Annalisa from my grip, and swoops her away from me. "Come on, darling. ABC News is ready to talk to you in the dining room. First let's freshen up your makeup." She quickly whisks Annalisa into the bathroom. And locks the door. I try the door and pound on it.

"You're going to explain what that meant," I say to the muffled sounds inside as Lopez drags me away by the arm. "I'm not done with you yet."

Chapter 26

WHEN I GET to my car, I check my cell. One missed call. Donovan left a message saying he picked up a night shift for a sick colleague and won't be home until late, so we can't get together tonight. Two nights in a row.

I'm still trying to figure out how to deal with the news that he was over at Annalisa's house last night. For one fleeting second, I wonder if he's having an affair with her. What if there is no sick colleague, and he's at her place again tonight? My stomach does a loop de loop, and I remind myself to call Marsha, my therapist. My jealousy is getting out of hand. I need to run all my fears and irrational thoughts by someone who is objective and can tell me whether I'm completely out of whack.

Later, at my desk, I take my time packing up. Being alone tonight sounds like a bad idea—an invitation for anxiety to creep up and clamp its fingers down on me. At the last minute, I dial Nicole.

JAX RESTAURANT IS the sheriff's favorite hangout and the spot I like to wine and dine my cop sources on the company credit card.

Sure enough, when I walk through the chandelier-and-candlelit room, past the piano player, I spot a few cops I know.

I head to the bar, but Art, the bartender, jerks his thumb toward the French doors. Nicole is waiting for me on the brick patio. Parisian cafe tables are scattered under a latticed pergola strung with vines and twinkling white lights. Nicole's eyes are sparkling, too, and she has a secretive smile.

"I've got some news," she says, shyly looking down.

"What? Did you scoop the *Trib* on your story?" I pull up a chair.

"I'm sorry I didn't wait to order, I'm starving," she says as a waitress drops off a huge chef salad for her. I gesture toward her soda and salad. "What gives? You worried about your liver still?"

"I have some news. I wanted to tell you in person . . ."

News? Fear spurts through me. "You got another job? Please, please, please don't tell me you're going to the *Trib*. I'll die. I swear. Please don't leave me!"

Nicole starts laughing. "No, but I will be gone for a few months next year."

"Huh?"

"I'm pregnant."

I look blankly at her.

"As in—having a baby. Knocked up. Bun in the oven. In the family way. Eating for two."

I leap to my feet and hug her. "Congratulations! That's—great. I had no idea."

"I wanted to tell you the other night, but I thought I'd wait until the doctor's office confirmed it at my appointment this morning."

"I just . . . I guess I didn't think . . ." *you guys were going to have kids.*

"Now that Ted has a new job, his traveling days are over. It seems like the right time."

"Wow."

Nicole beams at me. I force a grin onto my face—this is *her* night and *her* celebration. And I am happy for her, truly, so I don't know exactly what my problem is.

We spend the rest of the night talking about baby stuff. I try to act interested, but I'm relieved when she yawns, saying she's exhausted and has to go home. She never asks how my conversation with Donovan went the other night, and I don't bring it up.

Driving home, I try to wrap my head around her news. Nicole having a baby? Have I lost my tough, courts-reporter friend? Does this mean we have to talk about diapers and that kind of crap for the next nine months? And beyond? I know I'm being selfish, but I want my old friend back. I feel like I'm about to lose her. I want to pore over pictures of dead bodies and talk about horrific crimes with her. Not booties and bassinets.

Chapter 27

AFTER SAYING GOOD-BYE to Nicole, I head to Donovan's place and let myself in. I fall asleep before he gets home, only vaguely sensing him crawl into bed with me.

In the early morning, I wake, sensing something is off. Opening my eyes in the dim light, I'm half-asleep as I make out Donovan's silhouette standing in the doorway. It seems like he's watching me. He's so still, it sends a chill through me. I shake it off. My eyes are heavy, so I give in and fall back asleep. When I wake, he's already gone.

It's Saturday, but I head into the office to polish my Sunday story on Adam Grant. I give Donovan a call on the drive in, but he doesn't pick up. At work, I can't shake the odd, out-of-sorts feeling I have today. Everything in my life seems off-kilter, yet there is nothing I can really put my finger on that is wrong. My relationship with Donovan seems okay on the surface, but there is something beneath that sends a ripple of fear through me. Are we okay?

Later, in the afternoon, when I see Donovan's name on my cell phone, I clamber to answer it as fast as I can.

"Hey, Ella, I miss you." Donovan's husky voice on the other end of the phone line sends a happy thrill through me just like it has since the first time we spoke. He's using my family's nickname for me. It took a long time for me to feel comfortable with it, but now the name on his lips makes me feel wanted and safe and instantly erases my unease. "Seems like lately we only see each other when we're both asleep in bed."

"I miss you, too," I say, barely above a whisper. "You working tonight?"

The police scanners on the desktop beside me crackle loudly. I turn the volume completely down. I don't care if the Bay Bridge has collapsed. All I want to do is hear Donovan's voice right now. I haven't really talked to him since Annalisa tried to imply there was something between them. I need to see him to stifle this jealousy.

"Hell no," he says. "It's Saturday night! That's why I called. I was thinking about having dinner in North Beach. I've got a craving for Bocce's ravioli."

Perfect. I have to drop by my place to feed my cat, Dusty, tonight, anyway.

"Let's do it."

WE TAKE MY car. I move over to the passenger seat when I pull up in front of his place. He likes to drive, and I don't mind relaxing and letting him deal with Saturday night Bay Bridge traffic.

He gets in, gives me a sexy smile, and leans over to give me a long kiss.

"Geez, I feel like we haven't seen each other for a week. You've put a spell on me."

I smile, but inside I keep remembering Annalisa's words—that Donovan was at her house the other night.

I brush it off. I will not let her viper venom poison my relationship. If he was at her house, I'm sure it was for a good reason. I need to learn to trust him. If I don't, our relationship is doomed. I will not ask him about it. Instead, I lace my fingers through his on the gearshift as he drives.

I always get a thrill crossing the Bay Bridge with the city lit up before me. The skyline always energizes me and makes me feel like anything is possible.

Donovan drops me off at the entrance to my building and leaves to find a parking spot for the car. Parking in North Beach is a nightmare, especially on a weekend night, so I know he might be a few minutes.

My place is a fourth-floor walk-up. No elevator means that although it's a pain in the butt, it keeps me in shape since I'd rather eat than go to the gym. When I get to the top floor, I try my key, but it doesn't seem to work. Donovan arrives, fiddles with the key, and pushes the door. This time it yields, swinging open. Dusty immediately streaks out between my legs and barrels down the stairs. It takes me a minute to comprehend what I see on my bed. When I do, I scream.

A dead man with bulging eyes looks my way. I take him in as snapshots, as if a flashbulb is going off, giving me tiny glimpses of a crime scene. White man. Mid-forties. Duct tape over his mouth. Bullet hole through his forehead. Receding hairline. Shirt untucked. Too-snug khaki pants. Slight beer belly hanging out. Scuffed brown shoes. One shoe has its laces untied.

Before Donovan yanks me back, I take in another detail—something shiny stuck to the duct tape over his mouth.

Donovan shields my view and makes me wait in the hall while he searches my place. His voice filters through the crack in the door as he calls 911.

I vomit into a bag of recycling on the floor outside my door, then, worried about Donovan, I peek in. He's standing over the body, making the sign of the cross. In my detached-from-reality state of shock, I idly wonder if he does that over every dead body he investigates. Then, he does something else, something that sends confusion coursing through me.

WITHIN TWENTY MINUTES, police are tromping through my apartment. Donovan is somewhere inside with them. I'm huddled on the rug in the hallway with my back against the wall, clutching Dusty to my chest. I can't stop thinking about what I saw on my bed. *My bed.*

Now, sitting in the hall, trembling, I think about what *else* I saw. Donovan reaching over to the dead man's mouth, picking up the shiny thing, and pocketing it. It was a police badge—like the one I found on my windshield.

I don't say anything about it when a nice female detective questions me in the hallway later. I tell her everything that happened. *Except that.*

Why in the hell would Donovan tamper with evidence at a murder scene? I realize I haven't told him about the badge I found on my windshield. When Donovan comes into the hall and tells me it's time to leave, I stare at him as if I've never seen him before.

How well do I know this man? I've been fooled in love before. Not long after my wedding was called off, I found out that my fiancé, whom I'd known since childhood, had been cheating on me for a year. I had never suspected a thing. Within two months of our breakup, he'd knocked her up and married *her.*

I eye Donovan's back. What secrets is he keeping? Ones that keep him up at night tossing and turning?

The detective brings Dusty's carrier out in the hall. She tells me I probably won't be able to come back until at least tomorrow night. I put Dusty in it and set it down in a corner of the hallway. Donovan turns and takes my hand.

"Come on. Let's go to Bocce. We'll pick him up on our way back."

I draw back, surprised. "We're going to have dinner like nothing happened? Like I didn't just find a dead man in my bed?"

"You need a stiff drink," he says.

I can't argue with that.

Donovan turns to the detective. "We're going out for a bit, then we'll come back to get the cat if you have any questions."

"Sounds good," she says. "You should be able to get in here and at least grab a change of clothes by the time you get back."

He takes my hand and leads me to the stairs. He's so calm. I feel like I'm going to explode, but I follow him.

Detectives Jack Sullivan and Harry Gold are pounding up my stairs as we head down. It's hard to believe that it's only been a week since the mayor of San Francisco was murdered. I bet the cops are going crazy that the case hasn't yet been solved. On the stairs, Sullivan wiggles a toothpick that is sticking out of his mouth. Donovan slings his arm around me protectively. All three detectives pause on the stairs, giving each other looks.

It's like a standoff.

"Hey Sully, awful nice that you have Napa's help to investigate crimes in your city," Donovan says to Sullivan, whose neck flushes red at the insult.

"We were just in the area and heard the call." Gold's tone is friendly and casual as if he is trying to defuse the tension in the air. "Thought we should swing by when we heard you were here. See if you needed some help. Make sure everything was okay."

Donovan nods, accepting the peace offering.

But Sullivan clears his throat. "Detective Donovan, I'm only a wet-behind-the-ears detective and probably should mind my own business," he says, teeth clenched on the toothpick, "but it seems to me there are an awful lot of dead bodies connected to you and the women in your life."

It smarts hearing this detective lump Annalisa and me in one category as "the women" in Donovan's life. Donovan, who has been suspended twice for losing his temper on duty, clenches his fists. His face grows red. I grab his arm. Sullivan takes all of it in and chuckles.

"What, tough guy? You going to hit me? Maybe you get mad with your women, too, huh? Listen, darling . . ." He turns to me. "You—I haven't quite figured out. Either you're in it with him, or he's out to make you take the fall. You better watch yourself because the way I figure, you're going to end up in jail for murder or on a morgue slab as a victim." I feel Donovan's arm tense under my hand, and I'm afraid to look over at him. "I hope I'm wrong, though because I'd hate for your pretty little body to be the next one I'm looking at naked in the morgue."

That does it. Donovan's arm shoots out as he takes a swing at the detective. I shout and grab for his arm. Donovan's punch arcs through the air in a blur. Sullivan easily dodges it by ducking, and smirks. "Pretty slow, old man. That might have worked ten years ago, but I think you've lost your touch. Better stick to knocking around people smaller than you."

Meanwhile, the other detective, Harry Gold, has pulled Sullivan away. "Come on, Sully."

Sullivan's face is now red, but he begins backing up the stairs.

"*Adios*, Deteeective." He draws out the word with a sneer. "I'll catch *you* later."

Donovan is breathing heavy and turns and punches the wall. "That son of a bitch." He then turns and storms down the stairs, flinging the glass door open, leaving me to catch up.

Chapter 28

WITHOUT TALKING, WE start down Columbus Avenue toward the restaurant. Donovan walks ahead as if I'm not even there. Everything is surreal. Lights are too bright. Voices too loud. Colors bleed into one another as if I'm dreaming. I can't shake the image of the dead man in my bed. It's there glowing when I close my eyes. Finally, I stop and wait for Donovan to notice. He keeps walking for about half a block before he notices. He shakes his head and comes back with a sheepish look.

"Sorry, that smart-ass kid has me really wound up." He blows out a big puff of air and takes my hand in his.

I hate when he's angry. It doesn't happen often, but it makes me extremely uncomfortable around him. But now he's *too* calm.

"What about the dead guy?" My voice is incredulous. "The dead body in my bed? Doesn't *that* have you wound up?" I don't even try to keep the sarcasm out of my voice.

Donovan takes a deep breath and looks off into the distance, at the spires of the Bay Bridge rising up on the horizon. "Let's go eat."

"I'm not hungry," I say.

"I get that. But I haven't eaten since breakfast. I need some food, or I'm going to get really crabby. And you need a drink. You act all tough, Ella, but I know you're not used to seeing something like that. Not like I am."

"Fine." I grit the word out.

At Bocce Café, Donovan orders an antipasti dish of olives, mozzarella, prosciutto, and salami. I manage to swallow a few olives. Donovan eats most of it. I make up for my lackluster appetite by drinking most of the bottle of zinfandel we split. We don't talk. I stare at him as he wolfs down the food.

"I don't understand. Why is there a dead body in my bed?" I finally say, putting my head in my hands. A wave of hysteria rises in my throat. I swallow and close my eyes to tamp it down.

Donovan stands, his chair scraping back noisily and plops down a wad of cash. "I knew the guy." He heads for the door.

My eyes widen, and I jump up from my seat, scrambling after him. "What are you talking about?"

"Somebody's sending me a message."

He's already at the door. I snatch my bag and jacket and run after him.

"You think?" My voice is incredulous. "Is that why he was in *my bed*? In my place?"

A wave of dizziness from the wine hits me as I walk out of Bocce after Donovan, so at first I think I'm seeing things when I notice that detective, Sullivan, waiting at the end of the long, covered walkway leading from the restaurant door to the street. His voice echoes down the walkway as he places his hand on Donovan.

"Sean Donovan, you are under arrest for murder."

Chapter 29

SULLIVAN SEEMS ALMOST gleeful as he snaps the cuffs on Donovan. I'm frantic. I don't know what to say or do. Donovan doesn't say a word. I run down the walkway. "Don't worry. I'll get you out. I'll call Troutman."

I grab Donovan's arm.

"Come on, lover boy," Sullivan says. At the car, he rudely brushes me off and shoves Donovan into the back of the car.

"Don't you dare touch me," I say.

Sullivan ignores me and slams his car door shut, brushing up against me again. The wine makes me brave—or stupid—and I try to push Sullivan back but miss by a mile, sending me off balance. I land on my butt, my jeans firmly hitting the one patch of dirt for blocks around. I scramble to my feet and lunge for the window where Donovan sits just as the car pulls away. He is resolutely staring in front of him, his jaw clenched and his profile rigid. I've never seen that look on his face before. It's a mixture of fury and determination. He doesn't look my way as the squad car pulls away.

I brush off my backside and start the walk home alone, frantically dialing Troutman. Walking fast, I'm filled with rage thinking about that redheaded cop trying to pin this on Donovan. A group of tough-looking kids start to approach me on one deserted street, but my glare sends them retreating back into the shadows. Troutman tells me not to worry and says he's on his way to the jail to get Donovan out of there.

When I get to my apartment, the door is closed. I know whom I have to call. I take my key off my ring and slip it under the doormat. As I lean down, I hear voices inside. The cops are still processing the scene. I don't need a change of clothes; I'll borrow some of Donovan's jeans. Even thinking his name sends a sob into my throat. I grab Dusty's carrier and hustle down the stairs as fast as I can.

I dial Crime Scene Cleanup as I gun my car through the quiet streets of downtown San Francisco. That's one thing nobody ever talks about—who cleans up after a violent crime. The cops sure as hell don't do it. In many cases, Scott Dawson does.

I became friends with Scott after I did a story on his burgeoning business. I hung out with him for a week, going with him to all the crime scenes he cleaned up after the cops were through with it. Although his company name specifies "crime" scenes, Scott will do any dirty work you pay him for. He will come in and clean up after a flood, fire, you name it. During my ride along, the most disturbing call we went to was a suicide. A thirty-two-year-old father of two blew his brains out sitting at his desk in the study after his wife caught him sleeping around and threatened to take the kids and leave him. There were brain bits much farther away from the chair than I ever dreamed possible.

"I'll make it my priority," Scott tells me on the phone. "Your place will be shipshape by tomorrow night."

"Thanks." An image comes back to me—the dead man and the big blob of blood that had pooled on my pillowcase, seeped over the edges, and dripped onto the floor. There's no way I can sleep in that bed ever again. "Can you pick up a new bed for me, too, and bill me for it."

"No problem, Gabriella. You'll never see it again."

By now, it's late, nearly midnight when I take the on-ramp to the Bay Bridge. I don't want to be alone tonight, but I'm not about to go to my mother's and have to explain what is going on. I don't even know what is happening myself.

I'm halfway across the Bay Bridge when Troutman calls back.

He tells me what he's found out through official, and unofficial, channels: Early this morning, around 4 A.M., one of the neighbors saw a man with a gun running out of our building. The man's physical description matches Donovan's, but wasn't particularly specific—man six-one, average build, longer hair, baseball cap drawn down low, brown leather jacket. The little-old-lady neighbor, who lives on the first floor, says she heard running down the stairs and peeked through her peephole. Then she looked out her window and saw the man get into a small, dark vehicle that she says, yes, could have been a black Saab—the same car Donovan drives.

"They recovered the slug—it was fired from a SIG .40 caliber, duty weapon."

I don't answer. I don't have to. It is the same type of bullet that killed Sebastian Laurent. Standard-issue gun for cops and other law enforcement.

In the back of my mind, I remember Donovan's odd behavior last night and how when I woke the apartment was already empty. He was gone. I shake my head to dismiss the shiver that runs through me. Donovan is the best man I know.

However, I know from my work as a crime reporter that sometimes even the most decent, law-abiding people are put into circumstances where they start to believe murder is their only option. I've seen it again and again—the father who faces the possibility of never seeing his children again. The wife who kills to stop her abusive husband. The man who kills the young man who raped his daughter. It happens.

But I refuse to believe Donovan would let it go that far.

As I cross the Bay Bridge, I listen to what else Troutman has to say. His "unofficial sources" have some bad news. Although police are holding Donovan for the murder of the man in my apartment, they are, also, trying to tie him to the deaths of Sebastian Laurent and Adam Grant. They are painting him as a jealous lover who kills anyone Annalisa has contact with. Apparently, Annalisa and the dead man were seen together at a Mission District restaurant yesterday afternoon.

Troutman's voice seems a universe away. Donovan's killing men connected to Annalisa? Donovan's killing someone would be devastating. That he did it for another woman? It would destroy me.

Chapter 30

"I'm going to be late."

The silence on the end of the line makes my stomach hurt, then I hear Kellogg exhale loudly. "It's Sunday. Your day off."

I swallow hard and close my eyes as I say, "I can't sit home. I just can't."

Another long sigh. "Can't you go be with your family?"

"Good God, no!" I practically shout. "Please. Please let me come in. I'll work on that story about the dead body they found in the Delta on Friday. Maybe it will end up being Jimmy Hoffa."

"Fine. Come in," he says. "I'll be there, too. I'm overseeing the coverage of . . . you know."

The arrest. Of my boyfriend. For murder.

I hang up and close my eyes, fighting back the tears.

Of course he's going to be at the paper. A cop arrested for murder is huge news. And I get it. He's got a job to do. He can't ignore crime news because my boyfriend was arrested for murder. *My boyfriend arrested for murder.* Even thinking those words sends a sob rising in my throat. *Die before cry.*

I grab my things and head for the San Francisco jail.

THE DEAD MAN was a cop. Or former cop, I should say. He worked at the Rosarito Police Department. That's how Donovan knew who he was.

Donovan tells me this through the bulletproof glass at the jail. Seeing him in the orange coveralls makes my stomach churn. The last person I visited in jail who wore an orange jumpsuit was a monster—a serial killer who preyed on children. Now, Donovan is the one on the other side of the glass, wearing the jumpsuit.

"I didn't do it."

"I know," I say. "Who's the dead cop?"

"Carl Brooke."

"Wait a minute." The name is familiar. "Isn't that one of the guys who served on that task force with you and Flora?"

"Same guy."

"When's the last time you saw him?"

"Years ago."

Brooke had left the department on a mental disability a long time ago, Donovan says.

I point out that two members of that task force are dead within a month—Carl Brooke and Jim Mueller.

"That is not okay. What if the killer is targeting you?"

"Well, I guess I'd be safe in here."

I'm glad he has his sense of humor intact, but I don't think any of this is funny.

"I'm serious."

"I made some calls after I read that in the paper. Jim Mueller was a suicide. Does that ease your fears?"

I think about that for a minute. Will Flora killed himself, as well. Two guys from the task force committed suicide. That's not as surprising as people might think. From what I've heard, cops tend to be more prone to suicide than the average person. It would make sense based on what they deal with every day.

"Maybe we should check on the other members. Are you still in touch with any of them?"

He doesn't answer my question.

"I left the team when Flora . . . you know."

Behind him, a guard pokes his head in to give him a warning. Five more minutes. I need to speak fast.

"What happened to the team after you left?"

"It puttered around for a while, but that was the last I heard of it. It was very hush-hush. It wasn't really supposed to exist. Some of the methods used were . . . unorthodox."

I'm horrified to find that despite the circumstances in which I'm hearing this story, I'm intrigued. It's that reporter instinct. The idea that a top secret special team is out fighting child porn appeals to my superhero-liking sensibilities. "Unorthodox? Like what?"

"Well, let's just say that one place—a shithole where they were making films of kids, really, really bad films—burned to the ground. With the owner inside."

I'm stunned. Murder approved by the higher-ups? I'm not saying the guy didn't deserve to die, but I'm astonished something like this was sanctioned.

"This happened after I left the team," Donovan says, "but unlike most people, I knew they'd been investigating that house, so I put two and two together. They all left the Rosarito PD within the year. I think the higher-ups quietly encouraged them to find work elsewhere. They all got hired on at other departments. I hadn't seen any of them . . . until today."

"What if someone—maybe some relative of that guy in the fire—is seeking revenge on you guys?"

Donovan's eyes narrow. I stare at the scratched window between us. Somebody has kissed the window and left fuchsia lip marks on it.

The question I really want to ask is why he took that badge off the dead man's face, But I can't. Not if our conversations are taped like they are at the Contra Costa County jail. I don't see any cameras but I can't take a chance.

We sit there in the silence for a few seconds. The guard opens the door. Time is almost up.

"Hang in there," I say. "You'll be out on bail tomorrow. They would've arraigned you today, but it's Sunday. What a total rip-off. I bet that jerk cop planned it that way on purpose."

At my words, Donovan gives a wry smile. "Yeah, that guy hates my guts."

"You think?" I say, making his smile widen.

The guard says something to him, and Donovan stands. The guard looks sheepish and meek. I wonder if he knew Donovan before his arrest.

"I have to go," Donovan says. I see his Adam's apple as he swallows hard. "Wanted to let you know I got a visitor request from that reporter at your paper, May. I'm not going to talk to her."

He says it defensively. I feel irrationally jealous and disturbed that Kellogg has already pulled May into this.

"I don't expect you to," I tell him. "But I will kick your ass if you talk to someone at the *Trib*." That makes him smile.

Donovan's arrest was splashed across the front page of our paper—and probably every other one in the state—this morning. San Francisco PD didn't waste one single second before they sent out a press release last night, in time to make the morning paper.

I can only imagine the media frenzy that is going to occur if the cops leak that they are looking at Donovan in connection with Sebastian Laurent or Adam Grant's murder, as well.

Seeing Donovan in orange jail coveralls makes my stomach clench in knots. I try to hide my feelings from Donovan. I've got to be strong for him and figure out how to get him free. But I feel the small fissures that are trying to expand into a large crack. I am trying to keep it together but am starting to feel a little hysterical.

The guard leans in again. "Detective, time's up."

I speak fast. "Why would someone you worked with years ago end up dead on my bed? Why? I don't understand." I know my voice is verging on hysteria, but I can't stop. Troutman had said they were trying to pin all three murders on Donovan.

He's silent on the other side of the glass. The guard is standing behind him now.

I look right at him. "What the hell is happening to our lives? Because there's one thing I can say for sure—all this is centered on you. You." I slump into the hard plastic chair and blink back tears, putting my hands over my face. I manage to stifle the waterworks, and when I peer through my fingers, Donovan is standing.

He speaks slowly and dully. His voice has no emotion, and his eyes are dull.

"I'm going to figure that out. You're going to have to trust me." His words hang in the silence between us.

Chapter 31

WHEN I WALK into the newsroom, all conversation ceases. It's like a bad movie. People glance away or furiously pound their keyboards with heads bent low. Nobody looks at me. The walk to my desk is like the perp walk.

Thank God it's Sunday, and the newsroom has a skeleton staff. But even so, Kellogg has brought in people to work this story. The realization brings a lump to my throat.

At the cop-reporter station, May is on the phone and barely glances my way. Her voice drops to a whisper. I'm sure she's talking about Donovan.

Kellogg is the only one who has any balls in this operation. He immediately comes over to my desk and engulfs me in a big bear hug. It's awkward and embarrassing, but I'm grateful.

"Giovanni. You let me know what I can do to help." He leans in and lowers his voice. "I told everyone—you're off-limits on this. The other reporters are on their own finding out info about Detective Donovan."

Reporters? I was right. He's assigned more than one to this

story. I swallow hard and blink even harder. He notices. "You sure you want to be here? Maybe this is a good time for you to take a few days off? Some personal days, huh?"

I shake my head. "I can't. I can't sit around at home."

"Let me know if you change your mind."

He gives me a light punch on the shoulder and walks away.

May gets off the phone and gives me a look. "It's not my fault I have to cover this, so I hope you're not going to be a royal bitch to me about it."

"Fuck you, May," I say. "It wouldn't have hurt to say something compassionate, like you're sorry I have to go through this or how about this: 'I'm sure your boyfriend is innocent, and I'll try to prove that.'"

"I don't know what your definition of the cops reporter beat is, but mine doesn't involve proving a suspect's innocence. I report what the cops tell me."

"Fine." I jump out of my chair so violently, it tips over, making a loud crash. I stomp out of the newsroom glaring, daring people to look at me. They all keep their noses to their desks. Cowards.

OUTSIDE, MY HANDS are shaking so badly, one of the press guys lights the cigarette I bum from him.

"Bad day?"

"If you only knew."

I start pacing underneath a tree, restraining myself from punching the bark. That would be dumb. I'm on my second smoke and feeling dizzy. I slump down onto the picnic-table bench right when Lopez comes flying out the back door.

"Saw your car in the lot. Thought you might be out here."

I shake my head.

"I'm sorry, man." He stands there for a minute with his hands shoved in his jeans pocket. "Let me know if there's anything I can do." I nod and bite my lip. He goes back inside, giving me one last glance before the door closes. It's not the first time I've fought back tears today. *Die before cry.*

I grab a crumpled reporter's notebook out of my bag and start writing down possible suspects. *Annalisa,* I scribble. Then, I close my eyes. I have zero suspects. Who else would kill these three men? A dot.com billionaire. The mayor of San Francisco. A former cop. What is the connection? Nothing I can see besides Annalisa. She was seen with the cop the day before? I need to talk to her a.s.a.p.

How does that task force figure into this? I don't care what Donovan says—if the task-force members are dropping like flies, maybe that's the connection. It started out years ago with six cops, and now half of them are dead? Something is going on. I rush back to my desk and dial Troutman, glad that May is away from her desk.

"I think someone is targeting Rosarito cops." As soon as the words leave my mouth, I realize it's true. There *is* something to my theory. I just know it. "Can you get extra security on Donovan in the jail? Just in case."

Troutman clears his throat. "Gabriella, I've already got him in protective custody."

"You do?"

"He's a police officer. Cops are more at risk in jail than child molesters."

"Oh."

He clears his throat again, and I know I don't want to hear what he has to say next.

"You should probably know that when they booked him, they did a lineup." He pauses. I hold my breath. "That witness identified him as the man she saw at the scene."

"That's impossible." I shriek it so loudly, people stop what they are doing and stare. I lower my head, hiding behind the wall of my cubicle. I lower my voice, "Plus, everyone knows eyewitnesses are completely unreliable."

Pulitzer Prize-winning reporter Edna Buchanan once demonstrated this to a class of journalism students. She paid a friend to run into the class, snatch her handbag, and run out. As the students panicked, she yelled something like, "Freeze. Write a description of the suspect." When students' descriptions ranged from tall to short to blond to brunette, she told them this is why eyewitnesses are so unreliable.

"We'll figure this out," Troutman says, and hangs up.

On top of my worry about Donovan, I'm disappointed my anonymous source hasn't called again. Maybe that was my one shot, and now he'll disappear without my finding out what he knows about Caterina.

It was probably another dead end anyway. Still, my heart leaps every time my phone rings. It's always a false alarm. I try to lose myself in my work, ignoring everyone around me. I work on a short story about the dead body they found in the Delta—homeless guy died of exposure—and then start on an evergreen story. Evergreens are stories that aren't timely and can run anytime space needs to be filled in the paper. My story about scam artists targeting the elderly keeps me busy most of the day.

One seventy-five-year-old woman tells me how she lost her life savings after turning over her bank-account information to a "nice young man" who told her she had won $250,000 and he needed her account number to deposit the winnings. There's a special place in hell for people like that.

I haven't been able to eat at all, but around three my stomach starts making embarrassing noises, so I hit the newsroom cafeteria. Greasy pizza and a small salad fit the bill, and I bring it back to my desk. I only manage a few bites before I push it aside.

At seven, my phone rings, and I yawn, taking my time before I pick up. I've left several messages about my scam-artist story. But now that the story's done, I don't really have room for any more comments.

"Giovanni."

"Do you know who this is?" It's a deep voice. My heart starts thumping up in my throat. It must be the man with the information on Caterina.

"I'm so sorry I didn't show up for our meeting on Wednesday. I was . . . well, I was detained. Can we try again?"

The man is silent.

"Hello? Are you there? I won't bring the cops. Just you and me, okay? I really need to meet with you. Please. I need to know what you know about Caterina."

Again, there is a long pause before he answers. "Okay."

"Do you want to meet at the same place?"

"No." The quickness of his answer startles me.

I wait.

"Oakland Hills Park. Tonight. Nine."

My stomach gurgles at the thought of meeting in such a remote area at night, but it's my fault for blowing our first rendezvous. Or rather, it's the cops' fault.

He must sense my hesitation and says this before he hangs up. "If you want to know about . . . Caterina, you'll be there."

Chapter 32

THE ROILING CLOUDS whipping in from the Pacific Ocean turn a clear, starry night into darkness in an instant. I nearly miss the entrance to the park. My headlights catch a small wooden sign in time for me to sharply make the left turn. The road winds steeply up the hillside, flanked by tall pines and redwoods. Every once in a while, the moon peeks out from the clouds, bathing the looming trees in light, but for the most part, the forested area is coated a deep black full of even darker shadows.

On the freeway, I called C-Lo but he didn't pick up. I left a message telling him to meet me at the park as soon as he could. I've realized this past year that I need to be more careful and let people know when and where I'm going. I owe that to Donovan and my family.

As my old Volvo chugs up the steep road, I dial Lopez again. When his voice mail picks up, I leave him another message asking him to call.

My nerves are on edge tonight. And it's not because I'm worried about meeting this guy. He seems harmless. Sort of grandfatherly. And although I don't like his choice of meeting spots, I'm learning to trust my gut instinct—he wants to help me—not hurt me. I'm certain of it. Besides, this might be my last chance. If I don't show tonight, he might be scared off and never call back, disappearing forever with his information. I wish Donovan could be here with me. He'd drop everything. I know it.

Thinking of Donovan in jail makes my stomach hurt, so I push those thoughts aside. A thrill of fear and excitement makes me press my foot down hard on the accelerator. I'm about to get the answers I've been waiting for my whole life.

At the top of the windy road is a parking lot. My headlights illuminate one other vehicle in the parking lot, a Jeep Cherokee. I pull up beside it and peer into the driver's seat. It's hard to see much in the dark, but it's obvious the vehicle is empty. A water bottle and what looks like a jacket is on a picnic table a few feet away near the head of a hiking trail. A small wooden structure with bathrooms is to the right of the table. He's probably in there. I wait a few minutes. Nothing. Then, I roll down my window. The air is warm, still, without even the slightest breeze.

"Hello?" My voice echoes in the silence. A flicker of apprehension runs through me. I'm a few minutes early. Maybe he's not here yet and that Cherokee belongs to someone taking a night hike. It's been known to happen around here although I've never understood the appeal.

Keeping my gaze on the empty lot in front of me, I rummage in my glove box, hunting for a crumpled pack of old cigarettes. Bingo. They're probably stale, but I'll take it. A cigarette might subdue the butterflies in my stomach. What is this guy going to tell me about Caterina? I light my cigarette and get out of my car, closing the door softly behind me. I'll sit at the picnic table, smoke, and wait for my source.

For some reason, the eerie silence makes me hesitant to make any noise. My footsteps are inaudible as I make my way over to the picnic table. I'm almost there when my phone, in my jacket pocket, rings, startling me so much I jump. It must be C-Lo.

"Giovanni." I don't know why, but I whisper.

"Why didn't you show up the other day? I got better things to do than sit around a fishing pier waiting for you."

"What? Then who —?"

A hand clamps down over my mouth. I struggle and try to scream, but the sound dies in my throat as sharp pain overtakes me, and the world grows black.

Chapter 33

I WAKE IN a hospital bed. I can tell by the smell before I even open my eyes. The back of my head feels as if someone is using it as a conga drum.

"Giovanni?" A man's voice sounds like it is coming from far away.

I blink and try to focus. Why is Donovan calling me by my last name? As I focus, I realize the blurry shape in front of my face is not my boyfriend. It's Lopez. He's so close, it startles me for a second. He jerks back.

"Sorry, man. Wasn't sure if you were awake."

"C-Lo?" The word comes out thickly as my fuzzy brain tries to piece together what's going on.

Then I remember. Donovan is behind bars. I'm in the hospital. I came in an ambulance last night. Or was it yesterday?

"What happened? I was at the park to meet that man about Caterina—"

"You got a little whack across the back of the head. Lucky some hot-blooded teenagers were looking for a place to neck."

"Huh?"

"Some Orinda kids. Pulled into the parking lot in time to see dude standing over you. Man, he was up to no good. He had rope and duct tape. Jumped into his car and peeled out of there like a bat out of hell. The teenage girl is a sharp one. She tried to copy down his license-plate number, but there was mud smeared all over it. It was so dark, she couldn't even give the cop shop enough description for a composite. There's an APB out for the dude now, but they aren't working with much."

I vaguely remember two kids kneeling down over me when I came to. The girl covered me with her coat. I wonder if I can get her name to thank her. I remember her soothing voice and smoothing my hair back from my face so sweetly, telling me the ambulance was on its way.

"It was a Jeep Cherokee," I say, and try to sit up. A black fuzzy circle begins to close in around my vision. I lean back and close my eyes. "When can I leave?"

Lopez shrugs, then punches the chair beside him.

"I should've been there. I was hanging with my lady friend. Didn't answer my phone." A blush creeps up his cheeks, something I've never seen.

"Lady friend?" I say with a big smile. He grimaces, so I give him a break and change the subject. "What time is it?"

"Midnight. You got a concussion. They want to keep you overnight for observation."

"How could I be out for so long?"

"Dude injected you with some shit in a needle—docs say sodium pentothal."

The name makes me sit up straight, which sends a wave of dizziness through me.

"Didn't have a chance to give you all of it, those kids pulled up. Needle was sticking out of your arm. Only a little bit was in you. The girl yanked the hypo out, or you'd probably be in worse shape. Maybe dead."

I close my eyes for a minute. *Sodium pentothal?* Lopez doesn't say a word. I crack one eye to look at him. "What is it? What aren't you telling me, C-Lo?"

"Nothing, man." He looks away for a minute, chewing his lip, then turns to me. Here it is. What he was going to say. "It's just that it's too bad your boy's in the clink. I'm sure he's going to go ape shit when he finds out what happened to you."

There's not a lot of love lost between Lopez and Donovan, but I'm touched he feels bad Donovan's been arrested.

"He didn't do it, you know," I say.

Lopez shrugs. "Hey, man it's none of my business. Want me to call your ma or something?"

"Mother Mary, no. That's the last thing I need. You go on home to your lady friend. I'm going back to sleep. I'll be fine."

I'd already ignored calls from my mother yesterday. I'm not ready to talk to her about Donovan's arrest. Not yet.

"Sorry, *chica,* but I'm sticking around. I'm going down to get a refill on this black sludge they call coffee, then I'm going to sit right here reading my new Vince Flynn novel. You better call someone in your family."

I roll my eyes.

"That's not right. They need to know. If you don't, I will."

I can tell he means it. "Fine." My phone is on the table near my bed. It shows I have a message from last night. I press the phone to my ear and lean back into my pillow. It's a news clerk at the paper.

"Are you okay?" she says. "I got a really weird call. This man called and said he was talking to you on the phone, and it disconnected. He was worried about you. Told me to call 911."

At her words, more about what happened in the park comes back to me. The man who had information about Caterina wasn't the one who called and told me to meet him at the park. I wince, replaying our conversation. I made it so easy my attacker: assuming he was the informant and even going so far as offering to meet with him. So, who the hell was it? The killer? They found a needle with the same drug found in Laurent's blood. A wave of exhaustion hits me, and I close my eyes. "Let me take a little nap," I say to Lopez. "Then I'll call my brother."

The next time I open my eyes, the sun is streaming through the blinds. Lopez is beside me in the chair, tapping his fingers. "Morning."

It's a regular party in my hospital room. Moretti is here, probably on police business, and good Lord, my brother, Dante, is, also, here.

"Hey, kiddo," Moretti says. "How's the noggin? When you feel up to it, I'm here to get your statement. Hope you're not planning on making this a habit. This is round two for us."

He was the one who took my statement at the hospital last year after Jack Dean Johnson attacked me at the Oakland harbor.

Moretti is in his trademark Armani suit. And even though he wears his expensive black shoes with the built-in platform heels, my brother still towers over him.

Dante is glowering and pacing. He's wearing slacks and a blazer, but he looks like he's warming up for a boxing match, taking shots. Dante is a lawyer, but also an amateur boxer.

We've had a rough year. Last year, before beating me up, Jack Dean Johnson kidnapped Dante's daughter, my niece, Sofia, to try to get back at me. I found Sofia and stabbed Johnson to death to stop him from shooting Donovan. I was too late. Luckily, Donovan was wearing a bulletproof vest.

Sofia has always reminded me of my sister, Caterina, but in looks only. Sofia is fierce and stubborn and strong. Caterina was quiet and shy and meek. I always wonder if that difference is what kept Sofia alive until I could find her, but I'll never know.

Dante continues pacing. An unlit cigarette dangles between his lips. He's swearing in Italian. I guess I'm lucky my brother Marco isn't here, too. As if reading my mind, Dante brings up our oldest brother. "As soon as Marco and I get ahold of that *putano,* he's going to regret ever fucking with the Giovanni family."

"Dante?" I say. He ignores me. "Did you forget that Lieutenant Moretti is a cop? You better watch what you say."

"He's only saying what I'm thinking," Moretti says. Dante gives him an appraising look, then turns his attention back to me.

"Ella, going up to meet that guy was a knuckle-headed move on your part." His eyes narrow as he says this. Guilt instantly floods through me.

"I got caught up in the thought that he might be able to tell me something about what happened to Caterina."

"Yeah, well, it looks like he was trying to *show* you what happened to Caterina. In person like. You know?"

"But it ends up the real guy—the one who called and wanted to give me the information—that's a whole different man," I say. "And when he calls back—*if* he calls back—I'm going to meet with him. In a safer place, yes, but I am going to meet with him. No matter what."

Dante walks over and grabs my hand, rubbing my fingers in his. "Listen, I'm not going to chew your ass for this in front of everyone, but you need to promise me you'll be more careful. Okay?" His voice grows soft on the last word.

"Yes." My voice is firm. "I know. I promise I'll be more careful."

He smiles and starts to turn away, but then I add, "But I can't turn my back on information about Caterina. You understand this, don't you, Dante? You of all people—you understand this, right?"

His Adam's apple bobs as he swallows hard and nods. He knows what I mean. I won't be foolish, but I'm no longer putting my head in the sand, either. He turns away. We have an understanding.

Moretti leans in toward me. "Gabriella, do you feel up to talking about this yet?"

"Yeah, let's get it over with." Lopez reaches down and grabs my hand. "Stay out of trouble, man. You had me worried."

I gratefully squeeze his fingers good-bye.

Before he leaves, Dante leans down and whispers in my ear. "That guy better hope me and Marco never find him because we will fuck his shit up."

AFTER MORETTI LEAVES, a nurse and doctor come in. They tell me they are going to keep me here a day for observation and say I'm lucky there doesn't appear to be any permanent damage.

"We'll do another MRI tomorrow, and if everything looks good, you'll go home then," the doctor says. She walks out before I can protest. I need to leave this morning. Donovan's arraignment is today. I'm going to get dressed and get the hell out of here. I have to be there for Donovan. I pull myself up to a sitting position and realize I'm not going anywhere. The pounding in my head makes me lie back down.

I hate to admit it, but I know another day of drugs for this incredible pain in my head will be welcome. And I'm so tired I feel like I could sleep until tomorrow.

I CALL TROUTMAN and get his voice mail. I explain what is going on. I hate asking him to tell Donovan why I can't be there.

"I'm totally fine, really. Will you please tell him not to worry?" I say. "And tell him when he gets out that I'm in room 507 at the Pleasant Valley Medical Center."

I'm asleep later when my phone rings. It's Troutman. I blink looking at the clock, wondering why he's calling and why Donovan isn't here yet.

Donovan was arraigned. He pleaded not guilty. The judge denied bail. He was charged with first-degree murder. My hand involuntarily flies to my mouth when I hear this. Denied bail and charged?

It doesn't seem real. How could Donovan be charged with murder? It's a mistake. He's being framed. His preliminary hearing has been set for next month. It makes my stomach flip-flop to imagine him in jail that long. I can't understand why he was denied bail—he's a police officer, for Christ's sake. But Troutman says that is exactly why the judge thought he might be a flight risk. That doesn't make sense to me.

"What evidence do they have against him? I can't imagine they have a single thing on him besides their idiotic theory and that batty old blind lady witness."

"They got something else," Troutman says in a quiet voice. "They served search warrants at Sean's apartment and his locker at work."

"And?"

"They found a vial of sodium pentothal and a needle in his locker."

A cold chill races through me.

"Detectives asked to rush tox on the victim in your apartment. But there was a needle on the floor by your bed. Came back positive for the drug."

Heat races up my neck at the same time I shiver with cold. It's suddenly hard to breathe. I close my eyes. *No. No. No.*

Sebastian Laurent. Carl Brooke. Me. And maybe Adam Grant.

All of us injected with sodium pentothal. It points to the work of one man—or woman. The investigators have to see this. They have to realize my attack was connected to all these deaths and that Donovan is innocent.

Troutman quietly hangs up. I hold my hands over my ears, but I can't quiet the screaming in my head.

Pull it together.

Finally, I fall back asleep, freeing me from my tormented thoughts. I sleep all day, and the next morning, the doctor says my MRI isn't until nine, the earliest she could get me in. I need to see Donovan. I plead with the doctor, but she refuses to release me until they do an MRI.

As soon as the MRI is over, and I'm brought back to my room, I immediately strip off the hospital gown and throw on my jeans and sweater. I perch on the edge of a chair, waiting for the doctor or a nurse to arrive with my release papers. I feel a bit dizzy, but the nurse had given me some painkillers, and my head is only a little achy right now. The back of my skull feels like a gigantic bruise when I touch it. After a few minutes, I grow even more impatient, throw open the door to my room, and peek out in the hall. A few nurses are busy at their station. I look the other way. Nobody. I'm outta here. They can send me the release papers in the mail.

VISITING HOURS AT the jail don't start for another hour today. I don't know when—or if—I'll be able to sleep at my place again, but I should probably grab some necessities while I'm in the city. The thought fills me with dread. My apartment has turned into a place I fear. I hate that so much. Slowly, I push open the door to my apartment and peer in, listening for any movement. Nothing.

The place is spotless. Scott's right. No trace of a dead body. A new mattress, and he even made my bed with fresh sheets he must have found in the cupboard. Even so, my own apartment gives me the creeps. It's as if an invisible darkness lingers over it. I leave my door open to the hall and rush into my bathroom, grabbing my perfume, birth-control pills, deodorant, and a big jar of aspirin. My head is starting to hurt again. Locking my door, my heart is pounding as I race down the stairs.

"ARE YOU OKAY?" Donovan's eyes search my face.

His concern sends a surge of guilt through me. "I'm so sorry I wasn't here for you yesterday," I say. "The last thing I want is for you to worry about me. You have enough to deal with."

"I'm the one who's sorry. What kind of boyfriend am I? Can't even protect you?" He grits his teeth and his eyes flash in anger. I want to tell him this isn't the Dark Ages. It's not his job to protect his "woman," but I bite my tongue. He feels helpless, and hearing that I was attacked must make him feel even more so.

Even so, I figure it's time to come clean and tell him about my slashed tires and the badge left on my windshield. I briefly fill him in. His eyes narrow. I don't think I've ever seen that look in them before. Another ribbon of fear snakes through my insides.

"What? Why do you have that look? Do you know something?"

I want to let him know I saw him take a badge off the dead

body. But I'm too worried about the possibility that our conversation is being recorded. Plus, I'm afraid to ask.

Maybe that is why we are together—I'm the type of person whose job is to tease every single personal detail out of a perfect stranger, yet in my own personal relationships, I live and let live. I never push and never prod or pry. Which, apparently, is the perfect match for Donovan, who will only reluctantly share the most mundane details of his life. Is that what the attraction is? We are both terrible at sharing details of our lives.

I'm going to call my shrink as soon as I leave here and tell her I want her next available appointment. I'm foundering here and have no idea what to say or do. Is it my paranoia and insecurity, or is there really something for me to worry about? I haven't a clue. So, I clam up.

He chews on the inside of his lip for a second. "Can you do me one small favor?"

I nod.

"No more meeting strange men by yourself," he says. "Chris Lopez has promised that he'll be with you every time you leave the office on assignment. I've cleared it with Kellogg."

What? "I'm not a child," I protest. I'm a little bit stunned he has made arrangements with Lopez, whom he barely likes, and Kellogg. I try to interrupt to ask about it, but he keeps on talking. My anger dissipates when I see how wan he looks in that orange jumpsuit. Fine. I'll put up with a babysitter. If it makes him feel better, worry less, then I'll go along with it. The last thing I want is Donovan sitting in a jail cell fretting about me.

"At night, I've arranged for you to stay in one of the guest bedrooms at the rectory. Father Liam is going to give you the garage door opener, so you can pull right into the rectory garage every night."

For some reason, the image of having a priest as my bodyguard makes me do a half roll of my eyes. It doesn't get past Donovan.

"Don't underestimate Father Liam. Remember, he's from Ireland. He not only knows how to dance, he knows how to kick some serious ass if he needs to. He's going to loan you a gun."

That shuts me up. I've been taking shooting lessons ever since I found myself face-to-face with Jack Dean Johnson last year and had my gun knocked out of my hands by him, not once, but twice. It's not my having a gun that surprises me. What doesn't make sense is why the priest would have one to loan me.

The guard is standing behind him, and I'm about to leave when Donovan's voice makes me turn back around.

"There's something else—the way the cops are talking, I get the feeling they think you were in on it with me. They're after you. Watch yourself."

Chapter 34

"GABRIELLA?"

I slouch in the chair and avoid meeting Marsha's eyes. I look past her at the sunny plot of trees in the office courtyard. A small bird tugs at a berry. I called Marsha as soon I left the jail, and she told me to come straight in.

I drag my eyes back to Marsha. My shrink seems distracted, as usual, tucking her plaid skirt under her legs and glancing into her mirrored wall, running her pinky over an unruly eyebrow to put it in its place. But she is listening. And waiting for my response.

"I know," I say, looking up. "You're right. Every single thing you said."

I had spilled the beans about my jealousy about Annalisa and my irrational reaction to Donovan's possible proposal.

"You're never going to find true love or happiness in life unless you make yourself vulnerable," she says with a bright smile.

"I know." It's not the first time she's told me this. Maybe she figures if she says it enough, it will finally sink in.

"When you allow yourself to be jealous of another woman,

you are essentially telling yourself that you are worthless and not worthy of love."

"Yup." I nod. She's the expert. Who am I to argue with her logic?

But I think about what she is saying. Is my self-esteem that low? I've never been jealous in any of my previous relationships. But then again, I've never cared as much as I do now. Dating Donovan is a game changer.

In my rambling about my jealousy, I've completely ignored the, volcano-size issues in my life. Better fess up.

"Um, by the way, Donovan's in jail for murder."

Marsha stops her grooming and sits up straighter. She begins lightly tapping her pencil on her desk and peers at me over her cat's-eye glasses.

"Why don't we talk about that for the rest of your time."

"He didn't do it," I say. "But there's something else I should probably tell you."

She raises an eyebrow waiting.

"I got a call. From a guy who says he knows something about Caterina."

I tell her how I missed the meeting, but how nothing on this Earth will stop me from meeting with him if he calls back. I don't mention, however, that I got hit in the head meeting with someone I *thought* was that guy.

She nods, listening, then says, "Let's go back to your boyfriend."

"But . . . I just told you that after twenty-three years, I might find out what happened to my sister." I'm baffled until she responds.

"I do want to talk about how that makes you feel. Can you come in later this week?"

"But I want to talk about it. Now." I'm getting mad.

"Gabriella, we can talk about whatever you like. It's your dime, but I think it is only fair for me to remind you of something . . . will you indulge me?"

The hostility rising in my throat fades away. "Yes, I'm sorry."

She takes a deep breath and slowly exhales, enunciating her words carefully. "One of the issues we have been talking about is how sometimes in your life you have used the past—an awful, difficult, terrible past, yes, but the past—to avoid dealing with the present. I don't know if you realize what you did just then, but as soon as you brought up your boyfriend—the present—you immediately wanted to switch topics and talk about your past—your sister."

I open my mouth to respond. And then slowly close it and nod.

"Gabriella, I think you are avoiding what is happening in your life right now. I don't mean to be harsh, but you just told me your partner, the man you love, is in jail under arrest for murder. You said it like you were telling me the temperature outside."

My mouth crumples. She's right.

"Oh shoot!" she says, glancing up at the clock, "Our time is up for today, but I want you to think about what I said, and I'd like to see you back here sooner than later. Either this week or next week."

I nod and flee the room before I start to cry.

WHEN I GET to the newsroom, Nicole calls.

"Are you okay?"

She must have heard about the attack in the park. She's called me several times since Donovan's arrest on my cell phone, and I haven't had the heart to pick up. If I talk about it with my best friend, then it is all real.

"Yeah. Guess I got lucky. Again."

"Are you sure you're not Irish? You're awfully lucky for an Italian girl." She gets the laugh she was going for.

"Hey, I'm sorry about Donovan." Her voice is subdued.

"I'm sorry I didn't pick up your calls."

"No problem, as long as you know I'm always here for you, no matter what."

I gulp back another sob trying to escape.

"Thanks."

"Hey, anyway, don't worry. They won't be able to make the charges stick. They can't possibly have anything on him."

I bite my lip. But then I spill it, telling her about the eyewitness and the sodium pentothal. I also tell her how the drug was found in Sebastian Laurent's body.

She's quiet for a long moment. "Someone might be setting him up," she finally says. "What about Grant? Have you checked the autopsy?"

The mayor's death was only a little over ten days ago. "Morgue in Napa said they won't release the autopsy report until tox is back—six to eight weeks."

"That's total bullshit. You know they rushed tox on Grant."

"What do your sources say?"

"They've clammed up. Not a peep. Nobody will say anything now."

I think about that for a second in silence.

Nicole clears her throat, and her voice grows louder. "By the way, I did some research on Annalisa Cruz for you, like you asked."

"What's the skinny?" I stop twiddling the phone cord and wait. I've been wondering how Annalisa got the red phone to our publisher.

"Jordan in the D.A's Office told me that Annalisa has something over Coleman."

Nicole pauses dramatically.

"What?" I bite.

"Photographs of Coleman's new wife in a compromising position. Hear it's something involving handcuffs and restraints and Annalisa in a garter belt."

"Seriously?" Not Coleman. His wife? And Annalisa? I shake my head to dispel the image of Coleman's Chanel- wearing trophy wife in bondage gear with Annalisa looking on.

"God's truth. Probably before they were married, but still."

"Fuck an A."

"You took the words right out of my mouth," Nicole says.

That's why our paper hasn't printed one word about Annalisa.

Not long after I hang up, Lopez swings by my desk.

"I'm on your tail. Like white on rice, man. Donovan told me you're my responsibility."

I sigh. "I thought you guys didn't even like each other, and now you're taking orders from him?"

Lopez scoffs. "He's okay, but nobody gives me orders. It's a collaboration-type deal. We both want something in common— making sure that weirdo stays the hell away from you. He had duct tape and rope, man. I didn't think you were coming back home again."

"Well, I'm touched," I say, maybe a bit sarcastically, "but I still think you're both treating me like a child."

I probably would protest even more, but right then, my phone rings.

"Giovanni."

"It's Red, the guy who has some info on your sister? I heard you got hurt. I called your office when the line disconnected. Glad to hear you're okay."

The informant I *thought* I was meeting at the park. So, he's decided to give me his name. My palms grow damp, and I can feel my heart thumping in my neck.

"I was in a bit of trouble, but I'm fine now. Um, did you tell anyone that you were getting ahold of me?"

"Hell, no. You think I want to get labeled a snitch?"

There goes that theory. "When can we meet?" I look over at Lopez, who raises his eyebrows when he hears my voice quavering.

"How about five o'clock? Berkeley Pier?"

"Perfect. Red, I'm going to bring a friend with me, but he'll stay in the car. He's a little protective of me since I was attacked." I roll my eyes at Lopez, who is giving me the thumbs-up.

There is silence.

"Okay, I guess I understand that. As long as he stays in the car 'cause I don't want the word to spread I'm a snitch."

"Fair enough."

"Take a walk on the fishing pier. I'll find you."

I spend the rest of the day trying to track down possible sources of sodium pentothal. My initial research shows that someone would need a medical license and a DEA certificate to buy the drug. Unless you worked in a hospital or were a doctor, it'd be pretty hard to get the drug. In America. If you lived in Europe? No sweat.

Someone could smuggle it into the U.S., right?

Annalisa mentioned frequent weekend getaways to Europe. Thinking of Annalisa reminds me that I need to talk to her. Soon.

RIGHT BEFORE FIVE, I pull into the dirt parking lot at the Berkeley Pier. A few cars and trucks are parked, some with beds full of fishing buckets. Lopez followed me in his car. His passenger-side window is open so I lean in. "Okay, here goes nothing."

"Don't worry, man. I got my eye on you." He holds up his camera. "Nobody is going on or off that pier without my seeing him. Me and *my little friend*."

He says it with an accent straight out of *Scarface* and pats his side.

"Thanks." He flicks on the radio to the classical-music station, cranks up Bach and points his telephoto lens toward the pier. I straighten up. My head still hurts, and I feel a bit woozy, but nothing is going to stop me from meeting Red this time.

As I walk to the pier, the wind picks up, and I gulp in the salty, fishy cool air that whips my hair back from my face. In the distance, the San Francisco skyline makes my heart soar, and off to the right is Alcatraz, with the Golden Gate Bridge behind it. The sunlight reflects off the waves, licking them with silver sparks that match the billowing clouds overhead. I shield my eyes with my palm, take a deep breath, and step onto the worn wooden planks, heading toward the water.

Chapter 35

SEVERAL MEN LEAN over the rail at the end of the pier, either looking into the murky depths or casting a line. I plant myself between two men, propping my forearms on the wooden railing. The wind has lashed the water below into a gray froth.

A few feet away, a man with a heavily lined face, thick glasses, and a black stocking cap looks over at me. He gives me a wry smile and makes his way over to me. He uses a cane and looks to be in his sixties.

"I'm Red," he says, sticking out a leather-gloved hand. A wisp of gray hair sticks out from his cap. His square chin is grizzly, with a stubbly gray beard forming. His small frame is swallowed by a big, thick, blue down jacket and baggy jeans with workman's boots.

"Gabriella Giovanni," I say, gripping his hand. "Thanks again for meeting me."

"Like I said, I ain't no saint, but I can't abide people who hurt children."

I nod. My head is throbbing now, and I keep thinking about

the big bottle of aspirin in the car. I try to focus. This guy knows something about Caterina's killer.

"Well, I won't waste your time," he says, gripping the railing beside me and looking out at the Bay. "Here's what I know. I was serving a rap for robbery. I was locked up and down this coast since I was eighteen. I never knew any better, couldn't keep my nose out of trouble. I'm over all that now. I don't have much longer on this Earth, and I aim to make the most of it. I finally figured out, money isn't what I need. It's family. I'm going to move down south to be around my kids. That way I get to know my grandkids. Those little ones love me. God knows why. They don't care that I screwed up and wasn't the best dad. They are my chance to do it all over again. Know what I mean?"

I already like this guy.

"Well, as I was saying, I have been in many a jail cell. Not nothing against any people, mind you. Stupid stuff, like passing bad checks and so on. But there was one time, only last year. I was housed with this guy, Mickey. He was a good guy. A little goofy—he was a head case, you know, a little mental. But not violent. Serving time for burglary, nothing violent. At least that's the ways he told it to me.

"Anyways, he was a good storyteller. Made the time pass fast in the joint with all his yarns. One day he told me that before me, he'd been locked up once with a really bad dude. And this guy, name Frank, was about the worst of the worst if you know what I mean. He was bragging to Mickey that he liked to take little girls and do bad things to them, then—kill them."

Frank.

My stomach does a flip-flop, but I nod at Red to continue.

"So Mickey says one day he was reading the *Bay Herald*—he's from Pleasanton, like me, and liked to keep up on the hometown news. There was a story he was reading out loud to Frank. He read the title, then your name—Gabriella Giovanni.

"Well, when he says your name, Mickey said Frank jumped up off his bunk and ripped the paper out of his hands. He laughs and laughs. Then tells Mickey he was the one grabbed your sister all them years ago. He said, and I'm sorry to tell you this, but he said too bad you were all grown-up because he wouldn't mind meeting you one day, too. Sorry, but you ought to know that part, too."

I nod grimly. My knuckles are turning white from gripping the rail on the pier. "Go on. I can take it."

"Well, when Mickey tells me this story, I immediately recognized your name. Since I grew up here, I always read the *Bay Herald* even when I was in the can. You do a good job. I've even got myself a little choked up once or twice reading one of your stories."

"Thanks." I'm not sure what else to say to that. I look down at the water below, watching a seagull hovering right above the waves.

"Anyhoo, this Frank scumbag was laughing, saying that you or the cops would never figure out who took the little girl—your sister. He talked about all the horrible things he did, but I'll spare you those details." Red sighs and looks off into the distance. "Mickey didn't know anything else. He'd bunked with Frank maybe three years ago or something. He didn't know whether Frank was still locked up or what. I seen last year that you killed that guy—that serial-killer guy—cause you thought he had taken your sister. But he wasn't the one, was he? He killed all them other young innocents, though. Hope he's rotting in hell."

"I hope so, too," I say, watching as other seagulls swooped

down to join their friends. They keep getting closer and closer, hovering right in front of us, so close I feel like I can reach out and touch them even though I know they are actually several feet away. Then, I notice. It looks like they are all watching me out of the corner of their eyes. A shiver runs down my spine.

"That's all I know," Red says in the silence. "But I needed to tell you all of this." He clamps his lips together and nods. I turn to face him. His eyes are kind and tired.

"Did your friend ever mention Frank's last name?"

"Nope."

"Know how I can get ahold of Mickey?"

"All's I know is that he's from Pleasanton, and his last name's Menendez."

"Where was Mickey when he met this Frank guy."

"Napa." *The state psychiatric hospital.* "Told you he was a little goofy in the head."

The hospital admits severely mentally ill people who cannot make it in society, but also houses mentally ill criminals, including sexually violent predators who the court believes will attack others if they aren't locked up. Convicts are sometimes sentenced to the hospital as part of their parole.

"Were they in the MDO program?"

"Huh?"

"The mentally disordered offenders program."

"Probably."

"Did Mickey say what Frank's deal was?"

Red looks off into the distance, trying to remember.

"It was a burglary rap. I remember 'cause it was the same thing as Mickey. But it was more than that. It was something like him breaking into women's houses when they weren't home and doing nasty stuff with their underwear and leaving a mess for the women when they got back home."

"Lovely."

"I told you he was a piece of work. Well, there you go, then, you got a name—or part of a name. What you do with it now is your business. I have done my job."

I turn and gaze into the thrashing gray-and-white-flecked waves. The seagulls have left, swooping down to where a fisherman has dumped his bait bucket.

After twenty-three years, a new lead. A wave of excitement rushes through me, making me anxious to leave and go try to find this Frank fuck. I wonder if I'm foolish to get my hopes up. Jack Dean Johnson spent months taunting me—saying he had taken Caterina. It was all a lie. It's true that he kidnapped and killed twenty other girls, just not my sister.

"Well, I really appreciate your meeting me and telling me this, Red," I say, and stick out my hand. "And good luck with your new life in L.A."

"Thanks. I'll be packing up and leaving in the morning. You were the last thing on my list of things to do around here. I made some amends, and talking to you has helped clear my conscience. I hope you get that son of a bitch."

"Me, too."

Walking back to the parking lot, I feel spent, exhausted, as if I have cried my eyes dry. But at the same time, adrenaline is shooting through my limbs. I lean in the car window and give Lopez the abbreviated version.

Back in my car, I dial the newsroom, so I can catch the news researchers before they leave for the night. Now that I'm armed with my information, I'm eager, even though my so-called information essentially consists of one name: Frank. I know it's not much, but it's something.

On the phone, I tell the head librarian, Liz, everything Red told me. I ask if she can track down anything about Frank and his bunkmate, Mickey Menendez, who now lives in Pleasanton. Liz is the best news librarian west of the Mississippi. That's why I am crushed when she gives a big sigh.

"Menendez should be easy as pie, but that Frank . . . no last name, huh? Oh honey, that's like finding an honest man at a political convention. There are a lot of burglary convictions out there. I'll see if I can track anything down that has to do with women's underwear, though."

"Liz? This is personal."

Ever since I killed Jack Dean Johnson, everyone at the newspaper and probably everyone in the entire county knows about my sister. For years, I kept it to myself. It's a relief not to have to do that anymore.

"Figured," she says. "Don't want you to get your hopes up too high."

I'm stuck in traffic out of downtown Oakland. I see Lopez's car behind me. She's right. It's a long shot. But I won't give up. "Doesn't it help that we know a bit about his conviction and the fact that he was in Napa sometime over the past five years?"

"Sugar, you better believe I'll do anything to find this guy for you. You know I will," she says. "What about your boyfriend? Cops have access to all sorts of criminal databases, you know."

I'm thrown by her question. Heat flares across my cheeks. How can she not know that Donovan is in jail? It was splashed all over the front page of every paper in the state, including ours. Then she remembers. "Oh, that's right. Geez, I'm sorry. Let me get on this right now. I'll do my best," she says. I can hear the remorse in her voice.

I hang up, feeling low. I realize I may be no closer to finding Caterina's killer than before. And Donovan is in jail. Even though I know he didn't kill anyone, how am I going to prove he didn't? I don't know.

Chapter 36

THE SUN IS setting as I pull up to the rectory, not sure where to go and what to do. In less than thirty seconds, Father Liam is in front of me at the end of a long driveway. Lopez, who has followed me the entire way back from the pier, waves once he sees Father Liam and peels off to head home.

I pull down the driveway. At the back, a small garage backs up against the hillside. The garage door is slowly rising. Father Liam smiles and gestures for me to enter the garage. He follows my car on foot into the large garage and closes the door behind us.

"Hello, so nice to see you again," he says, opening my car door for me. "Hope you're hungry."

My head hurts so bad the thought of food makes me feel sick. All I want to do is sleep for a week, but instead, I smile. I feel less awkward once we are inside, and I realize I'm not the only house-guest. A visiting priest from India, Father Michael, is, also, staying in the rectory.

Father Liam explains that there are six bedrooms in the rectory: four downstairs and two upstairs. He and Father Michael are downstairs and he's put me upstairs to give me some privacy. I remember that the study, where he danced, is upstairs.

"Excuse us, Father Michael, I'm going to show Gabriella her room so she can freshen up for dinner."

I follow him up the stairs.

"I hope you don't mind. Sean told me you had a key under your mat, so I took the liberty of stopping by your house and packing a few of your belongings. And I picked up your cat from Sean's place."

My small duffel bag is on the bed, and Dusty is meowing from his crate on the floor of the attached bathroom. Small silver bowls, one with water and one with cat food, are already set up on the floor near Dusty's crate.

Father Liam closes the door behind us, then reaches into the top drawer of the nightstand and withdraws a big black handgun. The only thing I can tell about it is that it's a semiautomatic.

"This pistol is called a 9 x 19 mm Grandpower K100, Slovak. Hold it. I want to make sure you're comfortable with it."

He gives me a brief tutorial. When he is done, he sets it on the nightstand.

"I want you to sleep with it right here. Every night, when you go to bed, I want you to lock this door." He points to the bedroom door, which I realize with surprise is reinforced steel with two dead bolts.

"Don't worry," he says, leaning down and giving me a small kiss on my forehead. "You're safe as a baby, here. I don't mean to scare you. I want you to be prepared in the highly unlikely event that someone gets through me. But that's not going to happen. When you're ready, come down. Dinner is in twenty minutes."

I watch him walk away and am not afraid. I'd like to see anyone try to tackle this man of God.

I POP SOME more aspirin and go to unpack my duffel bag. Set gently on the very top of all my clothes is the picture of me and Caterina I keep by my bed. Tears sting my eyes as I set it gently on the nightstand by the gun. I hang my clothes in the small wood armoire. It's strange to think that the priest went to my place and packed my bag. He didn't do too badly. But remembering his designer duds, I'm not surprised. I have enough to last at least a week if I plan it right: He packed the essentials, which include my comfy flannel men's pajamas, a pair of worn and soft jeans, a white blouse, a floral blouse, gray pants, a blue, flowered dress, a bulky gray sweater, and a black dress.

After settling in, I change into the flowered dress, wash my face, and head downstairs. Father Michael is already seated at the large dining-room table. The aspirin has kicked in, and I'm now ravenous. The crystal chandelier and long, tapered candles softly light the rectory dining room. The mammoth mahogany table gleams, and I'm worried the condensation on my crystal water glass will mar it, so I scoot it over onto my lacy placemat.

"Voilà!" Father Liam says, coming through the swinging door from the small galley-style kitchen, balancing three soup tureens on his arms. He places butternut squash soup in front of me and pours a deep red cabernet into my wineglass.

I dip my spoon into the creamy, sunset-colored soup and raise it to my lips. It is so good I pace myself, so I don't slurp the entire thing up in one second.

"This is amazing."

"It's simple," Father Liam says with a shrug. "A little squash and milk."

"You're too modest. It's fantastic."

I'm filled with guilt, thinking of Donovan behind bars, eating jail slop, while I sit here warm and cozy, dining on a gourmet meal and sipping wine.

Father Michael, who is East Indian, but grew up in Rhodesia, regales us with tales of his life there. He had a pet crocodile named Samuel. As a child, he ran with the monkeys and played in the waterfalls for fun. The crocodile is now full-grown, living in back of his uncle's store in Rhodesia.

I want to learn more about Father Liam, but being the perfect host that he is, he expertly steers the conversation away from himself at every turn. He is an adept conversationalist, focusing on listening more than speaking. Few people have mastered this skill.

The most I manage to pry out of him is that he came to America after abandoning his dreams of becoming a professional dancer when he injured his foot. Apparently, the injury wasn't from dancing, either. Some kids in the neighborhood beat him up, hitting his foot with baseball bats until it disintegrated.

"Good God!" I say, forgetting for a moment who I'm talking to.

His parents immediately shipped him to America, where he first lived in New York City and worked for a distant uncle. He's a bit vague on what that job for his uncle entailed.

I try to steer to conversation back toward him.

"What happened to those kids? Did they get arrested?"

"I'd rather not talk about it, if you don't mind," he said with a sad smile. "Let's talk about you. You are a much more interesting topic, don't you think, Father?" He turned to the other priest.

"Fine, but one more thing," I say, not giving in that easy. "You have to admit you aren't a typical priest. I mean, the priests in North Beach are nothing like you. You are a lot different . . . than the others."

"Yes. Sometimes the archbishop gets very frustrated with me,"

Father Liam says thoughtfully. "But in the end, he always supports me. There aren't a lot of Catholic churches that welcome the diversity of people that I do. In his heart, he knows that we are doing the right thing by offering these people a spiritual home even if our methods are a bit unorthodox."

I remember Donovan's telling me that his church had openly gay couples with children, African-Americans who wore their traditional garb to Mass, and liturgical dancers at many Masses. I'm not sure how I feel about this. Part of me really likes that the church welcomes all types, but I crave the traditional Masses that I was raised on. I'm not sure I would like the dancers flitting around with their scarves on the altar.

I don't get the friendship between Donovan and Father Liam. To me, priests have always been revered—someone to have over for dinner, sure—but always held a little at a distance.

After he clears our soup tureens, Father Liam disappears for a few moments into the kitchen, only to reappear with a rack of roasted lamb that he sets in the middle of the table. A small side platter of roasted eggplant, zucchini, and peppers is nearby.

After we finish our main course, Father Liam brings out a green salad. The vinaigrette is the perfect blend of flavors. A plate of fruit is brought out for dessert with espresso.

"I'm glad that Donovan can turn to you for advice," I say, taking a sip of my espresso. "Right now, he needs that more than ever. But I'm still a little thrown off by your relationship."

"Gabriella, what you have to realize is that while I am a priest, I am, also, a man," Father Liam says. "I have chosen to spend my life serving God. It wasn't an easy decision, but it has brought me more gratification than I could have ever dreamed. But my life in Ireland was not simple. Or easy. If you had told the teenage me that I would turn to the priesthood, I would have laughed. But sometimes, these matters are out of our hands.

"I think that if you spend any time with priests, you will realize that they are like you in many ways. Except instead of pursuing a career, say in journalism, they have devoted their lives to bringing people to God. That doesn't mean that we are immune to all the temptations and foibles of being human."

Okay. I get it. It's a major paradigm shift for me to see a priest as somebody like me. I had a hard enough time reconciling that Donovan once wanted to be a monk, and say as much to Father Liam.

"Donovan's father's death really tormented him. He thought the way to make his mother happy was to become a monk, but then he realized it wasn't the right life for him. So he became a police officer."

"Those two professions seem like polar opposites. That's one reason I have such a hard time imagining him as a monk."

"They are not very different when you think about it," Father Liam says after a pause where he takes a bite of cantaloupe. "They are both professions of service. Donovan became a police officer because he felt that was the best way he could serve others in this world."

I am silent. Tears are ready to erupt. I clench my jaw until they go away. Crying won't help anything. Donovan is in jail. For murder. I feel so guilty sitting here when he is in a squalid, smelly jail cell.

"They've got to find the real murderer," I finally say, once I compose myself.

Father Liam closes his mouth and nods, looking at me. "Have faith, my dear. We know Donovan didn't kill anyone. Have faith that the truth will emerge."

I'm Catholic, and I believe, but I decide right then, I'm not going to wait around hoping the truth will emerge on its own. I'm going to make sure to give it a little push. Or shove.

Chapter 37

I'M RESTLESS. I need to do *something*. Donovan needs my help right now, but I feel like I'm spinning in circles. I'm not a detective; I'm just a reporter. And I'm not even an investigative reporter, either. What can I do to help?

I've never felt so helpless in my life. Not even when Caterina was missing. Then, I was just a kid and *knew* there was nothing I could do. I looked to the adults to do something. But now, I'm the adult, and if I don't do something, the man I love might go away forever for a crime he didn't commit.

It's late, but I try Annalisa's line once again. She doesn't pick up. I leave a message, another stab at reaching her. I've left messages for her all week.

I pace. But no matter how long I stay up at night, lying in bed, racking my brains and trying to figure out if there is some clue or some detail I've learned that could clear Donovan's name, I've got nothing.

I'm torn by two different pressing needs and desires—proving Donovan is innocent and finding the monster who killed my sister. I feel helpless to do either.

BLESSED ARE THE MEEK 215

Looking at the picture of Caterina and me on my nightstand, I realize that maybe there is something I *can* do. I have something. A name. A first name. I'm not sure what to do to help Donovan, but now that I have a name, a jail, and a crime, I can try to track down Caterina's killer. And if I don't act, that man might continue to kill, leaving a trail of bodies behind him.

I feel guilty, remembering what Marsha told me about using the past to avoid dealing with my present. Well, I have to do *something*. If I can't help Donovan, at least I can get some answers about Caterina. If I don't, I'll lose my mind.

Liz, the librarian, hasn't called and won't be in the office again until morning. I don't know if she's had any luck with finding a Frank, or Red's friend, Mickey. I know she has access to Lexis-Nexis, which means she can find almost anything on a person—their address, their criminal record, the year they got divorced or married, you name it.

I set up my laptop on a small table in my room. Father Liam has AOL service. I sign in with my user name and after a few minutes am connected to the Internet. I start to search: burglary, underwear, women, Frank. Nothing. Then search with HotBot and excite.com.

Nothing for a Mickey Menendez in Pleasanton. I grab my cell phone and punch in Moretti's number.

"Hey, kiddo. *Come stai?*"

"Not so good, Moretti."

Of course he knows what I'm talking about. "Anything I can do?"

"Prove he didn't do it?"

"Wish I could."

I can sense his sadness in the silence that follows. He's a good friend.

"Moretti, there's actually something else you could help me with. Something to do with my sister."

My words immediately change the tone of our conversation.

"Anything."

I tell him my story about Red. After a few seconds, Moretti clears his throat.

"I know a guy who works at Napa. Haven't talked to him in years, though," he says.

That's it. I can't sit still another minute waiting for someone else to do something about finding the man who killed my sister. "Well, I'm heading up there tonight," I say. "I'll be visiting the Napa hospital first thing in the morning. Can I use your name?"

"Ask for Lonnie Sandoval."

I CHANGE INTO jeans and the bulky sweater and throw my pajamas and extra clothes and a toothbrush into the duffel bag. At the last minute, I stick Father Liam's big black gun in, too. It's already ten, but I need to get out of the rectory right this minute before I go crazy. I need to feel like I'm doing something useful. Otherwise, despair is going to settle over me, and once it's made itself at home, it's hard for me to get rid of it. I've felt this way before. I know where it leads. It's not good.

I dial Lopez.

"Feel like going on a road trip?"

"Sorry, man. My ma just landed in the hospital. Her blood pressure was super-high, and she threw up. Doctors say she's probably cool now, but I'm on duty to sit with her tonight." I hear the hesitation in his voice. "But if you need me to, I'll call my sister."

"No. Give your mama a kiss for me. I'll see if Father Liam wants to come with me."

I hang up, feeling guilty for lying, but I'm not going to pull him away from his sick mother. And I'm not going to wake Father Liam. I'll just be extra careful.

Downstairs, I stop by the kitchen and scribble a note to Father Liam.

"I'm sorry to run out, but I didn't want to wake you. I'm tracking down something in Napa. I've got your gun, and I promise to be careful. Here's my cell number. Will call in the morning."

I feel like a teenager sneaking out of the house as I quietly pad my way to the door to the connecting garage.

Chapter 38

WHEN I PULL out of the rectory, a car parked on Lakeshore Boulevard turns on its lights and pulls out behind me, several hundred feet back. It gets on the freeway after me. I watch it in my rearview mirror. I've promised everyone I'm going to be careful, so if it stays behind me any longer, I'm pulling off and heading right to the Albany police station.

But as soon as I merge onto I-580, weaving in and out of traffic, I realize I'm being paranoid. Nobody is following me.

Besides, if anyone is tailing me, it's probably those damn detectives. Maybe they've been tailing me the whole time since I left the hospital, and I've never noticed. They can follow me all they want. Maybe they'll learn something that proves I'm not the killer. Even so, I keep a close eye on my rearview mirror every time I change lanes or freeways.

On Interstate 80, I'm sleepy and somehow miss the turnoff for Napa, ending up a bit northwest of the town. I'm too tired to care. I'll get a room and hit the jail first thing in the morning.

Nobody is behind me when I take the exit for the motel. I make sure. Maybe I'm being paranoid, but I'm not taking any chances. It's the least I can do since I already feel guilty about leaving without waking Father Liam. In my motel room, I shove a small dresser in front of the door. It won't stop someone but will at least wake me up if it topples or moves. I put the gun near my head on the nightstand.

It takes me a long time to fall asleep. I startle at every little sound At one point during the night, I hear voices in the parking lot and peek out the blinds. It's a couple that appears to have been drinking. The woman laughs shrilly and totters in her high heels, leaning heavily on the man. I close the drapes and lie back down. I feel scared, lonely, and guilty that I'm not doing more to help Donovan clear his name. But right now there's something concrete I can do to find Caterina's killer, so I need to follow up on it. I fall asleep toward dawn, but only for an hour.

Only once morning sunshine filters through the thick drapes and I'm showered and dressed, do I move the dresser aside to leave. I peer around the parking lot, but it's quiet. There are a few other cars, all empty.

I grab a bagel and coffee in the lobby when I check out. The map shows two different routes to the mental hospital One is a windy, mountain road. The other seems less daunting but is still a curving passage through steep hills. Either way, my old Volvo will strain chugging up the incline, but I opt for the slightly flatter route even though it will take me twice as long to get to the mental hospital I glance at my watch, but it's still too early to call Father Liam. Besides, he has my number.

The radio is blaring, "Pride" by U2, and the combination of

this song and the brilliant sunshine fills me with a mix of hope and excitement and makes me punch the accelerator as I navigate the curvy road toward Napa and the mental hospital. The road is cut out of the side of a hill that is a soaring chunk of land. Seeing a sharp turn ahead, I gently tap on my brakes. My foot presses down flat to the floorboard a little too easily. But my car doesn't slow. I press the brakes again. Nothing.

I lift my foot completely off the accelerator and grip the steering wheel, realizing my brakes are shot. I have nowhere to go. The mountain road, which has begun to climb out of the valley is already about ten feet above the ground. My side is lined with pine trees and a wall of dirt and rock, roughly hewn out of the mountainside, borders the other lane.

My car has slowed a bit since I took my foot off the accelerator, but it is still going too fast for the curve ahead, which is alarmingly close. Vaguely I register the radio is still blaring U2. At the last minute, I remember my emergency brake. I yank up on it and my car spins as the tires shriek. My car whirls violently and jerks around like a bumper car. The world around me is a blur of colors. I hear a loud crunch, then a rat-a-tat-tat noise. Then silence.

Distantly, as if I am watching myself in a movie, I note that my bagel is now upside down, cream cheese sticking it to the dashboard and my coffee with cream has disintegrated, coating the windshield in a weird light beige Rorschach pattern. My sunglasses somehow left my face, and I'm not sure where they landed.

At the same time, my cell phone rings, but I'm not sure where it landed in the chaos. I hear the beep indicating someone has left a message.

I can't see out my front windshield. My side window is surprisingly dark. The dark is actually dirt. My car and window is jammed up against the hillside. I'm in the wrong lane, facing the wrong way. I spring to action, releasing my seat belt and scramble out the passenger door. I don't want to be sitting in my car when an oncoming car rounds that corner.

I fish around on the floor and find my cell phone. I have to push past a piece of my bumper to open the passenger door. I quickly open my trunk. Then I run as fast as I can to set up flares several hundred feet up the mountain to give a driver coming down the hill warning. Then I do one more flare on the road coming up before I stop, catching my breath, and dial 911.

While I'm on the phone with the 911 dispatchers, another call tries to get through and goes to voice mail.

I try to piece together what happened, tracing back my trajectory based on my skid marks. Apparently, the pine tree trunks were so close to the shoulder of the road, they acted like bumpers on a pinball machine, keeping my car from plunging off the side. There are about ten trees that have the bark completely stripped at about the level where my car would have scraped against them.

My knee is howling. I think I whacked it on the steering wheel. My collarbone is chafed from my seat belt. My neck doesn't hurt, but I remember whiplash usually doesn't show up until the next day.

I give my poor car a look. The front is mangled. Seeing my hood munched up into a triangle, I make the sign of the cross. I thank God, the Virgin Mary, and the engineers who design Volvos.

I grab my duffel bag and catch a ride back to town with a nice friendly police officer. He offers to put my bag in the trunk, but I clutch it on my lap, hoping he can't tell that it has a big fat gun inside. I'm sure his colleague, Detective Harry Gold, would love to hear I crashed my car in his county and am packing illegal heat. He'd lock me up for sure.

I'm still a little nervous, hoping Gold wasn't listening to his police scanner when they ran my driver's information over the air talking about the crash.

At the garage, the officer is sympathetic when he sees the tow truck pull up with my crunched Volvo hanging off the back like a fish on a hook.

"Looks like she's totaled," he says.

I nod solemnly. She was a good girl who served me well.

"You were lucky," the cop reminds me. "Volvo's are tanks. Any other car would have probably collapsed like a tin can with you inside."

The tow-truck driver, who is peering underneath my car, calls the cop over to him. I wander over to listen in. The brake line was cut. Not a drop of brake fluid was left. A cold chill races across my scalp. Thank God I hadn't taken the steeper, mountain route to Napa. The attack at the park—and now this. Those weren't just warnings. I know for sure now.

Someone wants me dead.

A few minutes later, I eye an orange Dodge Charger circa 1980s with a for sale sign on it. It's only $400. I head to the ATM inside the nearby convenience store.

Within the hour, I'm motoring over the mountains in my new ride. I listen to my voice-mail messages. Father Liam. He doesn't sound happy. But I'm not going to call him back until I'm already at the mental hospital. It's too late to turn back.

The big orange car clunks, thuds, and even smokes a little, but keeps on puttering up the hill. The passenger door is completely crunched in. I'm sure that door won't open. The driver's side is spotted with bondo. The mechanic promised me the beater would get me from point A to point B. That's all that matters. My neck is now starting to hurt, and it seems like every muscle on my body is sore and aches, so I pop more aspirin and make the sign of the cross that I'm still alive.

When I pull into the Napa state hospital parking lot, I return Father Liam's messages.

"Good grief, child, you've had me worried sick."

"Father Liam, I'm so sorry, I didn't want to wake you last night to tell you where I was going. I couldn't sleep, but I, also, couldn't sit still and do nothing."

"Are you okay?"

"Everything is fine." I feel a surge or guilt lying to the priest, but I'm too embarrassed to tell him someone tried to kill me. "I'll be back to the rectory by dinner."

"Please call me when you leave." He doesn't sound happy.

COMMANDER LONNIE SANDOVAL'S office walls at the Napa State Mental Hospital are lined with a variety of awards and plaques. A big U.S. Marine flag takes center stage. His tight-cropped hair, crisp uniform, and posture smack of a man who is good at following orders. That worries me. He doesn't have to share any information with me.

And he makes that clear from the get-go.

"The only reason I'm talking to you is because of Michael Moretti. We go back a long ways, and if he says to tell you what I have, then I'm going to give it to you because I'm sure he has a good reason."

"I appreciate that," I say.

"Here's what I've found—looks like Frank Anderson might be your man." He taps a file folder.

My heart races. His last name is Anderson. Bingo.

"Was a resident here from 1993 to 2001," Sandoval says, reading. "From Sacramento. He liked to break into homes and—well there's no easy way to put this."

He hesitates.

"You don't have to censor it for me," I say. "I can handle it. Besides, my source already told me this Frank guy masturbated with the women's underwear or something."

"Wasn't women's underwear."

"Huh?"

Sandoval is clearly uncomfortable talking to me about this, despite my reassurances.

"You see, he targeted houses with young girls in them." Sandoval lifts his eyebrow at me. "He liked little girls' underwear."

Sandoval darts his eyes at me, gauging my reaction. He appears startled to see a smile spread across my face.

"That's him," I say, nodding. "It's got to be."

I briefly wonder if I should call the Livermore detective assigned to Caterina's cold case but dismiss the idea, remembering the cop's derision for my ideas. First I'll get proof, then I'll go straight to the Livermore police chief, bypassing the detective altogether.

According to what Sandoval tells me, Frank Anderson had broken into more than a dozen homes, leaving his semen on girls' underwear, before he finally got caught. The police somehow kept his perverted burglary streak out of the news, probably because the crime involved minors. He got caught one morning when a father returned home to retrieve a briefcase he had forgotten. The man, an ex–pro wrestler, found Anderson in his daughter's bedroom, with his pants around his ankles. He beat the crap out of

Anderson before calling police. Anderson, who had a documented history of mental illness, pleaded guilty by reason of insanity. He served eight years. He was paroled last year.

A thrill of excitement surges through me. Semen equals DNA. I wonder if they have any DNA from twenty-three years ago, when Caterina was killed? Since we don't talk about Caterina, it's a question that has never come up in my family. If he's the one, we might be able to nail him.

"Anything else on his record?"

Sandoval frowns and shakes his head.

"Current address?" I ask as if it's my right to have it.

"We last had him in Moraga. Parole officer lost track of him two months ago. But the good news for you is that his failure to check in makes him an automatic arrest for parole violation. Back in the big house."

Even so, my heart sinks. I'm trying not to be crushed that two months earlier, there was an address for Frank Anderson. An actual house. A place where I could . . . do what? I'm not sure what the answer to that is yet. What I do know is I'm not giving up until I look him right in the eyes.

Chapter 39

When Lopez pulls up beside me on the street in Moraga, he rolls down his window, eyes my orange beater, and snorts with laughter.

"Hey man, did you pick up this beauty for undercover work or what?"

"Hardy har har." I roll my eyes.

"No seriously, man. Too bad we aren't undercover narcs: White woman. Chicano man. Hooptie car. They would *totally* deal to us."

After calling Father Liam and filling him in, I'd called Lopez to check on his mom. She'd been released, so I asked him to meet me near the address I have for Frank Anderson. I thought I could take care of myself, but somehow someone managed to follow me and cut my brake line while I was asleep in the motel. I need to be more careful. I owe it to Donovan.

Lopez and I meet a few streets over from the house.

He nods at my car again. "What's up with the beater?"

"Car crash. Someone cut my brake line."

"What about the chappy?"

"What?"

"You know, the padre, man of the cloth, Holy Joe?"

"You mean Father Liam? He didn't come."

"Goddamn it, Scoop," he says, raising his voice. "You told me you were going to Napa with the priest. You're not supposed to be traipsing off in the middle of the night by yourself."

"I know. I'm sorry. I promise I won't do it again." I say the words, but a wave of resentment rises at being treated like a child. Is it because I'm a woman?

Lopez relieves my guilt by bursting into laughter when he gives my car another look. He leans over and unlocks his passenger door. "Why don't we take my ride, it's a little less . . . obvious." He stifles another snort of laughter.

We creep around the corner in Lopez's dark gray Honda. I am checking the addresses when I realize that Frank Anderson's house is the one with the FOR SALE sign in the yard. We park and peer through the curtainless windows, but, of course, the place is empty.

A voice behind us startles me.

"What business do you have with this house?" says a man with a baseball hat and tan jacket. His tone indicates he is not part of the neighborhood welcoming committee.

"We're looking for Frank Anderson."

His lip turns up a little into a sneer and his eyes narrow. "How come?"

"He needs to be behind bars." I say it matter-of-factly.

The man's scowl disappears. His arms unfold.

"That's a fact. The most we could do was drive that son of a bitch out of our neighborhood. A person like that has no right to live in a place where there's kids."

"As far as I'm concerned, he has no right to live anywhere. He should either be behind bars or underground." The man can tell I mean it.

He gives me an appraising look. "I like what you're talking."

"Any idea where he moved?"

The man shrugs. "One day I woke up, and the house was empty. Must have packed up in the night and left. Don't know why. Figured our prayers were answered. We found out about him 'cause of them notifications from the sheriff's office—you know those ones they send out for when a pervert moves into your neighborhood?"

I nod.

"This fellow moves in and sits there on his front porch, smoking and eyeballing the kids in the neighborhood. He's lucky he got out of here alive. John Snelling—he lives in that white house—comes over and tells him to get back in his house and quit looking at our kids. Snelling grabs Anderson and throws him into those bushes. He's lucky. If it'd been me, I'd a thrown him through his own front window. So you know what this pervert has the nerve to do?"

I shake my head.

"Calls the cops, he did. And Snelling, a hardworking family man, a Persian Gulf veteran, gets picked up on an assault charge. What the hell is wrong with this world? A pervert calls the cops and gets a decent man arrested? A sick son of a bitch can sit on his porch and leer over our children, and it's okay because they sent us some damn notice in the mail telling us he lives here?"

The guy is working himself up into a frenzy.

"What kind of car did he drive?"

"Piece of shit. Beat-up Chrysler LeBaron. Beige."

"Know if he worked?"

"No, that loser just sat around all day perving out."

I figure we've hit a dead end, so I turn to leave.

"You might want to ask around at the Depot. I saw his lady friend come home wearing a shirt from there, like she was an employee."

Lady friend? "Do you know her name?"

"Yeah. Only because that pervert was yelling at her in the driveway one night. It's Delilah."

THE DEPOT ISN'T half-bad. It's a run-down hamburger joint. Old posters are peeling off the walls, and the linoleum is black and scuffed in places.

Lopez orders a beer and my Absolut. The bartender looks like she's seen it all. I bet if a gunfight broke out right in front of her, she would yawn and check her lipstick. Her long, bouncy blond curls and her trim figure make her look youthful from behind, but when she turns around, her stringy neck, the puffy bags under her eyes, and her lined face reveal that she hasn't had an easy life. When she asks if we want another round, I pop the question.

"I'm trying to locate a friend of mine—Delilah. I haven't talked to her for a while, but last I heard, she was working here."

"You and me both, sister."

I raise an eyebrow, keep silent, and hope she'll keep talking. She obliges.

"She didn't show up for her shift last week, and she won't answer her phone," the woman says, plopping my Absolut down in front of me. "Had to pull a double three nights in a row until I could bring someone else in to take her place. She's got some explaining to do."

I do some fast thinking. "Well, maybe her mom will know where she is—lives over on Manzanita Way. I'll head over there next. Hey, I don't want to be disrespectful to her mom and not call her the right thing, but I can't for the life of me remember Delilah's last name."

The bartender gives me a look. "You ain't her friend."

Busted. Something I said blew my whole cover story. Her mother is probably dead or something. I can tell I better come clean if I want any information.

"You're right," I down my vodka. "I'm sorry I lied. I'm a reporter. I'm looking for the man Delilah was living with. He's up to no good. She's probably in danger if she's with him."

The woman starts drying some glasses. I know she's thinking about whether to tell me anything more. She continues swabbing water off the glass mugs. I wait. She doesn't look up.

"Can you at least call me if you hear from her?" I hand her my card but don't feel optimistic that Delilah is going to return to the Depot anytime soon—or that the bartender will pass on my message. Before I leave, I ask the bartender what gave me away.

"You said you couldn't remember her last name," the bartender said. "Oh please. Who can't remember a last name like Jones, for crying out loud?"

THE NEXT MORNING, I fill Donovan in during my daily visit.

"You're getting close, Ella," he says, smiling. "We're going to find him."

His enthusiasm for this makes me want to cry. He is sitting in a jail cell, yet he is excited that I'm making progress in tracking down my sister's killer. But his reaction fills me with guilt.

"But what about you?" I practically whisper it into the phone, wanting so badly for the glass between us to vanish. All I want to do is touch him and have him hold me.

"If there was something I thought you could do to help, believe me, I'd tell you," Donovan says. "I get it. I know you feel helpless. That has to be horrible."

Again, he is turning it around to me and not him. Not fair. "Who cares about me? I want you out of here. You're innocent, and they are crazy to have you here."

His eyes turn steely and the set of his jaw is firm. "I'm working on something. Troutman and I are getting close. You have to trust me on this."

"Can you please tell me?"

He slowly shakes his head.

"But why?" I know I'm pleading, practically begging.

He gives a long sigh, and says, "I can't. I'm already worried about you enough as it is. I can't put you in more danger."

The guard who has been standing behind him gives him a final tap on the shoulder. He stands. "I love you. Trust me."

He hangs up before I can say I love him back. I head for the door and the tiny hallway separating the visiting from the lobby.

Walking to my car, I go over everything I know about the three murders.

Troutman had told me Annalisa had lunch with the dead cop who was found in my room the afternoon he was murdered. That's the reason the detectives are looking at Donovan, painting him as a jealous lover killing men who are connected to Annalisa. What is the connection? How are Donovan, Annalisa, and the cop connected? The common thread seems to be that special-task-force team where Donovan met Carl Brooke.

How does Annalisa fit into all of this?

A long time ago, Donovan had said he'd tried to get back together with the girl he'd left the monastery for. He told me it was shortly after he became a cop, while he was still a rookie. Maybe I'm wrong, but what if all this took place at the same time, and that's how Annalisa knew Brooke? It might add up. I get excited thinking about it but then realize it still doesn't explain anything. For instance, how do Sebastian Laurent and Adam Grant fit into the puzzle?

Donovan won't—or can't—talk. Brooke is dead. That leaves Annalisa. She won't return my calls. Time to pay her a visit. I immediately turn the wheel toward Laurent's house on the hill, which I guess I should start calling her place. I pound on the doorframe. The door itself is covered in thick iron lattice. I yell, loud enough for the neighbors to peek out their second-story window at me. I'm hoping she will be embarrassed enough to open the door. No go. The garage has no windows, so I can't tell if she is even home, but something tells me she is just avoiding me.

After a few minutes, I stop yelling and dial her number non-stop, letting it ring and ring—she must have disconnected her answering machine. I listen to the continuous buzzing, then hang up and redial. I pound the door at regular intervals. There's no way to creep around to her steep backyard overlooking the city because the houses are fenced. Finally, after forty-five minutes, I leave, making a racket as I turn the ignition of the orange beater and it backfires. Driving to the office, I call Annalisa every five minutes or so. I've dealt with enough politicians before I got on the crime beat that I have pesky reporter down to a science.

Chapter 40

Pulling into Nana's curved driveway and seeing her sprawling house nestled in the hills of Livermore's wine country always brings peace to my heart. The slanting sunlight gives the house's white Carmel stone an ethereal glow. Giant, overflowing flowerpots and trailing vines add splashes of cheerful color to the front of the home. The extensive garden beds in the back are testimony to my grandmother's endless energy. In her eighties, she won't even consider slowing down. Her home has been the host to our family's big Sunday dinner for the past fifty years or so, ever since my mother was a little girl, and the family moved out of San Francisco's Italian neighborhood.

Donovan has been in jail a week. It's time for me to face my family. Father Liam and Donovan agreed it would be safe for me to spend the weekend with my grandmother. I've hardly come up for air all week. Every day I stop at the jail to visit Donovan. After, I head to Annalisa's, where I pound on her door for a few minutes before heading into work. In the newsroom, I spend my days churning out as many evergreen stories as I can before heading to the rectory late and falling into bed.

I'm so relieved to be at my grandmother's house. Lopez followed me to her long driveway, then peeled off, back to his place in Oakland. I know I'm lucky to have such a loyal friend, but I need my family at the moment.

My world feels so uncertain right now—I need some grounding. Nana has always been my confidant. And I need to confess.

"*Mi cara.* You make your nana so happy coming to stay," she says, giving me kisses on both cheeks. "I heat up some *pasta fazool,* we have some wine, and watch *Wheel of Fortune,* okay?"

"That sounds perfect," I say with a smile. That's what I need—something normal and mundane and wonderful with someone who loves me unconditionally. I need some relief from the despair I feel. Thinking of Donovan sitting in jail sends flutters of panic through me as if a heavy weight is pressing on me, and I can't escape.

I know tomorrow is "D" Day. The day I have to face my family about Donovan's arrest. If my Nana knows anything, she isn't letting on. By the way Nana is treating me, I have a feeling my mother didn't tell her.

For some reason, I always blurt out the things that are bothering me while my Nana and I do dishes after a big meal. Tonight is no exception. She hands me a glass to dry and I say, looking at the big colorful ceramic cross above the sink, "Donovan was arrested for murder last week. But he didn't do it."

Very little ruffles my grandmother, who has outlived one husband, three children, and one grandchild, and I find it comforting that this doesn't, either. She stops and looks at me, with her brow furrowed with thought.

"He has good lawyer? Does he need money? I have some money, okay?"

"He's got a really great criminal lawyer. One of the best. A friend of his family. Thank you. Save your money for your trip to Italy this winter."

"Then he should be set free." She dismisses the problem as if it were nothing, handing me a bowl to put away on a high shelf.

"It's not that simple. Someone has done something to make him look guilty, and I'm not sure we can show he's innocent without finding the real killer."

"So. You find the real killer," she says with a shrug. I find it refreshing that instead of trying to protect me and warn me off my own efforts like the rest of the world is doing, my grandmother has faith that I can do something to help.

I give her a big hug. I'm so lucky to have her.

Before bed, I sneak into the living room and dig out an old photo album my nana keeps in a drawer. Flipping through photos of Caterina and me as children is always bittersweet. I think of Frank Anderson. As far as I'm concerned, his days are numbered.

THE NEXT MORNING I attend Mass with my grandmother in Livermore, then we come home to stir the sauce for Sunday supper. It's been simmering on the stove since seven this morning. Two gigantic, industrial-size pots hold the red sauce, a dozen pork chops, three dozen meatballs, and two dozen Italian sausages.

My grandmother fixes the same meat sauce every Sunday, frying the meatballs on Saturday morning so they are ready to simmer in the sauce the next day. My back almost hurts just thinking about all the work involved in rolling that many meatballs every week. I'm glad I was there this morning to help.

People start showing up in small groups after they attend their own Masses at Catholic churches across the Bay Area. Everyone arrives with a dish to share. Aunt Lucia brings some green beans with almond slivers. My brother Dante's wife, Nina, has three loaves of fresh bread. Uncle Dominic comes bearing a platter with mozzarella, fresh tomatoes, and basil from his giant garden. I give my niece, Sofia, an extra long hug.

Children are racing around the backyard, and bright linens are flung on the long wooden-plank tables under my grandmother's grape arbor in the backyard. Each Sunday, more than thirty people, mostly family, but family friends, too, arrive to eat Sunday supper. It's my favorite day of the week and has quickly become Donovan's. My stomach flip-flops imagining him in a jail cell while we bask in the day's glorious sunshine and warmth. A wave of guilt makes my stomach churn. It puts a pall on everything today.

Shortly before 1 P.M., my mother arrives with a giant pan of tiramisu. I've been anxious, waiting for the sound of her sandals to enter the kitchen, where I've been helping my grandmother. At this point, Nana really doesn't need my help to stir the sauce. In reality, I'm hiding from my family and the questions in their eyes. When my mother arrives, she puts the dessert in the refrigerator and places her hands on her hips, looking at me.

"Guest bedroom. Right now."

I know better than to argue.

"I don't understand why you don't ever call me back," is the first thing she says once the door closes.

I shake my head. I don't know why I react that way. I wonder what my shrink would say? Which reminds me, I've ignored her phone calls about scheduling an appointment this week.

"You are a grown woman, Gabriella. I'm not going to scold you. I want you to feel you can turn to me when things are . . . difficult. Okay?"

She reaches over and hugs me tightly.

"Now," she says, standing up and straightening her beige linen skirt, "what is going on with Sean? How could they possibly arrest him for murder? Who is out to get him? What can I do to help? I will move the heavens and Earth to help prove he is innocent."

For some reason, a few hot tears form in the corners of my eyes when I see how my mother instantly defends Donovan and is ready to fight for his innocence. I don't know why this surprises me. It shouldn't.

I realize she is treating me like an adult. Talking to me as a friend, almost. I wonder if this has to do with her change of heart about visiting the cemetery. She's about to walk away when I lightly touch her arm.

"Mama, did you go that day?"

She knows what I mean. The anniversary. She turns to me with a smile so bittersweet that my chest hurts. She nods. "It was good. Really, really good." She presses her lips tightly together, and her eyes are glossy with tears. "I'd like it very much if you would go with me next time."

I don't answer, afraid I'm going to burst into tears. I nod back.

"Go fix your face, honey. My hug smeared your lipstick. Everyone is going to be wondering where we are," she says, giving me a small kiss on my forehead like she used to do when I was a little girl.

She's going to talk to the rest of the family, so they won't bother me with questions, she says, and walks out.

I'm grateful for her intervention. Nobody bothers me or even gives me funny looks. It works for everyone except my brothers. Not long after, Marco and Dante corner me in the living room.

"Oh no." I look for a way to escape, but they are standing in front of the only door out of there. "I thought Mama told you to leave me alone."

I catch Dante, the pretty boy in the family, checking his hair in the mirror over the hearth while Marco, our eldest brother, talks.

"I know you think he didn't do it, and hey, maybe he didn't, but I'm letting you know, if your boy is a killer, he's not only going to have to contend with the law, he's going to have to deal with us." Marco raises his eyebrow, as if I'm not already getting the point.

Dante turns around. "Yeah, we will fuck his shit up."

"Correction. We will destroy him," Marco says. He doesn't believe in swearing, saying only uneducated buffoons resort to cursing.

"Easy boys," I say, rolling my eyes. It's comforting to have two loyal, Italian-American brothers, but it can be a royal pain in the ass. Dating in high school was the ultimate nightmare because both of them thought they should play the asshole Italian father figure in front of all my dates. I know it's wrong, but I'm touched by their fierce loyalty in a little bit of a screwed-up way. I don't condone violence, but it's still nice to know in this crazy world my brothers will always have my back. *No matter what.*

"Why don't you save that energy for getting the guy who hit me over the head. You're wasting time worrying about Donovan when the real killer is out there."

"Don't worry. The guy who hit you on the head, he's going to regret that," Dante says.

"Then worry about him, not Donovan," I say. "You said Donovan was like a brother to you now."

"Yeah, well, that situation changes dramatically if it ends up he's playing around on you with that woman and whacking people," Marco says.

"Yep," Dante chimes in. "Whole new ball game then."

"Don't believe everything you read."

"That's rich, coming from you, little sister," Dante says with a smirk. "Big newspaper girl admits that what's in the papers is pure crap."

"Don't change the subject," I say. "Donovan didn't do it, and if you want to help, then please believe me. Come on. You guys welcome him into your homes. He hangs out with you and watches football. He's family now, right? I need you to believe in him."

Marco's face softens when he hears the pleading in my voice. Dante comes up, loops his arm around my neck, and ruffles my hair with his fist, like I'm in junior high school again. "Don't worry. If your boy didn't have nothing to do with it, he'll be cool."

"Yeah," says Marco, spreading his arms wide. "We'll welcome him back with open arms."

"Yeah, he's family," Dante says. "He's family—until he fucks with a Giovanni. Then he's dead meat."

LATER, THE OLD uncles are peeling their peaches and plopping the wedges into their wineglasses for dessert, when Marco's wife, my sister-in-law Sally, places my newborn niece in my arms.

"Would you hold Adriana while I use the bathroom? She misses her auntie anyway."

Adriana, unlike most babies in our family, takes after her mother, with nearly white blond hair. She looks up at me solemnly as I gently rock her, then sing, "Frère Jacques."

How can such a little thing seem so wise? I lift her up and smell her head. There is nothing like the smell of a baby. I inhale deeply and smile. Then I hear whispering. I look up to see Marco and Sally watching me. I didn't realize it, but they had been standing there for a while watching.

"I didn't mean to be hard on you earlier, but you're a good kid," Marco says. "You deserve to have a man who loves you more than anyone else, like I love Sally here. That's all I want for you."

Sally nods in agreement.

"Thanks." I stand and thrust the baby at them and rush off.

The rest of the afternoon is spent with my family and filling up on wine, coffee, and dessert. I squirrel away two small pieces of my mother's tiramisu so I can take them back to the rectory to share with Father Liam and Father Michael. When Lopez came to meet me at my grandmother's house to follow me back to the rectory, Nana loaded him up with enough leftovers to feed an army. Now she has a fan for life.

The family time has done me good. But my mood darkens as I grow closer to the rectory in Oakland, with C-Lo's car in my rearview mirror. I can't block out images of Donovan sitting in a jail cell. Or the thought of some, faceless monster named Frank Anderson plotting how to prey on his next victim.

Chapter 41

Donovan has been in jail for nine days now. But it feels like a lifetime. Visiting hours start in a few minutes. I drum my fingers on the steering wheel. I left the rectory this morning in plenty of time, but I'm stuck in traffic on the Bay Bridge. I bite my lip and watch the patterns of the cars, waiting for an opening in traffic.

Donovan has finally agreed that I don't need Lopez trailing after my every move as long as I promise to let him know when I'm pursuing more "risky" leads or stories. I feel like a kid let loose at recess. I gun my motor, switching lanes on the Bay Bridge like I own it.

I can't be late. I need to spend the full thirty minutes with him. Even that is not enough. I rush into the jail lobby fifteen minutes late, eager to get in to see Donovan, but when I hand my visitor request slip to the clerk, she tells me he already has a visitor.

Troutman? No, attorneys get special visiting hours, don't they? Donovan's mother? I've been meaning to call or go visit her, but for some reason I've avoided it. I think I'm afraid. I don't know her that well and find her slightly intimidating. After Donovan's dad died when he was ten, she single-handedly raised him and his six older sisters. He's always been the baby. Sometimes I worry she thinks I'm not good enough for her only boy.

While I wait, I get my chess book out of my messenger bag and study some moves I've been contemplating using against Tomas. I wait, tapping my foot nervously. I can't concentrate on my book. If his mom doesn't hurry, I won't get to see him at all.

It's nearly 9:50 when I complain to the clerk.

The woman behind the glass booth shrugs. "You'll have to wait for the next visiting hour."

"When's that?"

"Ten."

"Fine." I can't argue. I'll be late to work, but with all the extra hours I've put in lately, I know Kellogg won't complain. Besides, I can't blame Donovan's mother for wanting to spend the entire time with him.

After a few minutes, a stream of visitors begins exiting the interior of the jail. My heart sinks. It's not his mother.

Annalisa.

A surge of jealousy ripples through me. She's wearing a red wrap-style dress that leaves nothing to the imagination and stiletto, over-the-knee boots. My faded jeans and floral blouse feel provincial. Her face is somber. She is still beautiful, but she has dark circles under her eyes. Before she notices me, I catch a look of despair pass over her face. She clutches her closed fist to her mouth and stifles a sob. Right then, she sees me.

We both stare at one another without saying a word. She visibly pulls back her shoulders as she passes. Part of me is tempted to run after her and hold her down and ask her what the hell she meant by saying Donovan was "protected" and what does she know about these murders. All the things I've wanted to ask her. But if I do run after her, I'll miss the last visiting hour.

I can't do it. I can't miss seeing Donovan. It's like a drug. I need to see his face. Every day. If I don't, the careful façade I've erected to keep it together will crumble.

I don't get up until I hear the front door to the jail close behind me.

DONOVAN LOOKS GAUNT, and his skin has an unhealthy pallor that I have a feeling has nothing to do with his orange jumpsuit. His beard has grown, surpassing its normal sexy five o'clock shadow. He gives me a smile that doesn't reach his eyes. It makes my stomach churn to see him like this.

My visits are becoming increasingly depressing. He refuses to talk about what it's like in jail, but the purple shadows under his eyes tell me everything I need to know. I compose myself before I pick up the ugly beige phone to talk to him, wiping it off on my shirt, which is sadly, a trick a serial killer taught me during jailhouse visits.

The first words out of his mouth are about Annalisa. He knows me well.

"I'm sorry you had to wait. She usually comes in the afternoon."

Usually?

"How is she connected to all this?" I ask. "Please tell me. I've been going to her house every day trying to get her to talk."

"She won't talk to you. She's jealous. She knows how I feel about you."

"Then you tell me how she's involved. Please."

"I can't." He looks away as he says this. "You have to trust me."

I don't have a choice, do I? I don't want to waste my time here talking about her, anyway.

"Fine. Let's not talk about her. I put some money on your account."

He gives a wry smile. "Thanks. I'm thinking about taking up smoking."

"For food, silly! Or maybe a razor," I say, eyeing his scruff.

He rubs his chin. "Yeah, not my best look ever. Thought I'd grow a beard."

"I hope you're kidding," I say in a snooty voice.

He laughs. "Totally."

He's not going to be in here long enough to grow a beard. He can't be. I need to know he's going to get out soon. It's taking all my acting skills and what feels like enormous effort to have this lighthearted conversation when all I want to do is put my head down on the counter and cry. But I won't. *Die before cry.*

"What has Troutman come up with for your defense?"

He gives me a look. "He's working on something. I think he's getting close. I can't talk about it, but we might be onto the real killer." Donovan looks away when he says this, at something over my shoulder.

"Is this place bugged?" I remember how my visits to the Martinez jail were videotaped.

"I don't know."

"Why can't you talk about it? To me? I understand not telling others, but why not me?"

"I'm sorry. I would tell you if I could, but Troutman made me swear to keep it under wraps. For now. It will all come out at the prelim."

My heart sinks. That's not for weeks.

"How are you going to survive that long?" I try to hide the sob in my throat, but it escapes. Every day he is here makes it more real and less of something I can deny or pretend isn't happening.

For the first time today, Donovan gives me a real smile, a wide one. "What do you think? I'm some pansy who needs thousand-count percale sheets and lobster to survive? I grew up on the streets of Oakland. I know how to survive a few days in the clink. Don't worry about me. I'm more worried about you. How's it going at Father Liam's?"

"Fine. Great. I'm still a prisoner there. In a gilded cage. I think I've gained ten pounds!" I give a mock sigh of exasperation. It works. He laughs.

"Oh, what I wouldn't do for some of Father Liam's famous roast lamb. Or for some of your manicotti for that matter!"

He's trying to be a good sport, but I can tell it's hard. I'll play along.

"Don't worry. As soon as you get out, I'm going to spend the next six months fattening you back up!"

"That's my girl," he says, then grows serious. "How's your family? I thought about you all day Sunday."

"They're good. My mother is really worried about you. And Nana offered to help pay for your attorney."

I can tell this means something to Donovan. His eyes grow soft. "Tell Nana to save her money but that I am honored she offered. Give your mother a kiss for me, too." He looks down. "I hope they don't think —"

"No," I interrupt. "They have unwavering faith in you."

He catches something in my voice or the way I say it. "But your brothers . . . that's a different story, isn't it?"

I shrug. "They'll be fine." I try to act nonchalant, but I can see the pain in his eyes.

Chapter 42

When I get to the newsroom, I return a message from Nicole.

"Hey, mama, how are you?"

"Sick as a dog," she says with a moan. She doesn't sound good. "I want to yak all the time. I don't think I can hack this. I've got a prelim, an arraignment, and the Andrews murder trial to cover today, and all I want to do is lie down on the courtroom floor. Maybe I'll do that and lift my head occasionally to vomit. Actually, that's the problem, if I were able to throw up, instead of feeling like I wanted to, I would probably feel a hell of a lot better."

"Can't they get someone to fill in for you?"

She moans again. "Oh no, gotta go, my other line is ringing."

I hang up. Poor Nicole.

I scroll through the newspaper archives on my computer, looking for information on the special-task-force team that Carl Brooke was on. The news researchers have spent the past year trying to put the old newspaper articles online, in many cases tediously scanning them in.

Unlike microfiche, this method allows me to search for particular names. There's only one mention of Carl Brooke, where he is quoted about a traffic accident that tied up commuters for two hours. Nothing about his serving on the special task force.

So, I type in Donovan's old partner, Sgt. Will Flora. I've never known much about Flora. Only that he sometimes acted as the public information officer for the Rosarito Police Department and that he was a mentor and a father figure to Donovan, really only what my boyfriend has chosen to tell me.

About a dozen articles come up naming Flora as department spokesman for about a six-month period. I wonder what he was like and if he was cool to the reporters who turned to him for information. The department must have had him doing double duty—serving on the special task force and occasionally being called in to deal with the press.

Someone up high in the cop shop either loved him or hated him to assign him this extra duty.

I skim the articles. In one, the reporter—a name from years ago I don't recognize—quotes Sgt. Will Flora about a bank-robbery team that took a hostage.

Usually, bank robbers are bumbling thugs—amateurs who get their money and run. I read on. I start scrolling back to previous stories. Apparently, the bank robbers had been targeting banks in the East Bay at closing time, getting away with six robberies in as many weeks. Then, for some reason, they changed their M.O. and took a hostage. Obviously, something went wrong.

I find a story that explains it: Apparently, an off-duty cop was doing business at the bank and drew down on them. There was a standoff, and one of the masked robbers held a gun to a teller's throat so they could escape. The article included pleas from the teller's family for her return.

I search for articles on the bank robbers and the teller's fate. The only article I can find quotes some other cop saying police are investigating the possibility that the teller was actually an accomplice. It appears she recently divorced, had a string of DUI arrests, had lost custody of her kids, and was about to be evicted.

After he is quoted in the bank robbery article, the next one I find with Flora's name is his obituary. I'm puzzled. There aren't any articles about the special-task-force team. Maybe it was hush-hush, like Donovan said, under the radar. For fun, I search under Donovan's name for that same year. His name comes up, along with about ten others in a brief piece naming new cadets who graduated from the police academy. I was hoping to find a picture of him as a fresh-faced rookie.

Nothing in the archives gives me a clue as to what Carl Brooke, Donovan, and Annalisa have in common. I feel like there is something I'm missing. Something right in front of me, but I can't see it.

I'm staring off into space thinking when Liz from news research taps my shoulder. She wears what I consider fitting for a longtime Berkeley hippie—a flowing skirt and Birkenstock sandals. I have no idea how long she's been standing there.

"Got something for you sweetie." Her soft brown eyes widen behind funky purple glasses as she says this. Like me, she likes the thrill of the hunt. She hands me a phone number for Mickey Menendez, the man Red told me about, the man who shared a jail cell with Frank Anderson, saying it was unlisted. My heart races.

"Nothing on Frank Anderson or his girlfriend, Delilah Jones, yet," she says. "Coleman has kept me busy searching for information on duct systems for houses. Guess his new bride wants one. Why not have old Liz waste her time searching every blasted article under the sun that's been written about it." Liz rolls her eyes.

I wince and push back the image of the publisher's wife with Annalisa in bondage gear. "Sorry. That sucks."

Liz smiles. "No worries." Then her smile fades. She pushes her glasses back on her nose, and I see the pity in her eyes. I can't bear it right now. I look away. Liz lingers. I can tell she is wondering if I want to talk about it. I don't. She leaves, giving me a glance over her shoulder.

Once I'm alone, I hold the phone number for Mickey Menendez up to Caterina's picture. "See? We're making progress, sweetie."

Mickey Menendez picks up on the first ring.

"Yeah, yeah, yeah. I already have a subscription, so you're wasting your time, good-bye." Crap. He must have caller ID and saw I was calling from the *Bay Herald*.

I talk fast before he can hang up. "I don't want to sell you the newspaper. I need to talk to you about Frank Anderson."

Silence.

"Who gave you my name?"

"I'm sorry, I can't tell you that. But I do know you shared a jail cell with Frank Anderson a few years back. I'm trying to find him."

"Why the hell do you think I would talk to you?"

"Because I protect my sources. I'd rather go to jail than reveal who gives me information for a story. But this isn't for the newspaper. This is personal. My name is Gabriella Giovanni."

That changes everything.

"Bet it was Red you talked to. Don't worry, your secret's safe with me, toots."

Mickey says he reads me every day and that he's always felt bad for me because of what happened to my sister.

"That man you are trying to find is the incarnation of evil," he says. "Don't know if he was telling me the truth or not 'cause, let's face it—we were in Napa together, aka, the loony bin—but I'm on the right meds now, and I don't think he was ever interested in getting his head straightened out. I don't think there was anything medicine could do. This dude was born bad."

"Have you heard anything about him or seen him since you got out?"

"Saw him once a few months ago. At this one bar I sometimes go to in the afternoons before my night shift. Down by the Alameda shipyard. I pretended like I didn't know him and got the hell out of there. I want nothing to do with him, understand?"

He tells me the name of the bar: the Salty Sailor. It doesn't sound very tough, more like a Disneyland ride.

"You probably shouldn't visit that bar alone, nice girl like you. But if you want, I'll make a point to drop in there every once in a while and see if I can find out more about him for you."

I give Mickey my cell-phone number and thank him, looking at the clock. It's only three in the afternoon. I hang up the phone and immediately punch more numbers. "C-Lo! Want a drink?"

The Salty Sailor has giant fishing nets hanging from the ceiling and has a tilted floor, even when you are sitting at the bar, which makes me feel a little off balance. I've felt a little woozy off and on since my thunk on the head.

Lopez orders a beer and my Absolut. When our drinks come, we settle back, letting our eyes adjust to the dark interior. I wait until my second drink to ask the bartender if he knows a guy named Frank Anderson.

"Nope."

His fast response and the way he won't look right at me when he answers makes me pretty sure he's lying. I wish I had a photo of Frank Anderson to show the handful of customers at the bar, but they'd probably all deny knowing him anyway. It's that type of joint.

Lopez talks to a few of the rougher-looking characters and comes back, downing his second beer. "*Nada,* man. They aren't going to tell us shit. Let's get out of here."

I decide not to leave my card. If the bartender is lying, I don't want him to hand my card to the man who killed Caterina. The thought of that man's holding my card, with my name on it and laughing, makes me want to vomit.

Chapter 43

I'M RESTLESS AND don't feel like going back to work. I need to do something, find something to clear Donovan. Maybe there are answers or a clue at his place. When I pull up in front of Donovan's apartment on the shores of Lake Merritt, I almost expect to see his face peering out the third-floor windows. But, of course, the apartment is dark and the windows empty. I still can't believe he's behind bars. I haven't been back here since that first night he was arrested. Looking up at the windows, a twinge of guilt runs through me, but I ignore it. It's not snooping if he gave me a key, right?

For some reason, my hand is shaking as I unlock the apartment door. Inside, all the blinds are closed. I turn on a few lights, feeling like a thief. Drawers are open and papers flung everywhere, like someone had burglarized the place. The search warrant. I creep into the bedroom. The covers on the bed are on the floor. The contents of the nightstand drawers are on the bed.

In the living room, the couch cushions and pillows are on the floor. On the long bar in the kitchen the contents of the drawers are scattered, knives, spatulas, spices.

What jerks. They could've been more considerate about it.

But they didn't find his secret compartment. I reach down and find the latch to the hidden cupboard latch. I fiddle and it springs open. Inside, I find two guns, ammo, a wad of cash, and Donovan's laptop. Resting near the computer is a notepad and pencil.

I clear a spot and put the laptop on the counter. Eyeing the notepad, I wonder why it was hidden. Is it important, or was it just tossed in with everything else when he went to work one day? The top page is blank, but there is a slight indentation that shows writing. I do an old kid's trick and rub a pencil lightly over it. I can only make out a few words, but it's enough.

Tim Conway. Todos Santos. Cabo.

I know that name. That was one of the cops Donovan mentioned from the special-task-force team.

I turn on Donovan's computer and look at his history. Sure enough, his history tab shows he was looking at flights to Cabo San Lucas. I try passwords for his e-mail.

His first dog was named Trixie. He loved that little guy. I give it a shot. Nope. He would think that is too cutesy, anyway. His dad's name was Finnegan. No. I type in Finnegan and his lucky number 12. No. His gun? Sig40. No dice. Then I remember: he told me once that if he had a daughter one day he was going to name her Grace after his great-grandmother. I type in Grace. No. How about Grace and Sig40? No. Grace and the number 12?

Jackpot. I scroll through his read e-mails—a few boring ones from his work, but then I see two from Tim Conway. The first one is cryptic. Obviously in response to something, Donovan had sent him:

"You're right. Only one way to stop him. I'll be waiting for you."

Him. The killer. With trembling fingers, I click on Donovan's sent folder to find out who *he* is. But the sent folder is empty.

The second e-mail from Conway is unread. It is guarded and brief. It was sent yesterday.

"Haven't heard from you. Can't wait much longer. I need to go underground. It's getting too hot. Come soon. Alone."

Getting hot? What is going on?

I book the next flight to Cabo. It's for later tonight. A red-eye. Sort of. I have a ridiculous, nonsensical layover in Phoenix. I'll get in at nine in the morning. Absurd. Who makes these schedules? But it's still the fastest flight there from the Bay Area. Then I search on a map—about fifty miles up the coast from Cabo San Lucas is a beach town called Todos Santos. I search for restaurants or hotels in Todos Santos.

I hit reply to Conway's e-mail and type, "Barajas Tacos. Thursday 2 p.m."

I think the answer to everything lies in Mexico.

Chapter 44

BACK IN MY car, my cell rings. It's Liz from the newspaper.

"Got it," she says when I answer.

Records show that Frank Anderson opened a checking account with Delilah Jones last year. Another document shows Jones is listed as owner on the title to a small house in Concord. I drive right past the rectory where I was going to stop and grab some clothes for my trip and instead hop on the 580 freeway. At the last second, when a shiver of fear runs through me, I call Lopez and tell him to meet me there. Won't hurt to have him with me.

Concord is not far from Pleasant Hill, where the newspaper is based. It's dusk, and the deep blue sky has purple and pink streaks when Lopez and I pull into the neighborhood. We both park a few houses down, eyeing the address—Lopez with his telephoto lens, me with binoculars. The weeds are a foot high and the grass is brown and dead. Chipped paint on the brown house reveals ugly streaks of red underneath.

After about fifteen minutes of watching the house and seeing no movement, we decide to knock. I'm not sure what else to do. I'm too impatient to wait any longer, and I have a flight to catch. I have no idea what I'm going to say or do if Anderson opens the front door. Commander Sandoval said Anderson is an immediate arrest for not checking in as a sex offender. So, I know at the very least, I'll call the cops if I can confirm he's here. Who knows what else I'll do?

Just in case, I reach over to the glove box and stick Father Liam's gun in my jacket pocket. I've kept it there since my trip to Napa.

Lopez whistles when he sees it. "Wow, man, that's some piece. You aren't messing around, are you?"

"Like you're one to talk?" I know he's got his regular small pistol in its ankle holster and probably another gun under his jacket.

We hurry toward the front walkway leading up to the house. I keep my eyes on the closed curtains, but don't see anything move. There isn't any glow of interior lights, like in the other houses on the block. At the front door, I glance at Lopez. He stands back with his hand under his jacket, eyes darting back and forth at the windows, then nods for me to go ahead. I knock on the flimsy wood door and step to the side to wait. My heart is racing, thumping in my throat. I clutch the gun inside my jacket pocket. I know I can't just shoot him. But will I want to?

I eye the windows in the front of the house in case someone is peeking out. No movement. I knock two more times and press my ear to the door, listening. Silence. Lopez raises his eyebrows and gestures toward a small fence at the side of the house leading to the backyard.

The sun sets, and, as darkness falls, the streetlights and nearly full moon make it easy to see. I look furtively around the neighborhood. I don't see a soul. No faces peering out. Everyone is probably inside eating dinner or watching the news. Lopez, as sleek as a cat, effortlessly scales the fence and crouches against the house, holding his gun in front of him. Looking around, I follow. My skirt rips up the back, startlingly loud. I probably look like a track-team dropout, but I make it over the fence in one piece. My blood is pounding in my ears loudly. I keep expecting to either smell the foul breath of a child-killing monster over my shoulder or have a police loud-speaker ordering me to put my hands up for trespassing.

Lopez, a few feet away, silently chuckles at my less-than-graceful fence scaling. He holds his finger to his lips and gestures for me to follow. We crouch walk underneath the windows, which all are covered in thick drapes, and make our way along the side of the house to the backyard.

At the back of the house, a small brick patio is home to a ripped armchair and an ashtray overflowing with cigarette butts. In the moonlight, the small square yard reveals itself as brown patches of dead grass dotted with cigarette butts. The grimy slid-ing glass door doesn't have a curtain. Lopez peers in, holding his palm up for me to wait. Then he motions me forward. I cup my hands around my eyes and peer through the window. The moon-light behind me illuminates the interior. The kitchen is empty. The house seems vacant, which makes my heart sink. Did I come so close just to miss him again? But then I see a take-out pizza box sitting on the kitchen counter. The sliding glass door yields easily in my hands with a loud screech that startles us.

Slowly, we creep in, leaving the door open behind us. Lopez is in front, with his gun drawn, directing me to follow with his hand. My heart is racing, and my hand is shaking when I take my gun out of my pocket. Clutching it with two hands, I hold it with my arms outstretched. It is heavy, and the shudders running through my body make it wobble up and down in front of me.

Lopez pauses a moment, looking back at me briefly. He's listening, maybe waiting for someone or something to respond to the noise we made on entering. It gives me time for my eyes to adjust to the dim interior. After a few seconds, Lopez takes a step. I follow on his heels. The living room has a small lawn chair, empty pizza boxes, and beer cans—some crushed, others upright—used as ashtrays. It looks like a homeless person is squatting here. Anderson?

Lopez gently pushes open the first door we come to—a bedroom door. Empty. Then another. It's the bathroom. Vacant. Goose bumps spring up on my arms. Something has been bothering me, in the back of my mind, nagging at me, since I walked in. Then, it hits me. I assumed the house smelled like cigarettes because of the stacks of butts, but then I realize I smell smoke. Fresh cigarette smoke. That isn't stale. The hand holding my gun begins to shake. From fear or fatigue at holding it, I'm not sure.

A clacking noise startles me.

Lopez rushes into the room the noise is coming from. I hear him exclaim, "Son of a bitch!" and rush in behind him, gun held in front of me.

Inside the room, I lower my gun. There's no one else here. Lopez flicks on the light to reveal a small pile of blankets, a book splayed open, and there on the floor—the cigarette I smelled, still faintly smoking. A breeze rippling through the room is making the blinds clatter loudly.

"Holy Mary Mother of God!" I stare down at the smoking cigarette, a Lucky Strike, and the book, Hermann Hesse's *Demian*.

Lopez pulls aside the clattering blinds. The window is wide open.

He was here. I can feel it. His presence. I can almost smell him. He must have fled when I knocked on the door. We missed him by seconds.

Chapter 45

I'M POUNDING THE steering wheel in frustration. I'm pinned between what seems like a million cars in front of me and another billion behind me on the I-880 freeway. I'm already late. Going to Frank Anderson's house meant cutting it close getting to the airport and now this. What's the holdup? Where in the hell are all these people going at eight o'clock at night? Then I remember. There's a U2 concert at the Oakland Arena. Donovan and I actually have tickets, but in the chaos lately, it slipped my mind. Not that I would go without him, anyway. All these cars are headed that way. Damn. I'm frantic I'm going to miss my flight to Baja. The next flight isn't until late tomorrow morning. If I don't catch this flight, I'll miss my meeting with Conway.

I wipe the sweat off my brow and try to turn up the air-conditioning in the Dodge Charger, which I'm pretty sure doesn't even work. Warm air blows on my face. And why is it so hot this late in the day? Where is that famous San Francisco Bay Area cold this summer? My phone rings. I snatch it up impatiently. "Giovanni."

"It's Mickey."

It takes me a second to remember who he is, but his next words make that perfectly clear.

"I just left the Salty Sailor. When I walked out, guess who walked in?"

My stomach lurches. That's where Frank Anderson fled when we showed up at his house. I look in my rearview mirror at the line of cars behind me. The same length as the line of cars in front of me. Then I look at the clock in my car—8:15. My plane leaves at nine o'clock. I'm already cutting it as close as I possibly can.

"Are you still near the bar?"

"Nope, I'm on the freeway right now, heading home."

"Okay. Thanks for the heads-up." I hang up without waiting for a reply and punch in three numbers.

"Nine-one-one. What is the nature of your emergency?"

I feel my face flush. What can I say? A man I think kidnapped and killed my sister twenty-three years ago is sitting in an Alameda bar?

"Hello? Nine-one-one? Please state the nature of your emergency."

"Um, I'm sorry. I want to report that a parolee who has violated his probation is in a bar having a drink right now . . ."

Even to me, it sounds lame. I wish the detective assigned to Caterina's case wasn't such a jackass because I could sure use some help right now.

"You should call your local police department or the jurisdiction where he was paroled."

"Yeah. It's a bit more complicated than that. Can you at least send a squad car over there?"

"I'm sorry, ma'am, this line is for emergencies only . . ."

"Oh never mind!" I hang up in frustration.

I call Moretti. He doesn't answer. I leave a frantic message on his voice mail, telling him to go to the Salty Sailor. That Caterina's killer is there. It sounds crazy even to me.

Hanging up, I wonder whom else I can call? That lame Livermore detective. I try his number and leave the same information. I know nothing is going to happen.

I know who I *should* call. Lopez and Father Liam. They both think I'm on my way back to the rectory. I'll call them from the airport, as soon as I know I've made my flight in time. Conway's message said, "Come alone." I don't want to scare him off. He might have the answers to clear Donovan.

I look again at the traffic surrounding me, which has started to move forward. The exit to the airport is only a mile away. The next exit is about a hundred yards in front of me. If I'm really obnoxious, I can budge my way over to the right-hand lane and get off the freeway. From there it will take me about twenty minutes—if there is zero traffic—to get to the Salty Sailor.

I could do it. He could still be there. But I would miss my plane. I would miss my meeting with Tim Conway. If I miss it, he might become suspicious if he's not already. He talked about its getting so hot he needed to go underground. If he does that, I might never find him again. I might never find why Donovan was going to meet with him. Conway was on the task force. I can't help but think that task force is somehow connected to all of this. It must have something to do with the murders. And I need to find out what it was. If Conway becomes suspicious and hides, I've lost him for good because if someone wants to disappear, Mexico is the place to do it.

I pound the dashboard. "Damn!"

It breaks my heart, but I realize I have to let the demons of my past take a backseat to my life in the present. That means picking Donovan over Caterina. At least that's how my decision feels to me as I get into the lane for the Oakland Airport exit.

Chapter 46

Baja California

ARMED WITH A bottle of water and a giant latte at the airport, I gun my rented yellow VW bug and get the hell out of Cabo San Lucas—a crowded beach town full of drunken American college students. I called Lopez and Father Liam during my layover in Phoenix. Neither was happy. I promised to call them both tonight.

The paved road, laughingly called Highway 1, is narrow and has no shoulder for most of the drive. Each time a car or big truck comes from the other direction, I start praying to the Virgin Mary, anticipating a head-on crash. Instead of a shoulder, a deep ditch lines each side. When I encounter my first pothole, I come to a screeching stop, my heart pounding. The jagged hole is big enough to swallow my car. I look behind me and throw the VW in reverse. Then, scanning the horizon for cars, I gun the car and pass the pothole from the opposite lane, swerving back into my lane as soon as I can.

A few miles later, a big hulking truck barrels toward me, straddling both lines. At this spot, thank God, there's a shoulder—or at least some dirt I can swerve onto, kicking up a whirlwind of dust that doesn't settle until the truck, horn blaring at *me*, for Christ's sakes, is long past. My heart is thumping in my throat as I put my forehead down on the steering wheel for a few seconds, feeling dizzy and nauseous. I say a little prayer, thankful that I didn't die on this godforsaken road in the middle of Nowhere Mexico.

Small shrines of crosses, flowers, and stuffed animals mark spots along the road where other drivers weren't so lucky. If I didn't have a death grip on the steering wheel, convinced that my life depends on keeping my eyes on the road in front of me, I probably would enjoy the beauty surrounding me. In some spots, I pass fields of giant Cardon cactus majestically arching up nearly sixty feet into the deep blue sky. Other twists of the road give me glimpses of the azure sea to my left. Two hours after leaving Cabo, I see a sign that says I made it to Todos Santos. I make the sign of the cross.

Chapter 47

BARAJAS TACOS IS packed. Two sides of the restaurant are open to the air. A rattan roof shades diners from the blazing sun. Cheerful waiters in tie-dye T-shirts weave through the crowded tables, balancing round trays filled with food high above people's heads. My stomach grumbles. I didn't have breakfast. It's 2:05, so I'm a few minutes late, but I don't see anyone sitting alone at a table. I pull up a seat at one side of the bar, giving me a view of the rest of the restaurant, and order two fish tacos and a ginger ale to calm my stomach. Tim Conway will have to forgive me for ordering ahead of time, but if I don't eat, I'm going to pass out. Or be the crabbiest person in Baja, California.

Only a few of the tables are occupied by men who look American. One obviously American couple sporting big straw hats, sunburns, and designer beach duds are nuzzling each other. Another table of men looks too young—surfers in their early twenties. One man looks like a possibility. He has graying hair slicked back and weathered skin that looks like he's spent a lot of time outdoors. I give him a tentative smile when he looks my way, then remember that Tim Conway is expecting Donovan, not me. The man says something to his friend, who looks Mexican, and the guy looks over at me and shrugs. The men throw some bills down on the table and turn to the waitress. I hold my breath.

"Thanks, Carla, see you tomorrow."

"Thank you, Mr. Henry."

Damn. Not Tim Conway. Even if he were using an alias, he'd wait longer for Donovan to show up. Finally, I turn to the bartender who brought me my tacos.

"I'm looking for an old friend. His name's Tim Conway."

The bartender stops wiping the bar. "Mr. Conway has not been here for, oh, maybe two days. He likes to come for happy hour, but I haven't seen him since Tuesday."

"Oh darn, maybe he didn't get my message. Do you know where I might be able to find him?"

The bartender gives me the once-over. I slide a twenty-dollar bill his way. He tucks it into his apron.

"Camps at Los Cerritos Beach. Airstream trailer. San Francisco Giants flag on top."

Making my way through town, I pass an old butterscotch-colored adobe church nestled in a patch of palm and pine trees. Most of the town is laid out on white dirt roads dotted with squat white or brick buildings. The downtown area houses several art galleries and more than a dozen restaurants.

I follow road signs to Los Cerritos Beach and head for the campground area, which is on a plateau above the Pacific Ocean. The surf lies below the beach, down a steep incline. The beachfront is sprinkled with small tents on the sand. Surfers dot the huge waves that roar in the distance.

Several small trailers are parked where the parking-lot pavement meets the sand. A woman with spiky red hair and a colorful sarong is near a small trailer with Canadian plates. She gives me a friendly wave as I pass.

Then I see it. Conway's silver Airstream with a tattered orange-and-black San Francisco Giants banner waving in the breeze.

I park beside the trailer and bang on the door. "Mr. Conway? I'm Sean Donovan's girlfriend. I need to speak to you?"

Silence. I step back and watch the trailer to see if someone is peeking out the windows or if the trailer is swaying from movement within. It remains still. I knock a few more times. I walk over to where I saw the woman with spiky hair. She's shaking out towels as sand falls to the pavement and pinning them on a makeshift clothesline.

"Excuse me, I'm looking for a friend—Tim Conway."

Her friendly smile fades.

"Can I ask why you want to know?"

I sense she isn't going to buy any story I come up with.

"My boyfriend is a police detective who is friends with Conway. His name is Sean Donovan. He was supposed to meet him down here but was delayed. I'm here in his place."

She looks me up and down again. Her scrutiny makes me nervous. After a few seconds, she nods and speaks.

"Sorry to be so suspicious," she says, taking a clothespin out of her mouth and fastening a swimsuit to the laundry line. "The people who flock to Baja are protective of one another."

I don't get it.

"If you spend some time here, you'll find that a lot of the people living down here are either escaping their previous life or hiding from something," she says. "I think in Conway's case, it's both. He warned us that some less-than-savory people might come looking for him one day."

She smiles at me. "You don't fit that description. Plus, he's mentioned your boyfriend, Sean Donovan. So I think it would be okay to talk to you."

I give her a grateful smile. "Thanks."

"My husband Arnt and I haven't seen him for a few days. His girlfriend lives in La Paz, and he often goes to stay with her for a few days. He'll probably be back in the next day or two."

I think about this. Maybe he didn't get my e-mail yet? "Okay. I'll wait a few days, just in case. Can you recommend a place to stay in town?"

"La Vista is nice. Good food, too."

"Great. If you see Tim Conway, could you tell him that Sean Donovan's girlfriend is staying there? My name's Gabriella." I think of one other question. "Do you know how long he's been living here?"

"Well, let's see? My husband and I drive down from Vancouver every winter to surf. Let me think back. I think we met Conway four winters ago?"

I nod. So, he's been here a while. I thank her.

"Of course. Speaking of good food—are you feeling peckish? I'm broiling some fresh clams and scallops we dug up this morning."

"Wow. It sounds wonderful, but I just ate. Thanks anyway."

I walk back toward my car, but instead of getting in it, I take off my sandals and step onto the sand toward the water. Mammoth waves crash in the distance like a wall rushing toward me. No wonder this is such a popular surfing spot. When I get to the edge of the small plateau overlooking the water, I sit, hugging my knees to my chest. The surf crashes on the shore some five feet below.

The last few weeks have been a whirlwind. It feels like so long ago that my life with Donovan was normal. This search for the real killer is starting to feel a bit like a wild-goose chase. I wonder what Tim Conway has to say that is so important? Maybe I'm wrong, and it has nothing to do with the murders. Maybe Donovan was going to meet with him and talk about deep-sea fishing or whale watching, for crying out loud.

But then I remember Conway's e-mail: There's only one way to stop *him*.

That line is why I'm here—to make sure that happens.

Chapter 48

ON THE WAY to the hotel, I admire the flowering vines scattered on crumbling walls of the city. This time when I see the towering, butterscotch-colored church, I pull over on the white dirt road. A plaque above the door says the *Misión Nuestra Señora del Pilar de Todos Santos* was built in 1733. It seems like a good place to ask for help.

Inside, the way the sun is slanted makes the far end of the church, where the altar is, glow an otherworldly shade of gold that infuses every last corner, as if the white stone is lit from within. The altar itself has a small alcove with a statue and peach and pink roses framed by a sparkling stained-glass window whose glowing blues, reds, and greens are almost too brilliant to gaze upon.

Tours of the mission have ended for the day, but a small, locked box is set up for donations. I stuff twenty bucks inside and make my way to the altar. The wide aisle is made of polished marble, but the pews on each side are simple, well-worn, wooden ones. At the front of the church, one life-size statue of Jesus nailed to the cross is on my left, and to my right, Jesus stands on a pedestal gesturing to his crowned, flaming, and thorn-wrapped heart as he looks down at the red roses someone placed at his feet.

The mission is named Our Lady of Pilar Church, so I'm disappointed I don't see any statues of the Virgin Mary. She's the one I turn to the most. From the front of the church, I scan the recesses of the rest of the church before I spot her—a smaller statue tucked into a shadowy back corner.

This Virgin Mary statue has hair, a long blond wig that reaches to her calves, and is holding a baby Jesus. Both statues have deep grooves, almost like scratches through their blue-and-white robes, but the look on her lady's face is beatific. I drop to my knees and clasp my hands together, looking up.

I ask for her help in catching the real killer, so Donovan will be set free. I ask for her help in finding Caterina's killer and that justice will be served. I hide my deep, dark thoughts of taking care of the man myself, but they are right there below the surface of my prayer.

BY THE TIME I check into the hotel, I'm suddenly sleepy, having not slept on the red-eye. I return to my room looking forward to putting on my pajamas and crawling into bed to watch movies when I notice the phone light flashing. The front desk clerk reads a message to me. Tim Conway wants me to meet him at a lighthouse up the coast. In less than an hour. So much for bed. Excitement races through me as I hurriedly throw on some jeans and sneakers and grab a sweater. Finally, someone who can answer my questions.

Chapter 49

THE SUN IS setting when I pull onto the dirt road toward the lighthouse, checking the map I got in the hotel lobby. The road is carved through chest-high scrub brush and meanders along high cliffs overlooking the water below. I drive with my window down, and the brush rustles noisily and eerily as I pass.

The white, sixty-foot-tall lighthouse looks like an upended flashlight perched on the rocks. My window down, I can hear the waves crashing below the elevated road. Eventually, the little dirt road dips, and I drop down to a dusty parking lot that is nearly at ocean level. One other car is parked in the lot, a small, beat-up Fiat that must be Conway's.

I turn off the rattling VW's engine and crane my neck to look up at the lighthouse. I don't see any movement. I listen out the window but only hear the crashing waves. Am I supposed to go inside?

I get out of the car, tugging my sweater on now that the sun is growing low on the horizon. The brisk sea breeze whips my hair and gives me goose bumps. Holding my hand up to shield my eyes from the setting sun, I peer up at the lighthouse again but don't see a soul. The door at the base of the lighthouse opens a few feet with the wind, then slams shut again.

"Hello?" I say, holding the door and straining to see into the darkness inside.

Nothing. The only noise is an eerie sound of wind whistling throughout the huge concrete structure. I step in and let the door fall shut behind me. When my eyes adjust to the dim interior, I make out the beginning of curving concrete steps.

The creepy sound of howling wind makes me pull my sweatshirt tighter and keeps me from yelling out again. I'm almost tiptoeing as I make my way up the stairs. The scent inside the lighthouse is a vaguely familiar one, sort of like a musty basement, which makes the hairs on my arm stand up. The only light is a dim one that pours down in long fingers from windows high above me. I wish I had a flashlight.

About halfway to the top, I pause at a little observation area with windows and an old, wooden bench. I try to see out the windows, but years of dirt and grime make the view a blurry one. The curve of the concrete steps makes it impossible to see what's ahead. I jump when a gust of wind bursts through one of the old windows with a loose clasp, making it rattle and thump noisily.

My heart is racing. I'm too frightened to call out. I trudge up to the next set of windows. What do I know about this Tim Conway guy? Maybe he's the killer and lured Donovan down here to take care of him? What have I gotten myself into? I look back. Part of me is tempted to race down those stairs, get in my car, and peel out of here. But I have to see what Conway knows. It might be the only way to save Donovan.

I glance out the window at my shoulder, which is not as dirty as the other one. Then I see him.

A man on the rocky shore below. He's in a small cove hidden from the parking lot. It looks like he's loading gear into a rowboat tied up nearby. He's wearing a baseball cap pulled low, windbreaker, and khaki shorts. Conway. I start back down the lighthouse steps.

Behind the lighthouse, a steep dirt path inches its way between rocky crags down to the shore. The man is sitting on a big rock about ten yards from the water.

"Tim Conway?"

He doesn't turn around. My words are probably lost in the wind. The man is playing with the rope that leads to the anchored rowboat, yanking it up and down.

I go a few steps closer and am startled by his voice.

"So, you're Sean Donovan's girl?" He doesn't turn around. His ball cap is pulled low. But his profile seems familiar.

I walk over to his side and stick out my hand. "Gabriella Giovanni."

He doesn't look over at me or take my hand. A chill shoots up my spine. I take a step back when I recognize him—Adam Grant's friend, Mark. The man from the pool party who rescued that drunken guy. The one who was eyeing me at Adam Grant's wake.

When he finally looks up at me, my insides twist in fear. Without his dark glasses, I see everything clearly now. His eyes. I've seen that look before. In the eyes of a sociopath. The glassy, vacant look. Nothing there.

I remember how when he first touched Annalisa at the wake, she jumped. She was afraid of him. Her snuggling up to him was all an act. He's the killer.

Instinctively, I start backing up, but my heels stop on a rocky outcrop. My horror must show on my face. He lifts his other hand

and points his arm out straight at my face. All I see is the barrel of a big gun.

"Sit down."

Shakily, I crouch on a nearby rock, still an arm's length away from him. He relaxes and settles the gun in his lap.

"Who are you? Where is Tim Conway?" My voice is shaking. My teeth are chattering, and it's not only from the cold air.

"You'll see him soon enough. Up close and personal, even. He's not far. He's right over there in the boat."

I remember looking out the lighthouse window and seeing this man lifting a bundle into the boat. I'd assumed it was fishing gear.

"You know, it's a shame you're going to die over a scumbag like Sean Donovan."

"What?" I feel dazed, stunned. I don't know what else to say.

"It has to end this way."

He looks back out at the sea again. I steal a quick glance behind me, gauging how fast I can run to get away.

"Don't even try it. I'm a deadeye shooter, expert marksman, sharpshooter, whatever you want to call it. Let's just say I don't miss." He doesn't even look my way as he says this.

That's when I know for sure. Conway is dead. Bile rises in my throat. I know I'm next. But if he's not Conway, who is he? A guy named Mark who is Adam Grant's friend.

Out of the corner of my eye, I see Mark fingering a badge in his other hand, the one that doesn't hold the gun. A Rosarito police badge. He's talking about that special task force that Donovan was on. He keeps talking, not looking at me.

"Thanks for leading me to Conway. I've been looking for this guy for the last six months. And I couldn't have planned it better myself. People go missing in Mexico all the time. It will be weeks before anyone even realizes the two of you are gone. And I'll be somewhere far away now that all my loose ends are tied up. Except Donovan, the rookie fuck. But he's essentially a dead end, too. He won't be going anywhere anytime soon. I should have taken care of this years ago. But I thought they knew to keep their traps shut."

He *was* targeting the task-force members. But why?

He unties the rowboat's rope from a big rock and starts coiling it around his crooked arm in a circle.

"I don't understand," I say. I'm pretending to pay attention to him, but, also, frantically looking around for a means to escape. There is no way I can outrun his gun. I don't see anywhere to flee. Panic wells up in my chest. That's when I remember—the badge found with Sebastian Laurent's belongings. Laurent wasn't on the task force. The killer didn't leave the badges as a warning.

"You left those badges as calling cards, didn't you?" He doesn't deny it. "So, why didn't you leave one with Adam Grant?"

"How do you know I didn't?" What is he talking about? Is the Rosarito Police badge why the detectives are going after Donovan? Is that their evidence? Why target all the task-force members?

Then it strikes me.

He's one of them.

I reel through the names in my head: Flora. Dead. Brooke. Dead. Mueller. Dead. Conway. I gulp—dead. That leaves one guy—Mark. Mark Emerson.

His name really is Mark. That much is true.

"Come on, Emerson. If you're going to kill me, at least tell me why?" I try to sound brave, but my voice is shaking. He doesn't even flinch when I use his last name. I was right. He has unhooked the rowboat's thick rope from the rock it was tied on and is busy winding it around his arm.

"I don't understand how Annalisa is connected to all this."

He doesn't look over at me when he answers. "Listen, this isn't some movie where I'm going to confess my sins to you, lady. I could give a rat's ass what you know and what you don't know. All you need to know is by this time tomorrow, you and Conway are going to be fish food. Now stand up and put your hands behind your back. It's dark enough now. All the fishermen will have headed back to port. We'll have the water to ourselves."

I stall. When I said Annalisa's name, he paused, frozen for a second. She's always been at the bottom of this, but how?

"Let's talk about Annalisa."

He stops coiling the rope and fixes his gaze on me. "I don't want to hear her name come out of your mouth." He says it in a low voice.

"Are you an item?"

"She's mine. She's always been mine. She always will be." He gives a smile that sends a chill through my core.

That's it. He's obsessed with Annalisa, so he knocks off the competition—Sebastian Laurent and Adam Grant, but how do the others fit into this? The task-force members? Donovan? Is it because Annalisa is obsessed with my boyfriend?

Suddenly, Emerson is on me. "I said hands behind your back." The gun pokes me in the spine. "Hands. Now!" I can smell his breath, minty like toothpaste, as he leans in toward my ear. Irrationally, I think angrily that his breath shouldn't smell fresh and clean. It should smell like the walking corpse that his dead eyes reveal he is.

My arms are wrenched behind me and bound together by something that cuts painfully into my wrists.

"Now walk."

Holding my arms, he guides me down the path to the boat.
When we get there, I brace myself to see Conway's body. It is unnat-
urally splayed in the bottom of the boat, one leg bent behind him.
Bulging eyes look frantic, and his mouth is pulled into a frightening
grimace. Bloody brain matter is oozing out a huge hole in his head.
It's not really a hole; it's that half his head is missing. I lean over and
vomit, spewing what little bile remains in my stomach.

"Get in."

I nearly trip as I lift my legs to get into the boat. Emerson gets
in behind me and pushes me down onto a seat. He uses an oar
to push off from the shore. The waves rock us, and I worry that a
wave is going to submerge the boat, sending us crashing into the
rocks. Somehow, he manages to row us out past the rocky shore. I
look down at my sneakers, avoiding the thought that the jeans in
front of me are a dead man's legs. Could I disable Emerson enough
by kicking him in his groin? Then what?

His dead eyes look at me as if he knows what I'm thinking.

"I could put a bullet through your forehead right now."

His arms are rowing, but the gun rests on the seat bench beside
him. Even if my hands were free, I could never grab it in time.

I lift my chin. "What's stopping you?"

A furrow crosses his brow.

It doesn't go past me. "What? You going to tell me you have
some sick code of honor where you don't kill women or something?" My words are dripping disgust. "Or rather you kill them,
but not at your own hands? By cutting the brakes on a car? Sort of
a 'keep your hands clean' kind of murder.

He swallows and looks off to the side. "Something like that."

"What was your plan in Oakland Hills Park then? That seemed
pretty hands-on to me."

His lips close tightly for a second before he answers. "Wanted to see what you knew. What that rookie fuck told you. Maybe at that point, you would've lived. Who knows? Maybe we would've ended up friends."

He eyes my chest. I glare at him.

"Listen, lady, it'd be a hell of a lot easier for me just to shoot you, but Donovan would know that you died quickly and painlessly. That's not what I want. I want him to agonize for the rest of his goddamn life over your death. I can imagine his face when I tell him how you spent your last moments on this Earth. He'll be behind bars, and there I'll be—a free man—describing the death of his girl to him. And there won't be anything he can do. I can't wait to see the look on his face. He will remember my visit and what I tell him for the rest of his sorry life. It's something I want him to think about—how you suffered—while he rots in a prison cell. I want him to replay it over and over again and know there was not a damn thing he could do about it."

Not only is he going to kill me, but he's ruined Donovan's life—in so many ways. I picture Donovan growing old in jail, hating himself, blaming himself for everything. It breaks my heart. Emerson's voice interrupts my morbid thoughts.

"Plus, Annalisa wants you dead."

I know she hates me, but so much that she wants me dead?

He sees the confusion on my face.

"Haven't you figured anything out? How have you ever lasted as a reporter? See, once this is cleared up, Annalisa and I can start our life together." He actually smiles and gives a little laugh, which is almost more disturbing than when he is scowling at me.

Annalisa. She wasn't just the object of his obsession, but was in on it the whole time? I can't believe it. He's lying.

"Does Annalisa know of your big plans to ride off into the sunset? Somehow, I doubt it." I purposely make my voice drip with sarcasm. His scowl returns. I hit the nail on the head.

"She'll agree to it readily enough. She won't have a choice. You see, me and Annalisa have some history together. Now, nobody is left. Just the two of us."

He methodically eliminated the competition. Sick. But I'm surprised to hear him say they have a past together.

"What history?"

"We dated after your pansy boyfriend broke up with her. Dumb rookie fuck brought her to a cop party, and I met her there. I knew right then she was the one for me. And she must have known it, too, because right when they broke up, she came running to me. It didn't work out at the time. But she's mine. She always has been. She always will be."

"She's no more interested in you than a chicken is in eating an egg sandwich."

It's not my most cutting remark or the best analogy I've ever had, but it hits the mark.

Slowly, and deliberately, he anchors the oars. He's going to shoot me now. Fear fills my insides. At the same time, I feel a spark of rebellion and stubbornness. Shoot me now. Go ahead. Good. I'll have ruined his big plans. Instead, he leans over and slaps me so hard I see black for a few seconds. I taste blood and feel one of my teeth on my tongue. I wonder if I should try to save the tooth, but with my hands tied, there's nothing I can do. Besides, I'm going to die soon anyway. I spit it out on the ground.

"You won't kill women, but you don't mind smacking them around? Is that your code of honor? That's absurd."

Emerson ignores me and looks around with a frown. He squints in the direction behind me, then a grin emerges.

"Ah, there it is. I'm an expert navigator, too."

He paddles furiously and I see it—a few yards away, a small fishing boat is anchored in the middle of the sea. It's dusk, but I can still make out the name on the side: EL DELFIN. The dolphin. He ties up near a small ladder on the bigger fishing boat and turns his attention to me. For a split second, I'm tempted to just roll off the boat into the water, but I'm not brave enough to drown myself.

Emerson grabs some rope and ties my legs and ankles together before he lays me down on the bottom of the boat near Conway's body. My face is next to a dead man's. I squeeze my eyes shut and try to turn away, but I still retch. The boat bobs as Emerson steps onto the ladder. I turn my head to see him, relieved that he is leaving. I'd rather take my chances at sea with a corpse than spend one more second around Mark Emerson. With one foot on the rowboat, Emerson slowly lifts his big black gun and points it at me.

Chapter 50

THE GUN'S GOING off near my ear momentarily deafens me. It takes me a second to realize he didn't hit me. I do a quick inventory of my body to see if maybe I'm in shock and don't realize I've been shot. As I do, I notice a small hole in the bottom of the boat. Was he trying to shoot me but missed? My ears, still recovering from the noise of the blast, hear what he says next as if I am hearing an echo from across a vast space.

"There," he says. "Now your boat has a small leak. You'll sink within the hour. Then, if you're lucky, you'll drown before the sharks eat you. But I've seen some seals around here, and seals mean sharks. I don't think you'll get the luxury of drowning. *Adios.*"

I can't see him but feel the momentum as Emerson gives our boat a violent push. An engine starts up. I don't lift my head until the sound grows distant.

Trying to ignore Conway, and telling myself to pretend I'm lying next to a log instead of a dead man, I rub against the ropes. My hands are still tied behind my back. I buck and arch and try to free myself. And then I spend long moments recovering from my efforts.

Water is slowly seeping into the hole in the boat. I can feel its icy cold fingers licking at the bottom of my feet and my legs. I've been lying beside Tim Conway's body but now realize that I have to take drastic measures to survive. Maybe I'm being foolish to prolong the inevitable. The water is rising.

It makes me retch more, and I close my eyes while I do it, but I turn and wriggle around enough so that Conway's body is beneath me. Soon, his body is partially submerged in the water pooling in the bottom of the boat. There's enough slack in the rope that I'm able to twist my body so my face isn't near his or in the water. I shiver uncontrollably, both from cold and fear. I close my eyes and pray, but for once, words fail me. Finally, I settle on one word—*please*.

I hear a splash, and my insides turn to jelly. I've been afraid of sharks ever since I watched *Jaws* reruns on TV as a kid. The thought of sharks in the water nearby is almost unbearable. I think I would rather die about any other way. I resolve to take a giant gulp of water as soon as the boat submerges. Maybe I should try to stick my face into the water at the bottom of the boat? I try to remember what I've read about drowning. Is it peaceful? I seem to recall that, but then again, wasn't there something else about its being one of the most painful ways to die?

All of a sudden, the hairs on my neck stand up. It feels like I'm being watched. The softest whisper of a sound comes from the side of the boat, as if a gentle wave is lapping up against it. Slowly, I turn my head.

A giant, inky black eye is watching me in the dusk. I nearly scream. Then, I realize what I'm seeing. A whale. A giant gray whale has surfaced and is looking right at me. I don't know why, but I burst into tears. To hell with my mantra: *Die before cry.*

But now I let go and taste the salty tears that silently pour down my face and drip into my mouth. Behind the whale, the sky has turned a brilliant, sherbet-colored orange. I can't stop looking into this eye that glimmers with intelligence. It is the exact opposite of looking into Emerson's dead eyes. This big black eye is full of life. My tears abruptly stop, and I can't help it—a sense of calm fills me. As if I have seen an angel. I feel meek and yielding and peaceful—ready to let go of all the pain in my life. For the first time in my life, I don't feel alone. I know now that today I'm going to die. And I'm okay with that. I'm ready to go be with Caterina. The whale has allowed me to make peace with death.

"Thank you," I whisper. Then, as if it were a ghostly apparition, the whale slips back into the water. The boat dips slightly, and the sea around me is calm again. At the same time, I hear a boat's engine and shouting. At first, I panic, sure that it's Mark Emerson coming back to finish me off, but then I realize if that were the case, I wouldn't hear shouting.

Lopez or Father Liam? They must have come down to find me when I didn't call last night. I struggle madly to get free, so I can flag the boaters down, but all this does is exhaust me and splash water around. It sounds like the boat is going farther away now.

I lie back down, whimpering like a child. It's too late. They've gone. Then the noise grows louder again. I'm too exhausted to lift my head. The seawater that has seeped into the boat is covering part of my body now. I have to arch my neck a little to keep my head out of the water. The icy water makes my whole body shiver. My teeth are chattering. I try to scream "help," but my throat is so dry, and I feel so cold and weak that it comes out as a croak. I keep trying, anyway. My little raspy yell isn't much, but it's all I have. If they hear me, it will be a miracle. It's out of my hands now. That same sense of meekness in the face of fate comes back to me. It is not up to me anymore. If they see the boat, I will live. If they drive past it in the darkness, I will die. It's that simple.

Chapter 51

THE SPOTLIGHT SHINING down blinds me. They see me. But I can't see them. The tears slipping out of my eyelids aren't helping me see any better, either. I must be delusional because in the mix of Spanish-speaking voices I think I hear Donovan's voice. Absurd. I don't even think he speaks Spanish. It sounds like an argument. I'm cracking up, losing it, imagining Donovan's voice out here on the sea in Mexico. Even if he wasn't locked up in a jail cell in San Francisco, there is no way he would be on some boat in the middle of nowhere off the coast of Baja California.

Dark silhouettes are in front of me, leaning over my sinking row-boat, pulling it closer to them, tying it to theirs. A shadow leans over with something shiny, and I shrink away when I see it is a knife. Suddenly, the cords binding my feet and torso are gone. Hurriedly, I stand, planting my feet in icy water up to my knees, legs shaking so much I nearly lose my balance. An arm reaches down to steady me, firmly holding my shoulder. I blink. The man in front of me on the other boat looks like Donovan. My eyes focus. He reaches his hand out to me.

It *is* Donovan.

Chapter 52

WE SPEND MOST of the night at the police station in Todos Santos. Every time I look at Donovan, I'm astonished. "I don't understand. You're supposed to be in jail."

He keeps telling me the same thing with a big smile. "It's all over. I'll explain. Soon. Let's get you taken care of first."

Before questioning me, the police took me to one of their houses, where they let me take a hot shower and gave me a clean pair of men's work jeans, a soft T-shirt, and a heavy flannel shirt. An older woman fed me this amazing *albondigas* soup, which has meatballs and is served with warm tortillas.

Except when I was in the shower, Donovan hasn't left my side.

"How did you find me?" I whisper to him, while the woman smiles and watches me eat.

"Conway. It's a long story."

Back at the station, I slump at the table in front of me and put my head down on my arms. My limbs feel heavy, and I struggle to keep my eyelids open. Every once in a while, I drift off for a few seconds. Donovan hasn't left my side. Every time I try to ask him

how he got here, how he got out of jail, he repeats that word—
"Soon."

The Mexican authorities want me to go over my story several
times, using a translator.

Unlike my experience with San Francisco detectives, these
cops treat me practically like a princess. One serious man with
glasses takes notes while the other asks me questions. He asks me
to describe Mark Emerson. I do my best. I tell him the name of
Emerson's boat: *El Delfin*. The man is kind and smiles at me often.
I'm being treated like a victim and witness, not a suspect as I was
in California. Donovan doesn't seem surprised that Emerson was
the one trying to kill me or that he'd killed everyone else.

Finally, around 3 A.M., they let us go. Apparently, someone in
the State Department called to vouch for us, and the Mexican authorities gave us permission to leave the country as long as we
were available in the future if necessary. Some friend of Troutman's, I guess.

Donovan asks me if I want to stop back at my hotel for a few
hours of sleep or head straight for the airport to catch the next
flight. I can barely keep my eyes open, but I want to go home. The
duffel bag I left in my hotel room is history. I don't care if I ever see
it again. I just want to go home.

"Airport," I manage to say, as we climb into the VW. The cops
brought my car here. Surprisingly, as soon as the doors shut, I'm
wide-awake.

"Tell me now."

"It was Annalisa. She went to the D.A. and told them the real
story. There's a warrant out for Mark Emerson's arrest now."

"I don't understand."

"It's a long story. It all goes back to something that happened a long time ago," Donovan says. "Something I was afraid to tell you. I thought if you knew, you wouldn't want to be with me. That you would think I was a coward. But I've come to realize that this secret is what destroyed my first marriage. I know that we can't get married until you know everything about me—the good and the bad."

His words send a tremor of fear through me. Get married? Good and bad? What has he done?

He pulls over to the side of the road on a turnout that overlooks the sea. A small stone bench is set near a brush area, facing the ocean, which is turning a silvery gray as the night lifts. He leads me to the bench and begins his story.

Chapter 53

FIFTEEN YEARS AGO, a rogue group of cops decided to team up for a more lucrative side gig to enhance their meager cop salaries—bank robbery, Donovan says.

"Who could better outsmart investigators than a team of cops?"

I clasp my hand to my mouth, shaking my head. I remember the story I read on microfiche about the bank-robbery gang. Was he one of the bank robbers? One of the rogue cops?

"You were . . ."

"I'll explain everything," Donovan says, not looking at me. "It's about goddamn time you know the truth."

Is that my answer?

"The plan, as I understood it, was to do it for six months and stop," Donovan continues, looking out at the distant horizon. "That's how most robbers blow it—they don't quit when they're ahead.

"It seemed foolproof," he says. "But one day, things went terribly wrong, and a bank teller was taken hostage in the chaos. In the

BLESSED ARE THE MEEK 291

confusion, one cop slipped and used another's name. The bank teller heard. Mark Emerson figured the only way to save their necks was to kill the hostage. He shot her, then made everyone else fire a bullet so they were all culpable," Donovan says. "So, nobody would know who fired the fatal shot."

I try to remember the newspaper article I read in the archives. Did they talk about a death? No, just a hostage taken. And Will Flora was quoted in it.

"So, all of them, each and every one, fired a shot into the body. The body was weighed down with rocks and thrown in the bay. Nobody ever found it."

Jesus H. Christ. "I don't understand." I look out at the black sky stretching above the endless ocean. I start to get up, but he grabs my arm.

"I didn't shoot her. I was a witness. A bystander. In the law's eyes, maybe just as culpable."

I sink back onto the bench.

Donovan peers over at me. His voice is wobbly. "I was in a car. Flora asked me to meet him there to give him a ride. His voice sounded funny. I was worried about him so I got there early. I saw the whole thing, and I didn't tell anyone. I never told anyone. The only people who knew I was there were the guys on the task force. Flora told them I'd take the secret to my grave. And I guess he's the type of guy who, when he says something, people believe him. And for good reason. I intended to do that—never tell a soul— until recently. I felt I had to—to protect Will Flora. To protect his memory. After my father died, he was like a dad to me. He's the reason I joined the force."

"I read an article about it," I say in a monotone voice. "They quoted Flora."

"Yeah. He was a sucker for seeing his name in the paper. Volunteered to be the department flack while he was on the task force," Donovan looks down. "That bit him in the ass when he was asked about the bank robbery later."

His voice contains a mixture of anger, frustration, and despair.

I want to put my arms around him, but I don't move. He keeps talking, looking out over the ocean, which stretches for as far as we can see.

"Goddamn it! I watched a group of police officers—my colleagues who swore to protect the innocent—fire their weapons into someone who did nothing except be in the wrong place at the wrong time."

"Wasn't she already dead from that first shot?"

He shrugs. "Whether she was already dead is completely irrelevant. The point is that they were cops—men who had sworn to protect and serve. They were no better than the scumbags they worked to get off the streets. They were maybe even worse—including the man I looked up to most in the world. And I watched. I sat there and did nothing. So what does that make me?

"I haven't done anything about it for fifteen years. In the last few months, I realized that I couldn't take it anymore. I can't live with this on my conscience anymore. I told Troutman at the jail, but I couldn't rest until I told you. I could never be the kind of man worth marrying otherwise. The guilt is destroying me. And I couldn't tell you. I wanted so much to tell you that day at the lake—after we visited Father Liam—but it wasn't the right time. It would've made me feel better with the relief of having told you, but at the cost of putting you in danger. It was just too risky."

I feel foolish. Here I thought he was going to propose to me that day. But a tiny bit of relief fills me that he did consider telling me before today.

"I've wanted to tell you for so long. I could feel my secrets coming between us." He pauses. "Just like it did when I was married to Teresa."

He swallows hard. I know I should reach over and comfort him, but I'm reeling from his words. I still don't understand how this has to do with him. I'm not ready to offer forgiveness for something I can't even wrap my brain around yet.

"Hold on. Explain how you came to be in the parking lot again?"

"Will," Donovan says. "He asked me to meet him there that night at the harbor. He never told me why. I don't think he knew they were going to kill her. I think he had another plan, but Mark Emerson ruined it."

"Did they all know you were there?"

He nods, his lips pressed tightly together.

"Is that why Emerson framed you for murder?" I ask.

"Part of the reason."

I'm dead tired, but it is starting to add up. Will Flora. Jim Mueller. Tim Conway. Carl Brooke. Mark Emerson. They were all on that special task force fighting pornography. And they became rogue cops.

"Why? Why would they do such a thing? Those bank robberies?"

"I don't know for sure," Donovan says. "Will Flora never told me, other than saying he was trying to get enough money for a good lawyer so he could fight for custody of his kids."

Shortly after the teller's death, Will Flora, racked by guilt, blew his brains out in a Porta Potty, Donovan says. "He was trying to be considerate." His suicide note on the door outside warned people not to come in and asked them to call police. It further directed the company to simply throw away the whole contraption instead of sending someone to clean up his mess. Flora put a provision in his will naming the Porta Potty company as a beneficiary and stipulating that the money pay for the cost of disposing and re-placing the Porta Potty.

"That's the kind of guy he was," Donovan says.

Brooke? "He was hooked on coke. The rest of them? I don't know why they did it. But Mark Emerson? Because he likes it? I don't know. Troutman and I have been trying to track him down for the past three weeks. We knew he was the answer to all of this."

"Wait. That was before your arrest. You knew it was him?"

"We suspected it. We think he killed Mueller and made it look like a suicide. We're having that body exhumed. We were looking for Conway and Carl Brooke to warn them. Unfortunately, Emer-son decided to kill Brooke to frame me. Probably thought he was killing two birds with one stone, getting rid of two more people who knew the truth. Tim Conway and I were onto him. Tim had a plan."

Donovan rakes his hand through his hair. In the chaos, I'd for-gotten that he'd just lost a friend, too.

"Why now? Why would he go after everyone now? After all this time?"

"Because Annalisa blackmailed him."

Good God, that woman again. But I knew she was tied to all this. I just didn't know how.

Donovan explains.

Apparently, at the time, Donovan was so torn up by what he saw the other cops do that he took a week's vacation, went on a bender, and briefly got back together with Annalisa. He con-fessed everything he had seen to her and made her swear to keep it secret. Of course, as soon as vacation was over, and the alcohol haze lifted, he remembered how he didn't even like Annalisa and broke it off.

She began dating Mark Emerson.

"She told me later that it was to make me jealous. But it didn't work," Donovan says.

A few months ago, Donovan says, Annalisa apparently saw the end coming with Sebastian. She knew he was going to dump her, write her out of his will, and leave her destitute. In an effort to get some money to strike out on her own and maintain her lifestyle, she looked up Carl Brooke. She knew he'd be the one most likely to cave and give her the information she needed about the bank-teller murder.

When Annalisa got in touch with Brooke, he was living in a residential hotel with a stack of boxes for a bed and was working as a security guard in Chinatown. Carl Brooke had gotten off coke but paid the price for his role in the bank robberies and murder. He never got over shooting the teller. He was reluctant to fire the bullet and only did so when Emerson held the gun to his head.

He told Annalisa he was living in squalor to punish himself for what had happened. That he didn't deserve to live, but the only reason he didn't kill himself was so he suffered, like the bank teller's children were suffering.

He was not a good candidate for blackmail but was easy to seduce, Donovan says. Annalisa got him drunk enough to tell the story, naming names, and got it all on tape. Then she found Mark Emerson.

"Why him?"

"Somehow, she found out he was loaded. Had taken his share of the bank-robbery money and got in cahoots with some other crooks with ties to the Colombians."

Drug money.

"How loaded?"

"Let's just say he flew his own plane down here to Mexico."

"Holy smokes."

Annalisa isn't stupid. Before she went to Emerson, she gave her attorney a copy of the recording, along with explicit instructions to take it to authorities if anything bad happened to her." Donovan looks over at me. "Or if anything happened to me."

I nod. "Once, when she was drunk, she said something about protecting you."

"A few weeks ago, she came to me and told me she thought someone was after her. At first, I didn't believe her. Then her boyfriend, Sebastian Laurent, turned up dead. I still wasn't sure it had anything to do with her. When Adam Grant was killed, I realized someone was sending *her* a message. The problem was, she wouldn't tell me why. That's one reason I kept meeting with her, hoping she would tell me the truth. At the time, I had no idea it had anything to do with me."

"Why didn't she just marry the mayor? I heard he needed a wife before his presidential nomination anyway. He'd have kept her in the furs and sports cars she wanted. Plus, I think she really cared about him." I sneak a glance at Donovan to see if he reacts to my saying Annalisa cared about Adam Grant.

He nods. "I'm sure that's what she would've wanted. But Grant's family already had his White House wife lined up. Letty Ravencroft."

"You've got to be kidding?" Letty Ravencroft was the beautiful daughter of the House Democratic Leader. "That would've sealed the presidential election for sure. Totally playing both sides. The moderate candidate. Who could resist?"

"Exactly."

"So, is she in on it with Emerson?"

"That day you saw Annalisa at the jail, she broke down and told me she had done a horrible thing. But she still wouldn't tell me what was going on. Then, yesterday, she called Troutman, and he met her and her attorney at the D.A.'s office, where she confessed to blackmailing Mark Emerson. She knew she had gotten in over her head. She just didn't know how dangerous he is. She didn't know he'd been obsessed with her for years. He killed Laurent and Grant as warnings to her, but also to eliminate any competition. He kept showing up everywhere she went, intimidating her into silence."

I remember how scared Annalisa was at the Napa house, as if she'd seen a ghost. It was because Emerson had shown up at her party. And she couldn't tell Adam Grant that. She couldn't explain that she had blackmailed somebody.

"As soon as she told the DA her story," Donovan continues, "the ball started rolling, and they released me a few hours later."

"Thank God." I'm quiet for a minute thinking about what Donovan has told me. "You knew those murders were connected didn't you? Is that why you pocketed that badge?"

He stares out at the sea and nods. "I knew it was a message for me. He was warning me that he was coming after me."

"Why didn't Emerson kill you, like the others?"

"He knows that some things are worse than death," Donovan says, quietly. "He knows how much I love you. That was his revenge."

"Why did he single you out, though? I don't get it."

"Annalisa," Donovan says. "He's always been in love with her and always been jealous of me. Hated me on sight when I joined the force. Will Flora had been his mentor and partner, but I think

Flora knew something was off with Emerson and asked to take me on when I was a recruit. Then he dumped Emerson.

"He hated me for that. He started dating Annalisa just to get back at me, but then he fell for her—hard. Cops went to his place yesterday to arrest him. He had an entire room dedicated to her. Pictures of her with other people cut out. He had one picture made into a life-size poster. Pretty sick stuff."

"He's obsessed," I said. "We need to warn her."

"Done deal. She's agreed to be a witness so SFPD called her and told her to go stay with her family in Modesto for the next few days."

"You'd think they'd charge her with blackmail? Or something for putting us through this hell."

"Looks like they're more interested in what she has to say about Emerson."

My mind is spinning from his story. But there is still so much I don't understand.

"How did you find me down here? Did Father Liam or Lopez call you?"

He nods. "But they didn't know exactly where you were headed. But Conway did. He came back from La Paz. Didn't like hearing some woman calling herself my girlfriend was looking for him. Sounded fishy, so he shot me an e-mail. I'd just gotten out of jail. When I heard you were down here, I booked the next flight and told Conway to go find you and look out for you until I got here."

"Guess Emerson got to him first. I'm sorry," I say.

"His trailer was trashed. I knew something bad had happened," Donovan says, and swallows. "A neighbor heard a gunshot and saw a guy put something in the trunk of a car. She called the Federales, but they blew her off."

"Down the road, I saw a fruit stand. Grizzly old farmer guy was packing up his stuff, but he told me a man driving a Fiat paid him twenty bucks for directions to the lighthouse. When I got to the lighthouse, I saw some blood on the rocks down by the water."

He pauses and looks down for a second. "Ella, I thought I'd lost you for sure."

"I'm right here," I say, taking his hand in mine.

"I figured you were all in a boat out at sea somewhere. The Federales were a little more motivated by a stack full of greenbacks, and we were on the water within an hour. Thank God we found you when we did."

"It sure didn't seem like Emerson was trying to cover his tracks."

"He wasn't. He figured by the time anyone squawked about it, he'd be long gone. It's not unusual for people simply to disappear around here."

"So I'm told."

Chapter 54

"Do you forgive me?"

Donovan practically whispers the words.

The sunrise is painting the sea below us with pink-and-orange shimmers of light. I feel like I could sleep for a year. Everything that has happened seems surreal. It's hard to wrap my brain around what Donovan has told me. I nod without looking over at him. When he kneels down in front of me, I blink, confused, and yet know exactly what is coming next. But I'm too stunned to stop him.

"Going through all this the past few weeks has made me really do some thinking. I don't want to live without you. Will you marry me?"

My mouth drops open. I don't know what to say. I don't know. I don't feel anything but numb. Not happy. Not afraid. Nothing. He must see the look in my eyes. And when I don't answer, he sighs and stands up, brushing the dirt off his knees.

"I guess I shouldn't be surprised," he says, sitting back down and looking out over the sea. "I knew this might happen once you knew the truth. Why would you want to marry someone who has kept something like that from the authorities? I'm basically complicit in the crime. I abetted them. I covered up for them. They said they'll forget about all that if I testify against Emerson. I understand why you wouldn't want to be married to me."

"You don't understand," I begin, trying to explain. "I do love you, but I don't feel like I know you right now. It's not that you kept this a secret from the authorities. It's that you kept it a secret from *me*. You never told me. Even when I begged you at the jail to talk to me, you never trusted me enough to confide in me."

He slumps back onto the bench. "You're right."

I wait, watching the water before us churning and swirling.

"Keeping it from you was wrong. But you have to understand; I was trying to protect you. I meant to tell you. I wanted to tell you, I tried to tell you—I knew keeping it a secret could destroy us, but I was certain I'd lose you if you knew the truth about me." He jumps up and begins pacing in front of me, running his fingers through his hair until it sticks up.

"We've been dating for more than a year," I say. "I've seen how haunted you are at night. But I never dreamed you were keeping such an awful secret. I just thought you didn't love me anymore. How could you keep something like that from me? Don't you know me enough to know I love you and would help you? You didn't trust me. You didn't trust me enough to confide your darkest secrets to me. I've trusted you with the worst horrors of my life. But you wouldn't let me do the same for you. You never gave me a chance. That's why I can't marry you. At least not right now. You don't trust me enough for me to be your wife."

When he looks at me, his eyes are haunted. "I understand that. I really do. But I hope you give me a chance and try to understand why I did it." He leans over to me, putting his hands on my shoulder and looking into my face. "But I think there's something else."

He's right. I can't lie to him. I put my head in my hands. I haven't even wanted to admit this to myself. I don't want to say it out loud. I'm so weary. All I want is to sleep. I look up. He's told me his deepest fears about our relationship. Now it's my turn.

"I don't think I can be a mother." Saying it brings tears to my eyes. "And I know you want a family."

"That's where you're wrong."

I look up. Has he changed his mind about having kids?

"You *can* do it. You're just afraid to do it." He says it softly.

I look up after a few seconds of silence. He's gone. He's tromping back to the car, his shoulders stooped.

Deep down inside, I know he's right. I'm not just afraid to love a child of my own. I'm terrified.

Chapter 55

DONOVAN STARES STRAIGHT ahead as I get in the car and strap on my seat belt. Without looking, he reaches over and squeezes my hand. I squeeze it back. When he starts to drive, I lean my seat back and start to drift off. Despite everything, my overwrought emotions and my exhaustion, I smile when I remember the whale. And I remember Annalisa's story: "If you ever look a whale in the eye, you must immediately return to shore and go to sleep. So you can dream."

I did return to shore right away after seeing the whale, so maybe it will still work if I go to sleep now.

I DREAM A dream that is so beautiful and terrifying I jolt to consciousness gasping. Donovan has his hand on my shoulder. His eyes have turned soft again. "Are you okay?"

I nod. I dreamed about a little girl. Unlike other dreams, this one was not about a missing Rosarito girl. It was not even about my sister, Caterina.

This little girl was someone I've never met before, yet she was disturbingly familiar. More familiar even than Caterina's face. And yet, her eyes—they were Caterina's dark brown eyes. She had Caterina's pouty pink lips. But instead of my sister's sleek blue-black hair, this little girl had a mop of brown curls. Unruly curls and freckles across her nose. Is it me as a little girl?

This shard of the dreamworld coming back to me in the car makes my mouth curve in a smile. But then fear courses through me as I remember the rest of the dream.

The girl, who was wearing a flowered swimsuit, was playing in the sand on a wide stretch of beach. She appeared to be alone. The beach stretched empty for miles in both directions. The girl laughed delightedly and filled her sand bucket repeatedly, patting the sand, then overturning it. She had built quite an impressive little city of turrets and moats.

Then, a long shadow fell across her small figure.

She was so busy, it took a moment for her to notice, but when she looked up, an expression of pure terror overtook her face.

That's when I woke. I can't shake the overwhelming sense of foreboding and dread left over from this dream. What does this mean? Two weeks ago, when Annalisa told her story about the whale at Grant's house, a heckler cut her off before she finished.

She never said what the dreams were supposed to mean.

Chapter 56

OUR PLANE BACK to California gets in late, and I gratefully fall into Donovan's bed. By the time I wake, it's nearly noon.

I find a note from Donovan on the night table. He's meeting with his union representative, the department's public-information officer, and the chief—working out details about a press release announcing his innocence in Carl Brooke's murder.

"Rest up," he wrote. "We'll have a nice dinner when I get home."

I put in a piece of toast and slowly sip some coffee. My stomach is doing loop de loops. I pour the coffee down the drain and toss the toast in the trash. I'll eat later.

There's a message from Lopez on my phone. Delilah, the missing waitress who lived with Frank Anderson, was found dead. Overdosed in a dingy motel room in Concord. I make a note to call the morgue and tell them to look extra carefully for signs of foul play. Anyone who ends up dead around that monster is probably his victim.

Now that Donovan is cleared, I need to focus all my energy on finding the man who killed Caterina, even if it means moving next door to the Salty Sailor until that bastard shows up again. But first to wrap up this nightmare.

I call Kellogg and tell him I'll have an exclusive story for him on the murders. With Liz the librarian's help, I track down a phone number for the bank teller's daughter, who is now in her twenties. Moretti already told me the police visited her this morning, but I want to make sure that I talk to her so that when I write my story, we do her mother justice.

She cries when I tell her why I want to write a longer story.

"Can we meet next week? I'd like to find out everything I can about your mother. Do you have pictures and maybe other people I can talk to? I think this story is going to take a long time to unravel, and I don't want her to get lost in the details. She's the true victim in this story."

The line is silent for a second, then I hear a small, quiet sound. "Thanks. Thanks for saying that."

Looking over my notes. I write the main story about Mark Emerson's killing spree and the rogue robbery team, editing out all the personal information about Donovan that nobody else needs to know about it. Sipping coffee, I read over it, nodding. The story seems wrapped up except for one thing—Emerson is still on the loose. The story will run with a description of him and a phone number to call police if he is spotted because he's considered armed and dangerous. I'm sure he's deep in hiding in Mexico.

I decide to take a shower and get ready, so I look presentable when Donovan returns home. After I'm showered and dressed, I see the light blinking on the answering machine.

Annalisa's voice sounds triumphant on the message.

"Don't worry, Sean. Everything should be over with soon. I'm meeting Mark today. I'm going to give him the tapes, the originals. He'll leave us alone now. It's over."

I close my eyes for a second.

Foolish woman. She has no idea who or what she is dealing with. So, Emerson was able to sneak out of Mexico without anyone's noticing? Well, police here will be happy to know he's back in town.

I dial 911. The line is busy. Unbelievable. But what would I tell them anyway? I don't even know where Annalisa is meeting him.

I click off and dial Donovan. Annalisa will listen to him more than me. But he doesn't pick up his cell. I dial the front desk at the Rosarito Police Station. The receptionist tells me Donovan and the lieutenant went out to lunch after their meeting. Seriously? I dial Annalisa. I don't wait for her to speak.

"Where are you? Aren't you supposed to be in Modesto?"

"What? Who is this? Is this Gabriella?" She sounds confused. "You're calling from Sean's line?"

"Annalisa, I'm going to ask you again. Where are you?"

"I'm on the Golden Gate Bridge, for your information. I'm meeting someone at the Marin Headlands. It's an extremely important meeting, so I don't have time to talk to you."

She doesn't even realize I listened to Donovan's message.

"Turn around right now. Let the police handle it. You don't know what you're dealing with, Annalisa."

"Oh, whatever. You wanted to be the one who saves Sean, but guess what? I did. I'm the reason he's out of jail. I saved him. He's free because of me."

"You're the reason he was in jail in the first place."

"I don't have time for you."

"Annalisa? Turn around!" I'm practically shouting, but she has already hung up. I dial her again, and it goes straight to voice mail.

"Annalisa, he's going to kill you! Please don't meet him. Talk to

Donovan. Call Donovan and tell him. Please. This isn't about you and me. This is about Emerson. He'll kill you."

I hang up and look around, frustrated. I'm the only one who knows about this meeting and I'm the only one who can possibly stop her.

I race down the stairs, jumping in the orange beater. I yank the gun out of the glove box and put it on the seat beside me before peeling out, leaving a long trail of black skid marks as I head for the freeway.

In my car, I steer with one hand, redialing Annalisa's number with the other. In between, I try Donovan's line. I leave a message for him, telling him where Annalisa is headed—the Marin Headlands. I don't mention I'm halfway there, as well.

A temporary traffic jam getting onto the Bay Bridge has me pounding the steering wheel in frustration, wishing I could will the traffic away.

If I only knew exactly where I was headed, I could call 911. Where would Emerson meet her? I rack my brains. The Marin Headlands is home to abandoned military installations that were used to protect against enemy ships from entering the San Francisco Bay. It contains old WWII bunkers, gun batteries, and antiaircraft lookouts, even a Nike missile silo. The shelters built into the hillside were designed to protect military personnel from chemical, biological, and nuclear attack.

I'm sure that's where he is meeting Annalisa—at one of the old military installations. But which one? I have to figure it out, so I can call the cops. I can't swoop in and rescue her alone. I've learned that. I need help. But right now, I'm all she's got. And the clock is ticking.

He's going to kill her. I know it. If she refuses to run away with him and be his woman, she's dead. And Annalisa is stubborn. She's going to turn him down. I know it. He won't be satisfied with her handing over the tapes she made with Carl Brooke, the ones that incriminate him. He'd rather take her out than have her reject him. I've looked in his eyes. They are dead. Vacant. He's soulless. A sociopath. Looking at my gun, I say a prayer that I can make it there in time.

Chapter 57

MY ORANGE BEATER starts to sputter as I cross the Golden Gate Bridge. It's already been thirty minutes since I spoke to Annalisa.

"Please don't die on the bridge," I pat the dashboard. "Come on, baby, you only have to make it across to the other side. You can do it."

I have been running through all the old military installations in my head, trying to determine which one Emerson would pick. Where would be the easiest place to get away with murder? Not Fort Cronkhite or Fort Barry, too touristy. It must be Wolf Ridge. I remember my uncle took my cousins and me there one summer. It's the least accessible area in the Marin Headlands. You have to park and hike to the ridge. On a day like today, where the fog is seeping in across the Bay, you won't be able to see anything up there unless you're at the top yourself, some eight hundred feet above the breaking surf below. And a lot of people won't be out in today's cold wind and fog.

When I was ten, and my uncle took me to Wolf Ridge, I thought it was cool but creepy. Giant cement platforms dozens of feet in the air were once home to target-tracking radar systems. Old Cold War bunkers were dug into the hillsides, with their rectangular openings slanted like big, black, gaping mouths. Some bunkers had collapsed into caved-in piles of timber and dirt. My older cousin, Sal, had dared me to go inside one. I got as far as the first few steps inside, then I came out at a run. It reminded me of a basement.

That's it. Wolf Ridge. It has to be. I dial Donovan's number again and get his voice mail.

"Donovan, I think Emerson is going to kill Annalisa. You have to send some help. I'm heading to Wolf Ridge. I'm pretty sure that's where she's meeting him. Please, please hurry."

I hang up. Last time I was going after a killer, I didn't call Donovan. This time, I want him and need him here, and yet, he's not picking up his phone.

I dial 911 again. This time I get through.

"There's going to be a murder at Wolf Ridge. I need officers there right away. If you think I'm a nut job, contact San Francisco Police Detective Jack Sullivan and tell him Gabriella Giovanni said there's going to be a murder at Wolf Ridge! Tell him it's about Mark Emerson!" I hang up. I know I sound crazy, but I think that by dropping Sullivan's name, they will take me more seriously, and maybe the message will get to him. And he won't be able to resist. He'll show. He might get here faster than Donovan. I have a gun, but I know I need more than that. I need cops here to help me. When I went after Jack Dean Johnson, I thought I could do it on my own. That was a mistake. This time, I know I need help. But if I wait for the cops to get here first, it's going to be too late for Annalisa. I can't wait and take that chance. I don't like her, but I don't want her death on my conscience, either.

On my way to Wolf Ridge, also known as Hill 88, I slow near the path leading to Hawk Hill. I doubt this is the meeting spot, since it tends to be more popular with tourists, naturalists, and bird-watchers. I look for Annalisa's car in the line of cars parked on the side of the road before the tunnel to the lookout point. There are only about a dozen cars. In a few months, the trail of cars will stretch all the way down the hillside because each fall, bird-watchers come to see tens of thousands of hawks, falcons, eagles, and vultures fly by this area of the Headlands, following warm thermal winds directly through the area.

I continue on. As I round the corner, at the base of Fort Cronkhite, Annalisa's gleaming Ferrari emerges through the fog, which has grown thicker with each turn. It's the only car parked here. If Emerson's here, he must have walked.

I park, tuck my gun into the big front pocket of my thick sweatshirt, and grab my backpack out of my trunk. I'm going to need the flashlight inside it. I peek into the Ferrari's windows and spot a tube of lipstick on the floorboard. I touch the hood. It's still slightly warm. Good. Maybe I can get to her before Mark Emerson arrives.

The fog prevents me from seeing anything very far ahead. I scramble upward, glad I wore my sneakers. The path to Hill 88, once a paved road, is washed out in places where landslides ripped out huge chunks of concrete and sent them plunging into the rocky surf below. My limited visibility in the fog reveals hillsides of damp, droopy wildflowers that scent the air when the wind blows. The path is dotted with wooden staircases and chaparral-torn pavement.

At the top of Hill 88, a crumbling guard shack greets me. The antiaircraft pallets rise in the fog like ghostly specters some twenty feet in the air.

The only sound is the distant clanging of a fog bell far below me. Occasionally, the mist parts, giving me glimpses of a building not far away. I creep closer, listening for any sounds while trying not to make any noise myself. At the entrance to the building, I stand to one side of the door and draw my gun before peering inside. Nothing but broken timbers and walls covered with colorful graffiti.

A scream breaks the eerie silence. Oh no. Emerson's already here somehow. The scream came from somewhere to my right. I run, following a steep path leading down a hillside. The fog lifts a bit and reveals a gaping black entrance to a bunker. I stop, panting. My heart races with fear. I can't go inside. Not underground. I hear more screaming and shouting.

I take a big breath and, heart pounding, pause by the entrance. I rummage around and dig my Maglight out of the backpack, turning it on. My hand is shaking as I point it at the big, black, yawning hole in front of me. I close my eyes and steel myself to enter. I put one foot inside and pause.

I can't. My fingers clutch the edges of the door, fingernails biting into the old rotten wood. My vision starts to narrow. I can't get enough air into my lungs.

She's going to die if I don't do something. Maybe Donovan got my message and is on the way. Sullivan should be sending his troops. Maybe I can lure Mark and Annalisa out of this bunker. Maybe not.

Another scream pierces the silence.

As much as I wish I could, I can't wait around for somebody else to rescue Annalisa. I throw my backpack on the ground at the entrance. I hope it will be a sign I'm inside to anyone else who arrives—Donovan or Sullivan or other cops. A small flight of worn, stone steps lie before me. I press my back against the wall, and, as if my foot is leaden, I force myself to take a step.

Just one step. Okay, now I'm just inside the entryway. Half of my body is shrouded in darkness—the other half remains in the dim fog. Already, I can feel the chill of underground—the difference between above earth and below. My nostrils can smell the damp, musty, earthy smell of the bunker, which has never seen the light of day or had sunshine pour down and warm it. I close my eyes for a moment and try to concentrate on my breathing. In and out. Just like Marsha taught me. Calm your fears and anxieties through deep breathing. I know it works, but why is it so hard to do?

In and out. In and out. I hear a small whimper. Annalisa. He has her.

No more breathing exercises. I don't have time for this nonsense. The gun is heavy in my front pouch. The weight is reassuring. I slide down the next step, one hand on the flashlight, which I click off. I don't want whoever is down there to see me coming. My other hand gropes the slick, slimy wall, which gives me zero traction. The steps are slippery under my feet, as well. I take a step and land on my butt with a thud.

Another whimper and what sounds like ghostly whispering. A chill spreads across my scalp as an eerie wailing sound pierces the stillness. I freeze, eyes widening in the growing darkness. I crouch against one wall, pressing my back against the wet slime. The sound starts up again, this time accompanied by an icy breeze. The tension whooshes out of my limbs. But it's just the wind. It's whistling through cracks in the bunker. For a second, it is silent, then whimpering and that creepy whispering sound again.

I remember Marsha's telling me to try to stifle my fears and anxieties with rational self-talk. *This is not your childhood base-ment. Your dad is not dead down there . . . but if you don't get your shit together, there* will *be a dead body below!*

My teeth are chattering. I can't tell if it is because of the cold or my fear. My back scrapes along the wall as I stand, legs shak-ing. I'm starting to imagine seeing things in the dark. As my eyes adjust, I see a glow at the bottom of the stairs. I turn and look at the entrance to the stairway. It's only a few feet away, but it is as if the bunker is a black hole, and the light seems a mile away. I feel the dark closing in on me. I can't stand it any longer.

I click the flashlight back on, keeping my other hand cupped over the end so only the smallest beam of light is at my feet. I peer down into the darkness. How far do these steps go? I slowly make my way down the steps, with my back scrunching along the wall. A few steps more, I accidentally dislodge a rock that noisily tumbles down the stairs.

A wave of anxiety flattens me. I feel weak, as if my knees are going to give out. I press my back hard against the slippery wall and close my eyes, trying to calm my breathing and my heart, which is thumping loudly in my ears. After a few seconds, I open my eyes, and it seems as if the dark stairway has grown lighter. The pounding in my ears has subsided, and now I hear other sounds.

More whispering and what sounds like scuffling. I click my flashlight off and freeze, holding my breath, waiting for some-thing or someone to come rushing up the stairs. Nothing hap-pens. No sound. My breath returns to normal. I tuck the flashlight in my pocket slowly and my fingers wrap around the cold metal of the gun as I draw it out.

In the dark silence, another small whimper. My arm holding the gun is pointing toward the bottom of the stairs, with my finger on the trigger. The click of the safety coming off echoes in the silence.

"Sean! Don't shoot! Please. He's holding me in front of him." Annalisa's frantic voice sends chills through me. They think I'm Donovan. Good. Maybe that will scare Emerson into letting her go.

Annalisa says something else, but it's muffled, as if Emerson is holding his hand over her mouth. A sudden, deafening blast drops me to my knees. I scream.

Mary Mother of God! He fired at me. He thinks I'm Donovan. Clumps of dirt and dust rain down on my head, dislodged by the shot. I sprawl on the step, with my cheek on the cold stone. My heart is in my throat, thumping madly. I press myself as flat as I can, with my knees curled in front of me. I hold the gun down, toward the bottom of the stairs. I'm waiting and listening, but the echo of the gunshot has made my ears ring. The only sound is the eerie wailing of the wind whistling through the bunker again and what sounds like more whispering.

"Don't shoot," I say, my voice echoing down the stairwell. "It's Gabriella. I'm not here to hurt you or arrest you, Mark. I just want to get Annalisa and go home. The cops are on their way. They aren't here yet. You still have a chance to turn this around, Mark. You can still get away. But you have to leave now. If you stay down there, you'll be trapped. Send Annalisa up. We'll leave. You can get away."

I wait, straining my ears to hear his answer. But the whispering has stopped. Then, a sound—something else. At first I question whether I'm imagining it, but after a few seconds, I'm certain. Somebody is creeping down the stairs above me. My eyes have adjusted slightly, but as I squint toward the opening, it is still too dark to make out any shapes.

"Donovan?" I say, barely above a whisper.

Bang. Another blast. This time a jagged chunk of concrete hits me in the shoulder. I try not to scream from the pain.

"Game over, Emerson."

It *is* Donovan. His voice sounds firm and confident. Relief rushes through me. "Send Gabriella and Annalisa up, and you'll get out of here alive."

"Fuck you, rookie!" It's hard to believe how much venom Emerson can put into three short words. I can almost hear the spittle flying out of his mouth. I clutch my gun, finger poised near the trigger.

More scuffling, but my ears are ringing from the echoes of gunfire in the stairway. I can't tell which direction the sounds are coming from. I feel cold metal against my neck and whispering in my ear. "Don't say a word. Down the stairs."

Emerson.

I make a move to shove my gun into his stomach, but before I can, he head butts me. I see bright shards of light zigzag across my closed eyelids. My gun clatters down the stairs as my hand goes limp, and I collapse in a heap. In my dazed state, Emerson yanks me downward by one arm, nearly tearing it out of its socket. I painfully clump down the stairs until I land with a thud at the dirt bottom.

For a second, I'm free, and I scramble to my feet before a claw like grip clamps down on my arm.

"Not so fast." He shoves me. I crash into a warm body. "Annalisa?"

I'm answered by muffled sobbing.

A bright light is shining in my eyes. I blink, unable to see beyond it. Annalisa is crouched in the dirt beside me. A dirty rag is covering her mouth. Her eyes are wild with fright. A small, purplish bruise is forming around one eye, and her cheek looks like it has a rash on it. I reach out and tug the gag out of her mouth.

Emerson sees me and kicks me in the thigh. "Annalisa, here's your prize. Have at her."

Annalisa gives him an incredulous look, eyes wide.

"*¡Te voy a matar! ¡Pudrete en el infierno!*" My Spanish is rusty, but I'm pretty sure she just told him to eat shit and die—or something along those lines.

"I did it all for you," he says, giving her a flirty smile.

Annalisa watches him in horror, with a hand pressed against her mouth and her eyes wide.

"Everything has been for you." His eyes are glassy. The deadness suddenly gone. "You never had to bring those tapes. You never had to try to get money from me. Don't you understand? Everything, everything I have is yours. I give you everything willingly. I will treat you like a princess. Don't fight me, my love.

"Do you finally understand how serious I am?"

A small noise echoes from the stairs. Emerson jerks around and fires off a round up the stairs. I gasp, holding my breath, praying and hoping Donovan wasn't hit. Emerson acts like nothing has happened and continues speaking to Annalisa, who glares at him.

"I forgive you for everything. You were confused. But now you can see how much I care. How we are meant to be together. I even took care of everyone on the task force so we could be together forever. With all of them dead or put away, there'd be nobody who could dredge up the past to hurt us."

Annalisa's face scrunches up with fierce concentration as she spits into the dirt at the same time she gives him a look that would have withered a lesser man. The veil drops from his eyes again.

He looks like a little boy whose mother has scolded him for something he didn't even realize was wrong—devastated and confused.

Although my ears are still ringing, I hear Donovan's voice shouting my name, seemingly from a long distance away. Thank God, he's okay.

"Stay where you are, rookie scum. One step down here, and I'm going to pull the fucking trigger. I'll blow their fucking heads off. You know I will." Emerson turns his head and shouts again, "Stand down, rookie fuck."

Silence.

Then he turns to me. "Tell him to back off!" He turns toward the stairway and crouches, creeping closer to it. He's trying to provoke Donovan. My body is now shaking uncontrollably. I start to feel as if I'm going to pass out. The walls and the darkness are closing in on me, and I start to hyperventilate. But I'm not going to cooperate.

"Say it!" he says, looking back over his shoulder at me. I shake my head in refusal. It happens so fast I don't have time to duck or react. Emerson is back next to me and his fist lands on my jaw. An acrid metallic taste fills my mouth. Blood. My head reels, and it takes me a moment to focus. I'm relieved I didn't pass out.

"Tell him!" He hisses the words. "He's the last thing standing in our way."

Emerson kneels before Annalisa. "Nobody will ever love you like I do. You are my queen. Please—"

She regards him with disgust, shrinking away.

Out of the corner of my eye, I spot movement in the shadows behind him, near the stairs, and hear a small sound. Emerson must hear it, too, because he whirls around, but it's too late. He is yanked off his feet by some seemingly invisible force in the dark.

The light goes clattering out of his hands and shines on a graffiti-covered wall. The reflection creates enough of a glow to dimly light the small chamber we are in.

I jump to my feet and grab the flashlight, shining it around in the darker, shadowy corners, frantically searching for my own gun. The light briefly illuminates Emerson and Donovan. The two men are struggling. Emerson is trying to put his gun up to Donovan's head. Donovan is pushing Emerson's arm down and away

I scan the chamber with the flashlight, looking for my gun. I hear Annalisa beside me, scrambling to her feet.

There it is. At the base of the steps. My gun. I set the flashlight down and dive for it. Once it is in my hands, I roll over, aiming for Emerson. In the blur of bodies illuminated by the flashlight, I can't be certain whom I will hit, so I don't pull the trigger. I can't take the chance of hitting Donovan.

"Get away from him, Mark." My voice wavers as much as my arm.

A blur heads toward the two men. Annalisa. She brings a large piece of wood down on the back of Emerson's head. The blow stuns Emerson into lowering his gun to his side. He staggers back a few feet. Donovan retreats a few feet back, as well, and reaches for his gun.

But before he can, Emerson steadies himself, lifting his arm and aiming his gun at Donovan, who is still reaching for his own weapon. In the shadows, I see Annalisa rushing toward Donovan. I only have a second. I raise my arm, gun pointing at Emerson.

Time slows.

In small snapshots, I take in the scene. It's too late. Emerson's finger is squeezing his trigger. Donovan is reaching for his holster. It's empty. His gun is on the ground, lost in the struggle. He knows it at the same second I do, and our eyes meet. I fire my gun at the exact same moment as Emerson. The simultaneous gun blasts are deafening in the small space. I rush toward Donovan, but I'm confused by what I see. He is looking down in horror. At his feet lies Annalisa's crumpled body. A hole right between her wide eyes.

Donovan takes the gun out of my hand. I continue to stare at Annalisa, slowly comprehending what has happened. She threw herself between Emerson's bullet and Donovan.

I reluctantly turn my head to where Emerson had been standing. He's on the ground. Blood is gurgling out of his mouth and nose and throat, and yet he reaches both arms out toward Annalisa's body. "No. No. No." The words are thick with blood. A look of intense pain blankets Emerson's face.

Donovan crouches and says something quietly in Emerson's ear. A second later, when Emerson's heart ceases to pump, the blood stops. His eyes remain open, glued on Annalisa's body.

All I can hear is the faint wail of sirens in the distance.

Chapter 58

I'M A TERRIBLE patient. All I want to do is throw on my clothes and run out the hospital doors. Instead, I'm sitting here feeling foolish in this flimsy hospital gown waiting for the okay to flee this joint.

The doctor said the lump on my head didn't even land me a concussion. I must have a tough skull. Emerson's punch in Mexico did more damage when he knocked out a tooth, giving me a goofy gap off to the side.

But because I violently threw up in the ambulance on the way here, the doctor gave me an MRI and took some blood. He told me not to worry, it was probably from drinking the Mexican water, with all its "assorted little critters" my body's not used to having inside.

"That's *not* reassuring," I say to Donovan with a frown.

I yawn.

"Relax. You have time to take a nap, even," Donovan tells me. He's sitting in the chair beside my hospital bed.

"Maybe I'm anemic."

"Here. Meat." Donovan scoops up some of the meat loaf from my tray, holding the spoon up to my mouth. "I know this is slop, but have a few bites, and I'll grill you a big, fat juicy steak when we get home."

"If you don't move that spoon, I think I'm going to vomit all over you," I say, trying not to retch from the smell. It doesn't work. I grab the ugly, yellow, U-shaped tray and vomit.

Perfect. That's exactly what I want my boyfriend to watch me do.

But Donovan is holding my hair back from my face. When I am done, he gently wipes my face off with a wet rag, then sits back down and rubs my arm soothingly.

"I'm sorry," I say with a sheepish look.

"You've been through a lot. But it's all over now. I promise. Try to rest for a few moments. We'll be home before long."

Home. He didn't say his place or mine, he said home. I think about Annalisa. She must have truly loved Donovan to throw herself in front of that bullet. Maybe he was the only person in the world she loved more than herself. I wish I could say I was sad about her death, but right now, I have too many other emotions. It was her fault all this happened in the first place. I don't wish anyone dead, but I can't say I regret her actions. She did, ultimately, save Donovan's life.

Exactly like she told me she had done.

A chill runs through my body when I remember Emerson's face. He loved Annalisa obsessively, violently, more than he loved life itself. He died knowing that love was not returned, but it didn't diminish his love for her.

Now, he's on a morgue slab because of me. I have the blood of two people on my hands. I feel my heart thumping under my chin.

Does that mean I'm no better than all the killers I write about? Who or what gives me the right to take a life? And then I scold myself. When I borrowed a gun, what did I think would happen? If you have a gun, you better expect to maybe use it one day. I was a fool to think I could play with it as a toy.

I put both hands up to cover my eyes. I feel the weight of Donovan's arm slung across my shoulders.

"Two men. It's a mortal sin. I don't know how I'm going to live with this." My voice is thick with tears.

"You didn't have a choice."

"That doesn't help. I can't take it back, Donovan. I'll have to live with it forever. With myself. I've done the worst thing you can do to another person. How can I possibly ever consider myself a 'good' person again?"

Now, I'm flat-out crying. He takes me in his arms and lets me cry until the front of his shirt is soaked. When I finally pull back and look up at his face, I see the pain in his eyes. He knows how I feel. He understands.

He purses his lips grimly. "Let's stop and talk to Father Liam tonight," he says. "He's counseled me about these things before."

I would like to see Father Liam, but I doubt he can tell me anything that will help me feel better about what I've done. Tomorrow, I'll have to come back to the police station and deal with the shooting. San Francisco detectives, not that jerk Sullivan, but another pair, briefly questioned me at Hill 88 before the ambulance came. I promised to visit the station for additional questioning.

Scenes from the bunker flash through my mind. I flash back to the image of Donovan crouching and whispering into Emerson's ear.

"Sean," his name feels weird on my lips but I go on, "What did you say to Emerson?"

Donovan shrugs. "There wasn't much I could say . . . he was going fast. I just said I forgive him."

The mercy of these words makes tears spring to my eyes.

Donovan's phone rings right when the nurse arrives. He steps into the hall to take his call. The nurse says the doctor will be in with my results in a moment, then leaves. I waste no time yanking my IV out, ripping off my hospital gown, and scrambling into my regular clothes. I'm lacing up my sneakers in a chair by the bed when the doctor walks in. Crap. I wasn't fast enough. I give him my sweetest smile.

"Can I go home now?"

The doctor eyes my uneaten lunch tray. "I'll release you, but you have to promise me you're going to try to eat better."

I look at him in confusion. "Huh?"

"I want you to start with crackers and try to keep them down. Once you do that, see if you can stomach more substantial food. Maybe some toast will work. This shouldn't last more than three months. Most women start to feel better around then. And stay hydrated. Lots of water and juices."

What the hell is he talking about? "I don't understand?"

At that moment, an image of my birth-control-pill container flashes into my mind, right when the doctor says:

"Ms. Giovanni, you're pregnant."

Chapter 59

THE ENTIRE CEMETERY, nestled in the rolling, green, Livermore hills, is bathed in a surreal glow from the sunset, brushing the Virgin Mary and angel statues with peach, pink, and orange strokes. Standing at the grave today, my mother and I have no words. Instead, we wrap our arms around each other's waists and look down at the headstones, which are side by side.

LOVING FATHER AND HUSBAND
GIACOMO DOMENICO GIOVANNI, 1941–1977
ADORED DAUGHTER AND SISTER,
CATERINA MARIA-THERESE GIOVANNI, 1970–1977

I silently say a prayer for my sister and father. My mother fishes a small rosary out of her bag. I know she's going to be a while. I tell her I'm going for a walk, and I'll meet her back at the car.

I haven't told my mother I'm pregnant. I'm having the baby but want to wait until I'm further along to share the news. Donovan is bursting with excitement, but he understands why I want to wait to share our news. We got pregnant right before Donovan was arrested, so I'm only a few weeks along and want to wait just a little bit longer before I tell everyone. I hate being so cautious, so wary. But it's because I'm afraid. The thought of losing this little life inside me is already devastating. What it would do to my mother, I don't know, but ever since Caterina's death, I've vowed to protect her from as much pain as I could.

I came early to the cemetery, before my mother, and told Caterina everything. Sitting with my back leaning against the headstone, I confessed that she was the reason I've been terrified to have a baby. How could I ever love another child as much as I loved my sister? How could I go through the pain of loving someone that much again? And then losing them? What if I loved my baby more than Caterina? What if that love took the place of the love I felt for my sister? My serene, meek, and loving sister, who only wanted to make other people happy—the last person on the planet who deserved the hand of fate she was dealt.

I spilled it all out to the cold gray headstone. And when I was done, and the tears had dried, I felt that subtle shift in the world. It would be okay. It was almost as if Caterina has given me her blessing.

Giving one last glance at Caterina's gravestone, I hug my mother and head toward a hilly area, making the sign of the cross as I pass Baby Land, with its bears and balloons atop tiny graves. Alone now, there is no longer even the threat of tears. Instead, I feel full of light and joy. I surprise myself and start singing The Verve's "Bitter Sweet Symphony."

The air is crisp, and my voice carries across the empty graveyard. I sing as loud as I can. I can't stop myself. If a deranged man held a gun to my forehead and told me to stop singing, I don't think I could. A car passes, and the driver, an elderly man who has his window down, does a double take, looking at me like I've lost it. Maybe I have. I keep singing.

I decide to walk the perimeter of the cemetery and loop around back to my mother. I head over to the chain-link fence and tromp through an area the lawn mower has neglected. It is dotted with tall dandelions, and for some reason, it feels good to have left the manicured lawn and tidy sidewalks.

As I walk and sing, something happens.

With every step I take, I trigger a mini explosion of small butterflies that take flight from the overgrown grass and flutter before me and around me. Orange and black monarchs, small white ones, and larger buttercup yellow ones tipped with a black stripe. They all dance around me. I laugh with delight.

As I walk, more butterflies take to the air in my path. And so, I continue on, laughing, singing, and walking with the butterflies.

Acknowledgments

On the day my rock star agent Stacey Glick offered to represent me, I asked her if she had an editor in mind for my book, *Blessed are the Dead*.

She did.

The editor she had in mind was terrific to work with, very smart, and extremely skilled at what she did.

As things turned out, that editor, Emily Krump, was the one who ended up buying *Blessed are the Dead* and this book, the second in my Gabriella Giovanni series.

I could not be more thrilled. I'm very grateful to have both these smart, super cool, talented women in my corner.

So first off, I want to express my heartfelt thanks to Stacey and Emily!

Stacey is a superstar agent. Emily is the kind of editor every writer dreams of having—I don't think there was even one small suggestion she made that I didn't absolutely love.

Danielle Bartlett and Dana Trombley, at HarperCollins, are

wonderful and I want to thank them for their expertise and help on the marketing end of things.

Writing groups are invaluable and I was lucky enough to be involved in two of them while I wrote this book—my first writing group, Mickie Turk, Laurie Walker, Alex Kent, Susan Hastings, and Carolyn Ore—all took a peek at *Blessed are the Meek*. After that, the members of Supergroup: Jana Hiller, Kate Schultz, Sean Beggs, Sarah Hanley, Coralee Grebe, and Kaethe Schwehn, all gave me extremely valuable input in to how to make this novel shine before I passed it on to Emily. In addition, Sarah Henning and Sam Bohrman both provided keen insight that helped get the novel in shape for publication.

Thanks to Lynn Cronquist for clearing up some cop procedural questions and just being overall super cool.

The L.A. band Wood & Smoke has been a source of endless inspiration to me since the late 1980s. Lead singers/songwriters Gary Williams and Lance Whitson are two of the most talented musicians I know. Their song, "Annalisa," inspired my character's name.

And last, but not least, I want to thank my fourth-grade teacher at Ponderosa Elementary School, Mrs. Ward, who encouraged me to pursue my dream of writing a book one day.

About the Author

KRISTI BELCAMINO is a writer, photographer, and artist. In her former life as a newspaper crime reporter in California, she flew over Big Sur in an FA-18 jet with the Blue Angels, raced a Dodge Viper at Laguna Seca, watched autopsies, and interviewed serial killers. She is now a journalist based in Minneapolis, and the Gabriella Giovanni mysteries are her first books.

Friend Kristi at www.facebook.com/kristibelcaminowriter or follow her on Twitter @KristiBelcamino.

Visit www.AuthorTracker.com for exclusive information on your favorite HarperCollins authors.